Tom West is the pseudonym for an internationally bestselling author of nine novels. *Private Down Under*, which he co-wrote with James Patterson under the name Michael White, is the latest in the Private series. Tom West lives in Perth, Australia.

THE
TITANIC
ENIGMA

TOM WEST

PAN BOOKS

First published 2013 by Pan Books
an imprint of Pan Macmillan, a division of Macmillan Publishers Limited
Pan Macmillan, 20 New Wharf Road, London N1 9RR
Basingstoke and Oxford
Associated companies throughout the world
www.panmacmillan.com

ISBN 978-1-4472-1033-7

1 3 5 7 9 8 6 4 2

A CIP catalogue record for this book is available from the British Library.

Typeset by Ellipsis Digital Ltd, Glasgow
Printed and bound by CPI Group (UK) Ltd, Croydon, CR0 4YY

PROLOGUE

375 miles SE of Newfoundland. Present day.

When the call came to get him to the bridge to begin his shift, Captain John Curtis was enjoying a very pleasant dream. As he opened his eyes and stared at the metal bulkhead above his bunk, he felt about ninety-five years old and told himself, for perhaps the fiftieth time, he would definitely take early retirement . . . just as soon as he got back home.

He pulled on his fleece and hat, yanked open the door to the cabin and hauled himself onto the deck of the *Ottawa Dawn*. It was a stunning morning – a clear, cloudless sky, a pinch of cold in the air, the ocean as still as a cup of coffee. They were steaming towards Newfoundland at their top speed of twenty-seven knots, anxious to get to shore with their catch of North Atlantic cod. Curtis ascended the metal ladder to the bridge, leaned on the handle and stepped inside. His first mate, Tony Saunders, was alone at the helm. Curtis said 'Hi' and then started rummaging around in a cupboard, removing charts and instruments.

This was when Saunders noticed something through the front window. Without a word, he lifted up his binoculars and surveyed the horizon. Curtis was still half in and half out of the cupboard sorting through things in preparation for the long day ahead. He had to steady himself occasionally as the ship swayed gently. It was quiet, the only sound the almost subliminal rumble of the trawler's engines and the rhythmic splash as the vessel sliced through the water.

Saunders mumbled something and bent forward, trying to make sense of what he was seeing through his binoculars. His face contorted in disbelief.

'Holy Mother of God!' he exclaimed suddenly.

Startled, Captain Curtis lifted his head and banged it on a low shelf inside the cupboard. 'Crap!' he yelled and then emerged, rubbing a spot just above his forehead. 'What's up, Tony?'

Saunders ignored him, transfixed by what he was seeing. Curtis came up to his right. 'What's wrong?'

'Look!' The first mate pointed through the glass.

Curtis screwed up his eyes then reached for another pair of binoculars resting on the radio console. He brought them up and let out a whistle.

To the naked eye, it looked like a single silver mass, but through the binoculars the view was very different. 'Take us down to five knots,' Curtis snapped. The boat began to slow, but it was carried by inertia straight into the leading edge of the thing they had seen. Saunders kept the helm while Curtis sounded the alarm and dashed through the door on to the steps and down to the boat deck, just as the crew emerged into the bright light of morning.

All about the boat, as far as the eye could see, lay dead fish bobbing gently on the surface of the water.

The five crewmen leaned over the rails and Curtis shouted to Saunders to kill the engines. They all heard their throb descending down the scale, leaving the trawler to drift with the current. The air stank, the ammonia of decaying fish cutting through the tang of brine.

'What the fuck's going on?' one of the crewmen managed to say, turning to his boss.

Curtis was about to reply when they all heard a low rumble. For a fraction of a second, the captain thought Saunders had kicked in the engines again, but this was a different sound, deeper, fuller. The sound grew in volume but kept the same note, a low sub-woofer throb.

The surface of the ocean began to tremble and churn. The fish started to vibrate. Giant bubbles broke the surface as though the Atlantic was boiling. And all the time, the sound was growing louder and louder. A couple of the seamen turned to the captain, the fear clear in their faces. Curtis felt himself break into a cold sweat.

One of the crew rushed through a door leading below deck. A few moments later, he emerged clutching his iPhone. Bracing himself with one hand gripping the rail, the other working the controls of the screen, he began to pan round.

And when it broke the surface, its giant slimy grey head first, the seamen could hardly believe what they were seeing. The sperm whale was a big one, at least fifty feet long. It roared through the surface of the water, half its body shooting above the fish-smothered sea before crashing belly-first onto the shuddering mess of silver. As it smacked down onto the surface, great plumes of water shot thirty feet into the air. The giant, stone-dead whale trembled as the energy of its ascent through the ocean was counteracted by buoyancy and gravity. Then it rolled onto its back, revealing great red furrows along its underside contrasting starkly with the bleached white of the guts and blubber spilling from it.

1

Bermuda. Three days later.

Everything was going pretty well, he thought. They'd checked the diving gear. All fine. The remote cameras had come up with some very cool pictures of the four-hundred-year-old wreck of the pilgrim ship, the *Lavender*.

He and Kate slipped off the side of the boat and began their descent. The *Lavender* was in only two hundred feet of water but there were hidden dangers. The ship was fragile, there were sharks aplenty, not to mention stingrays and freak currents.

He saw Kate just a few feet below him. 'Everything cool, babe?' he asked through the comms.

She gave him the thumbs up.

A few minutes later they had reached the ocean floor. The wreck was directly ahead. It really did look like something from *Pirates of the Caribbean*.

'Take it slow here, Lou,' Kate's voice resounded in his headset. 'I'll lead the way in through the port side. Everything OK with you?'

'A 1.'

He saw Kate glide through the water. Then he felt something thump his back. A surge of irrational anger swept through him. He twisted and saw two black circles through the whipped-up water, an opened mouth, rows of triangular teeth.

A great white shot past. Lou swung round, swept his arm up through the water, and as the shark went to snap he slammed his fist into its skull, right between the eyes. It slipped down through the water, stunned for a moment.

He screamed into his comms, but Kate seemed totally unaware of what was happening, as though their radio link had severed. He waved frantically. She turned, raised a hand, nodded . . . totally oblivious. He looked down and saw the shark rocketing up through the water. It twisted and headed straight for Kate. She had her back to it.

From ten yards away, Lou could see the huge fish open its mouth and slither to one side, grip Kate about the middle, close its mouth and start to shake its prey.

Blood plumed outward like a mushroom cloud rising from a nuclear explosion, Kate's body a rag doll mauled by a rabid dog. Then, as he watched, the water becoming opaque with blood, he saw Kate's body snap in two, her legs slipping downward slowly to the ocean floor.

*

Lou Bates woke screaming, covered with sweat. He sat bolt upright gazing around, elemental dawn seeping its way between the blinds and into the darkened room. The sheets were soaked. He took a deep breath, forcing his heart to slow, then looked at his shaking hands, just visible in the gloom. He couldn't still them, couldn't escape how real his dream had seemed.

But it was a dream.

2

Lou Bates pulled onto the North Shore Road in his rented US Army jeep. The sun's iridescent orange rays sparkled on the ocean – real holiday brochure stuff. His long mousy-blond hair was swept across his face by the warm breeze. He glanced at his watch. It was coming up to 9 a.m. Leaning forward, he flicked on the ancient radio.

'On this morning's programme,' the presenter said, 'as civil unrest grows, what next for Thailand? And the election in Croatia . . . no clear result expected. But first . . . At an emergency meeting in New York this morning, the UN Security Council passed Resolution 44 allowing a NATO force to police a five-mile exclusion zone around what the military are calling "Marine Phenomenon REZ375", otherwise known as the *Titanic* site. In the three days since the odd phenomenon was first brought to public attention by the crew of Canadian trawler *Ottawa Dawn*, conspiracy theorists have had a field day – not least, of course, because the location of the peculiar incident is directly above the site of the final resting place of the *Titanic*, which sank on 15 April

1912. Now, though, cranks aside, many respected organizations and individuals are asking some pretty uncomfortable questions about the cause of the incident. Late last night, a few hours before the Security Council meeting, Greenpeace issued a statement claiming they had proof the phenomenon has been caused by an unknown source of radiation. Although they have offered no evidence, they are already pointing a finger at the US military.

'This claim has been strenuously denied by the White House, and the United States government has repeatedly reiterated expert opinion . . . that the destruction of marine life in the vicinity of REZ375 has been caused by a mysterious, but nevertheless entirely natural, effect. At the same time, it has taken extraordinary diplomatic efforts on the part of the US and the UK to quell the concerns of the other three permanent members of the Security Council. I have on the line from Moscow Professor Dimitri Karasov from the Soviet Institute of Natural Sciences . . .'

Lou flicked off the radio impatiently. He was growing sick of the whole story. It was obvious to any idiot the incident was caused by something entirely of human doing. All this talk of mysterious natural effects was pure spin. He gazed to his right seeing shearwaters diving for fish and the breakers on the beach, the white foam like chintz curtains draped over a turquoise silk. The road skirted the sand and then weaved inland a few hundred yards before descending towards a rocky peninsula, surveyed by hungry seagulls. He started humming an old tune, called something like 'Photograph of You', by some eighties band whose name escaped him, and from the jeep he could see the clutch of tin-roofed, white stone-walled buildings that constituted the team's work base and lab.

He'd been here in Bermuda three months now; him, his team leader, Kate Wetherall, and a group of six technicians. And, as much as he loved this beautiful island, he was missing his one-bed apartment in Hampton, Virginia, a mile from the Institute of Marine Studies. He also pined for the cozy lab he shared with Kate at the institute. He knew that when this assignment was over, he would hanker after the constant tropical sunshine, but in exchange he would once again have reliable broadband, live baseball, a lab he did not have to share with herons and lizards, and, most crucially, he could give back the jeep and slide into his pride and joy, the 1959 T-Bird he had spent five years restoring.

He pulled the jeep into the car park of the lab – a level concrete rectangle as big as a football pitch twenty yards from the road along a narrow gravel lane. A path led down from there to the buildings close to the top of the rocky outcrop protruding from the cliff face. Pulling to a stop on the ocean side of the car park close to the precipice, Lou yanked the keys from the ignition and snatched up his worn brown leather satchel from the passenger seat. He descended the fifty-seven stone steps cut into the rock face and strode into the outer prep room of the lab. Through a huge glass window facing north, he could see the sweeping ocean and sky.

He still got a thrill from this purest of vistas. He still loved the smell of this makeshift lab, the feel of his chair tucked under the workbench in the section of the lab where he spent most of his time, and, above all, he loved, absolutely loved, the job itself – every damn moment of it.

Admittedly, it had all been a bit rocky to start with. It had nothing to do with the work, he had been fine with that. With a degree in archaeology and a PhD in marine science, he was more than qualified for the post. Indeed, he had spent his entire life fascinated by marine archaeology, the romance of the shipwreck, the mystery of doomed voyages. What could be learned from these relics told the researcher so much about bygone centuries, about the ordinary, everyday lives of ordinary, everyday people.

No, none of this had been a problem for him; the problem had been Kate, Kate Wetherall, Kate and him. They had fallen for each other almost instantly. It had been a really freaky thing. He had never experienced anything like it before. He had walked into his interview a week before starting the job, and that was it. The two other interviewers behind the table had faded to insignificance; all he could focus on was the woman in the middle of the three, the Head of Research. He'd been headhunted from Massers Marine Research Facility in California. The post was to work with her, to be her number two.

Later, post-coitally, Kate had told him that she had tried her damnedest to have her way in vetoing the choice of the other two interviewers – both board members who controlled the purse strings of the institute. She knew he was the best qualified for the job, but she also knew he would be trouble, because she had reacted to him in exactly the way he had to her. The sparks had been almost visible. He had never met anyone like her.

Kate had only lived in the United States for three years. She was a Brit, from an academic family, very stoic, tough, straight down the line. Her mother, Geraldine, had been a biochemist who died of breast cancer at fifty-one. Kate's father, Nicholas Wetherall, had a been a world-class evolutionary biologist, an Oxford don and later Emeritus Professor at Princeton. He had also died young, from a brain tumour when Kate was fourteen.

Kate, Lou knew, was a damn fine marine archaeologist. At the same time, she was overmodest and self-deprecating, and possessed a sense of humour he could not fathom half the time. She was so utterly different from him. It wasn't until they had been together for a month that Lou had wheedled out of Kate that her grandfather had been a super-wealthy industrialist and she had been educated at Benenden – Princess Anne's alma mater.

But that was all now in the past. They had shared a beautiful, if overheated, relationship that had lasted six months. It had almost destroyed their ability to work together, disrupted the team and had driven him into depression. He had pulled himself back from the brink at the last moment and salvaged his career. With Kate's help, he had brought their relationship to a new, healthier place.

*

Lou burst through the doors to the lab and was surprised to see that Kate had got there before him. She was seated at one of the computer monitors so absorbed it took her a few seconds to acknowledge Lou's boisterous arrival. She had a large lab beaker filled with cereal in one hand, a plastic spoon in the other.

He strode over to where she was sitting. 'And good morning to you!' he said.

She kept watching the screen, flicked a strand of her shoulder-length blonde hair behind her ear and lifted the spoon to her mouth without moving her head. 'Have you seen this?'

'What?'

'This film shot by the fishermen on that Canadian trawler.'

'Oh, God, this is so tedious!'

She turned from the screen. 'Why are you being so negative?'

'It's obvious the navy has screwed up. There's been some sort of accident with a nuclear sub, or a cargo vessel has dumped something they shouldn't have.'

'Directly above the *Titanic*? Bit of a coincidence, Lou.'

'Yes, it is. But, honey,' and he smiled sweetly, 'what was that famous song by Elvis Costello, "Accidents will Happen"?'

Kate stood up. She was five-ten in trainers, just an inch shorter than Lou; her lab coat swished around her slender, toned body as she turned. She had a runner's physique and maintained a regime of at least forty miles a week, usually before 6 a.m. each day. If she missed exercise for more than a day, she could be very hard to talk to.

Lou watched her and could not stop a memory. A summer night in Virginia, his apartment. Kate nestled into his shoulder, a sheet barely covering their naked entwined legs. Nowadays he could no longer say it aloud, but he missed her.

'Say what you like about this,' and Kate tapped the screen, 'I think there's something very odd going on.'

'Yes, and you're not the only one. All the crazies have come out of the woodwork over this, Kate. You're in very good company!'

She sighed and gave up. 'So, do you want to know what I've just discovered?'

'Of course!' Lou pulled a stool up to her monitor.

During the three months the pair had been on Bermuda they had been trying, day by day, to unravel the mystery of why a ship, the *Lavender*, carrying ninety-six pilgrims from Plymouth had run aground on a calm evening in July 1615 a few hundred yards from where they now stood. Kate and Lou had been down to the wreck some two dozen times. They had retrieved an array of artefacts, photographed and filmed the wreck from every conceivable angle and catalogued everything. In their island lab they had studied tiny fragments of porcelain and metal under the microscope, conducted infrared spectroscopic analyses and run a multitude of chemical tests on items ranging from metal casks to the remnants of four-hundred-year-old Bibles partially protected inside rusty chests. But they were still no nearer to knowing the cause of the accident. Now they had begun to consider the idea that the voyage had been doomed because of a clash of personalities aboard the *Lavender*.

Kate tapped her keyboard and the image of a fragment of paper appeared on the screen. It contained some text, but it was almost completely illegible. At the top, above the edge of the piece of ancient paper, a label read: *Sample # BZ081*.

'This is the best of the Bible fragments we found in the captain's chest.'

'Yes, I recognize it.'

'I ran it through an enhancement program.' She moved the mouse and clicked an icon. 'At maximum resolution, I got this.' The new image was a much clearer copy of the original fragment.

'You can almost read it,' Lou said.

'You can read it – a few words anyway.'

'Yes, I see . . . there . . . what does it say?'

'A snatch of Latin: *Magna*. Then a gap: *vitas . . . praevalet*.'

'*Magna est veritas et praevalet*,' Lou muttered and glanced at Kate.

'How on earth did you . . .?'

'Kate, baby . . .' He held his hands out wide apart, palms up.

She laughed. 'So you get the relevance of it?'

'Er . . . No.'

'Hah! Well, smart ass, in English *Magna est veritas et praevalet* means—'

'I know what it means! "Great is truth and mighty above all things".'

'But more importantly,' Kate said, 'it's from *I. Estras*, a book of the Apocrypha from the Old Testament. The pilgrims aboard the *Lavender* would have only read the King James Bible, and that definitely does not contain the Apocrypha. They would have abhorred such a thing.'

'So you reckon the captain was a Catholic? Oops!'

Kate was about to reply when they both heard a strange sound from outside. They looked at each other and headed towards the doors leading to the corridor and outside. A dark-blue Harrier was settling onto the tarmac of the car park.

*

By the time Kate and Lou reached the plane, its engines had begun to quieten. The passenger canopy rose and a tall, well-built man in naval uniform and clutching an aluminum attaché case began to clamber down a fuselage ladder. Reaching the ground, he made his way over. In his mid-thirties, the man had cropped hair, a hint of grey at the temples, black eyes and a strong jaw.

'Lou Bates and Kate Wetherall?' he said. His voice was deep with just a trace of a southern drawl to it.

'Guilty,' Kate said.

He took a step towards them. 'Captain Jerry Derham, United States Navy.'

Lou snapped his heels and did a mock salute.

Kate gave him a dirty look.

Jerry smiled and stuck out his hand. 'I'm sorry to turn up unannounced. I hope I haven't interrupted your work. Can you spare me ten minutes of your time?'

Lou made them coffee using what he and Kate referred to as the 'sacred coffee machine' – a Miele espresso maker that had been shipped over from Virginia and was their lifeline on slow days.

Captain Derham removed his cap and took a sip. 'Good coffee,' he said appreciatively. 'I guess you're wondering why I'm here?' He took another sip. 'I'm Section Commander at the Norfolk Naval Base, Virginia. It's about ten miles from your facility at the Marine Research Institute.' He nodded westward. 'We're heading up the investigation into Marine Phenomenon REZ375.'

'I've just been watching the film of the trawler,' Kate replied. 'It's quite something.'

'It is.'

'Although,' Kate went on, 'my colleague –' and she nodded towards Lou '– thinks it's the navy's fault.'

'I didn't say that exactly . . .' Lou began.

'Believe what you like,' Derham replied. 'I'm not the Inquisition. But I have something I'd like to show you.' He plucked an iPad from his case, switched it on and handed it to them.

'That,' he said as the film started, 'was taken by a deep-sea probe we sent down to the *Titanic* two days ago. You've probably seen similar footage from the remote submersibles that visited the wreck back in the mid-1980s. But note the digital display in the corner.'

'Yeah, I was wondering what that was,' Lou said.

'It's a readout from a Geiger counter.'

'It's reading . . . what? Two times ten to the power of twenty curies? That's ridiculous!'

'Almost off the scale.'

'So Greenpeace and the others have been reporting the truth – there is a radiation source down there,' Kate said without taking her eyes from the screen. The digital display kept climbing. 'What happened to the crew of the trawler?'

'Radiation sickness, but they'll all survive – they got out of the area pretty damn quick.'

'What sort of radiation are we talking about here?' Lou asked.

'Alpha and beta particles, gamma rays – pretty conventional, but our probes show that the combination of the three types of radiation is unusual. It's possible we're dealing with a type of source we've not seen before. There's certainly nothing in nature that produces this radiation profile, even if we ignore the intensity.'

'But if it isn't a natural source, it has to be military hardware, surely?'

'It's not ours,' Derham said.

Lou looked sceptical.

'As far as we know, it isn't,' the captain added.

'Russian, Chinese?' Kate offered.

'We simply don't know.'

'So, what now?' Lou said, handing back the iPad.

'We've isolated the source to somewhere in the bow section of the wreck. But we have no precise coordinates yet. It's a big ship. We're working on it, though, and hope to have it down to a few square yards in a day or two.'

'Then?'

'Well, that's why I'm here. We need your expert help. The story has broken across the Internet and the world is watching. You two come highly recommended; experienced marine archaeologists – a rare commodity.'

'But we're in the middle of our own project,' Kate said.

'I understand that. We wouldn't be bothering you if we knew anybody better qualified; and time is of the essence.'

'I'm listening,' Lou said. 'But we're –' he glanced at Kate '– close to a breakthrough here. What exactly do you want us to do?'

'We're zeroing in on the precise location of the radio-active source.'

'But then what?'

'We have to get people into the ship to find out for ourselves what it is.'

Kate and Lou both burst out laughing and turned to the naval officer in unison. 'Get people into the wreck! The *Titanic* is on the ocean floor . . . What, 13,000 feet beneath the surface of the Atlantic?'

'12,600 feet to be precise,' Derham replied calmly. 'That won't present a problem.'

3

'Let's just say for the moment,' Derham said, 'that we do have the technology.'

Lou turned to face Kate. 'You'll catch flies.'

She closed her mouth. 'I'm sorry,' she said. 'That, I did not expect! For a start, how can you overcome the pressure at a depth of 12,600 feet?'

'I'm afraid I can't talk about it right now. If you decide to join us, you'll each need to sign a Defense Department non-disclosure agreement. He nodded towards his briefcase. 'I have them here. We've already done security checks on you . . .'

'Hang on,' Kate interrupted. 'Aren't you jumping the gun a bit? She looked over to Lou who was studying the captain's face.

Derham had his hands up. 'Apologies. Of course you need some time to think about it.'

'I don't,' Lou said avoiding Kate's eyes. 'How long would we have to delay our work here?'

'Two days. Three, max.'

Lou gave Kate a questioning look.

She shook her head slowly and sighed. 'Three days?'

'Absolute tops.'

'OK, well I guess you can count us both in.'

*

The VTOL aircraft ascended into the clear blue morning sky, roared over the group of white buildings with their tin roofs, swung round and headed out over the ocean.

From a pair of seats behind Derham and the pilot, Kate and Lou had an amazing view. When they were in level flight, Derham unbuckled and came back to the two researchers. He gave them each a folder containing everything NATO had ascertained about the radiation leak, along with facts, figures, schematics and maps relevant to the wreck of the *Titanic*.

They already knew most of the basics from Lesson 101 of their training as marine archaeologists. The *Titanic* had set sail for New York from Southampton on its maiden voyage on 10 April 1912. Four days into its journey, she struck an iceberg and sank. This resulted in the deaths of 1,517 of the 2,223 passengers and crew. It was the greatest peacetime disaster in maritime history.

The report contained a map of the ocean floor and described the current state of the wreck scattered over two square miles. The vessel had broken into two sections as it sank. The larger, bow section, was located at precisely 41° 43' 57" N, 49° 56' 49" W; about seven hundred yards away lay the stern, which was now in far worse condition than the bow section. According to the report, no trace of any soft furnishings, carpets, wooden objects or indeed human bones remained, as these were long ago consumed by marine life. What remained was frail. Parts of the deck of the stern section had collapsed and many of its metal structures were heavily corroded. The final page of the document covered what little was known about the radiation leak itself, reiterating the phenomenal radiation levels measured by the probe that had filmed the footage of the wreck.

*

An hour later, the US Navy aircraft touched down on a pad a hundred yards from the nearest buildings. Derham led them from the aircraft. A grey Pontiac was waiting for them, a guard at each of the rear doors. The servicemen saluted briskly and snapped to attention as the captain approached. Kate and Lou were shown into the back seats of the vehicle and Derham sat in the front. A silent driver in naval uniform drove the car across the tarmac to a squat building at the edge of a cluster of ugly concrete and steel hangars. A fighter jet screamed low overhead as they stepped out.

The car park beside the squat building had been built on high ground a quarter of a mile from the Atlantic Ocean. From here, Kate and Lou could see part of the military base spread out before them – the dry docks and the harbour, and a long line of piers. Lou counted sixteen massive warships, great grey lumps of jagged metal, stark against the blue. The naval base was one of the largest in the world. At any one time, seventy-five ships and over one hundred and thirty aircraft were stationed here.

The two scientists followed Jerry Derham towards the squat building. He flashed his ID at a guard close to the main door. Inside, they crossed a wide reception and entered a lift. It dropped quickly. Lou and Kate noticed a digital display counting off the floors in rapid succession. It slowed and stopped at B17.

'It's a bit of an iceberg – if you'll pardon the terrible pun,' Derham said, turning first to Kate then to Lou. 'There are nineteen levels below ground. This building is the main research hub for the station – and indeed for the entire United States Navy.'

The lift opened onto an administration area. They could see uniformed staff busy at computer terminals and consoles. In one corner, a small group of officers sat in comfy chairs going over some notes, iPads and clipboards in hand. There were at least a dozen naval personnel in the room; all of them seemed oblivious to the new arrivals.

Derham led the way to a large steel door on the far side of the room. He placed his palm on a pad to the left of the door. A light strip over the pad turned green and a computer voice said, 'ID confirmed.' The door slid sideways into a recess and opened onto a long, brightly lit, white-walled corridor that curved to the right. Ahead was another door and a second sensor pad at head height. Derham stood in front of it. A narrow horizontal light beam moved slowly from the top of the rectangle to the bottom like a flat bed scanner. 'A retinal reader,' he said without moving his head as the light followed its course. 'ID confirmed,' the computer voice said.

They were in a room the size of an aircraft hangar. In the centre stood two metal cylinders the colour of aged pewter. At the rear of each cylinder was a large jet nozzle. Two fins, one each side of the tubes about a third of the way from the front, made the machines look like very strange aircraft, but it only took a few seconds for Kate and Lou to realize they were looking at some form of submarine.

They could see a small maintenance crew working on the sub furthest away. One of the men was wearing a protective mask and held a welding tool blazing in his gloved right hand.

'*Jules Verne 1* and *Jules Verne 2*,' Derham said. 'These subs each carry four people and a half-ton payload at speeds up to thirty knots. They can comfortably go to 15,000 feet beneath the surface, and if the crew are really great friends, *JV1* and *JV2* can stay submerged for up to a year. They're completely pressurized, so the crew don't need to decompress. The guys are attaching additional anti-radiation shielding to the hulls.'

Neither scientist knew quite what to say. Lou took a couple of steps towards the nearest sub and ran a hand along the smooth hull. It felt like silk. 'How?' he said, shaking his head slightly.

'How what?'

'How did you build this? I've never seen anything like it.'

Kate walked over to the end of the jet nozzle and peered inside. A pair of technicians approached and she stepped back, rejoining Lou and Derham.

'These vessels, along with everything else you see in this construction hub today, are top secret. These are the only two such vessels in the world. They cost over a hundred million dollars each to build and they employ technology that will not be released into the civilian world for at least twenty-five years. They come from the drawing boards of the Defense Advanced Research Projects Agency.'

'DARPA,' Kate said, 'of course.'

Derham nodded. 'We have DARPA to thank for the cell phone, pilotless aircraft, the Internet, digital technology and microelectronics, to name just a few things we now take for granted. But thirty or forty years ago all those things would have been as far-fetched as these babies seem now.' He waved a hand towards the subs. 'DARPA had the technology to design these back in the 1980s – primitive versions, for sure, but they worked.'

'Necessity being the mother of invention,' Lou remarked.

'Exactly. The military need to be not just one step ahead, but half a dozen steps. When something is improved or replaced by even better technologies, the older ones are released to the public.'

'And these have been tested?' Kate asked. 'They can definitely reach the depth of the *Titanic*?'

'Yes,' Derham replied. 'But there's more. Come this way.'

He took them through a door. A small group of over-alled technicians were coming towards them along a corridor and the three newcomers stepped aside to let them pass into the construction hub. Derham then headed off towards a door at the end of the corridor. It led into another large room, alive with activity. Desks and computer terminals lined the walls to left and right. Lab-coated figures and more technicians in differently coloured overalls worked at stations or stood in groups deep in discussion. A glass cube dominated the room. They could see two or three figures moving around inside. They were wearing white hats, latex gloves and shoe covers, and masks over their mouths and noses.

Lou and Kate followed Derham to a secured door that opened with a card from the captain's pocket, and he led them into a small antechamber. Here they found a collection of plastic parcels. Derham plucked one up, ripped open the packaging and pulled out a gown, a hat and the other paraphernalia needed to go into the sterile room. A few moments later, the three of them were suited up and inside the glass cube.

A circular metal rail had been suspended in the middle of the ceiling of the cube. Dangling from it by wires were a dozen or more metallic-coloured suits. At first glance, they looked like the sort of spacesuits worn by NASA astronauts on the first orbital flights of the early 1960s. But a closer examination showed they were made from a strange silk-like fabric similar to the outer shell of the *JV*s in the construction hub.

'These,' Derham said, 'are the LMC suits.'

'LMC?' Kate asked, eyeing the suits.

'Liquid metal carbon. It's a revolutionary new material the eggheads tell me is somewhere between a solid and a liquid. I think the nearest analogy is the element mercury; at least that's how they describe it.' He walked over to one of the technicians standing close by, said something and nodded towards the rack of suits. The technician took one down and clambered into it. Pulling on a helmet, he ran his fingers over a panel on his left sleeve, the suit emitted a single low note and expanded. He looked like a Michelin Man.

'Whoa!' Lou exclaimed and stepped back. The suit shimmered like a mirage. It had the appearance of moving water, held together in a human shape by some miraculous power.

The technician took a few steps towards Derham and stomped back the other way. Breaking into a brisk walk, he turned just before the far wall and paced back again. They could see the man grinning through the visor of the helmet.

'It's not possible to swim in them – they're too bulky – but these suits,' Derham explained, 'allow the wearer to leave the *JV*s and walk on the ocean floor under pressures in excess of 480 atmospheres – the sort of pressure experienced at the depth of the *Titanic* wreck. They double up as extremely effective radiation suits.'

'No way!' Kate declared. 'That's impossible.'

'No, it's not,' Derham replied, a faint smile flickering around his lips. It was clear he was enjoying showing off this stuff. 'The LMC gives under pressure. Think of it as a blob of mercury with a human inside it. In theory, the LMC can take almost unlimited external pressure – it simply moulds itself to the form inside.'

'My God!' Lou exclaimed and walked over to the technician in the suit. 'May I?' he asked, turning to Derham.

'Sure.'

Lou touched the shimmering material and Kate came over to try it too. 'It's like nothing I've ever felt before,' she said. 'It's like . . . like . . .'

'Like it's not actually there?' Derham said.

'Yes,' Kate replied. 'Yes, that's it, exactly.'

'So,' Lou said, turning away from the technician. 'This means you really can get down to the *Titanic* and inside it. I still can't wrap my head around that idea. I envy you, man.'

'Why?' Derham said, turning first to Kate and then back to Lou. 'Aren't you coming with me?'

4

Five miles outside Lyon, France. Present day.

Smoking a fat Bolivar, one of her favourite cigars, Glena Buckingham, the CEO of Eurenergy, sat up from her chair as her Polish executive assistant, Hans Secker, came into the drawing room at her European home, the magnificent Louis XIV country estate of Château Chambourg.

Secker was a small man dressed immaculately in a blue suit and a lightly patterned purple tie. He had worked closely with Buckingham for almost four years and was her most trusted lieutenant.

Buckingham drew on her cigar. 'I hope this is as urgent as you made it out to be on the phone, Hans. I have to be in Strasbourg in forty-five minutes.' Her voice was cut-glass Home Counties.

'I think it is, Glena,' he replied and leaned down to open his briefcase. He was one of only a handful of people in the world who called her by her Christian name. When he straightened, he had a small folder of papers in his hand. He passed it to her.

The top page was a photograph showing segments of a shipwreck. Buckingham recognized it immediately. '*Titanic*,' she said. 'It's been all over the news.'

'Officially, Marine Phenomenon REZ375 has been caused by some natural radiation leak.'

She shuffled through the papers and stopped, read a paragraph, lifted another photograph and studied it as she walked towards a massive window trailing cigar smoke behind her. Sunlight splashed onto the marble floor.

'The source is in the ship itself?' she exclaimed. 'And the radiation levels are rising.'

Secker was at her elbow, nodding slowly, a brief cynical smile playing across his lips. Buckingham turned and stared down at him.

'How can that be?'

'I don't know . . . yet. But I intend to find out.'

Glena Buckingham studied him without expression as she worked through the possibilities in her mind. 'It could still be a natural source.'

'It could; but, if you look here.' He gently turned a page and tapped the bottom paragraph. 'A precise sensor sweep from one of our satellites in geosynchronous orbit over the site has established that the source is not from the ocean floor or beneath it, but close to twenty-five yards above it, which puts it within the bowels of the wreck.'

Buckingham stared again at the papers. 'I can see why NATO have set up an exclusion zone . . . and why you have brought it to my attention, Hans. It could be a natural radiation source, but if it's not then it has to be an alternative energy source, which definitely presents us with an unacceptable threat. You've done well.'

Secker merely nodded.

'And NATO is basing the operation in Norfolk, Virginia? Do we have anyone there?'

'We do.'

'Good. Contact him right away.'

'No need. He has already called us. The navy has enlisted specialists. He's not sure what they are planning, but they are very keen to get to the root of what this is all about.'

'Of course they are. Give your contact free rein. I want updates as they come in, Hans. Got that? Also, get Sterling Van Lee onto it. He's our best . . .'

'I took the liberty . . .'

Buckingham nodded. 'Good.' She looked back down to the photograph of the *Titanic* lying broken in two on the floor of the Atlantic Ocean and drew on the fat cigar. 'Who could have imagined such a thing?' She handed the papers to Secker then strode across the room, through the hall and out onto the gravel driveway towards the waiting chopper.

5

NATO Exclusion Zone, 375 miles SE of Newfoundland. Present day.

NATO had deployed four surface warships to patrol the perimeter of the Exclusion Zone – two destroyers, the USS *Brooklyn* and USS *Toledo*, along with the Australian ship HMAS *Darwin* and a British aircraft carrier, HMS *Ipswich*. An AWACS Boeing E-3 Sentry patrolled the skies over the region and was in constant communication with HQs on both sides of the Atlantic. The Exclusion Zone itself was an area of twenty-seven square miles centred on the point above the wreck of the *Titanic*.

All vessels were operating under Extreme Radiation Risk status, which meant that no crew were allowed on deck unless they were wearing full radiation suits. The ocean was strewn with dead and decaying marine life ranging from a host of tiny minnows to larger fish, octopuses and plants. The stench was ferocious.

Only twenty-four hours had passed since Captain Derham had walked into Kate and Lou's lab, and now they were inside the Exclusion Zone aboard USS *Armstrong*, the mother ship for the *JV1* and *JV2* deep-ocean subs. The ship was a small, purpose-built vessel, with a crew of just twelve. Heavily shielded to protect it against high radiation levels, it was only lightly armed with two 5-inch/54 calibre mark 45 guns.

'These are the latest probe images just in,' Jerry Derham said. He, Kate and Lou were alone in the ready room of the *Armstrong*. There was a knock on the door and a woman wearing a naval commander's uniform stepped in. She had short auburn hair and a hard face. Kate and Lou had met her briefly at Norfolk Naval Base. Commander Jane Milford was the navy's number one *Jules Verne* submarine pilot and had put in over five hundred submersed hours in *JV1* and *JV2*. She had been in the Exclusion Zone for twenty-four hours before Derham, Lou and Kate had arrived, and she had already made a surveillance dive to the *Titanic* wreck in a conventional deep-ocean submersible.

'Sorry I'm late,' she said, 'last-minute checks on *JV1*.'

Derham looked up. 'Commander. Please, sit down. I was just showing these guys the latest probe images. The wreck looks kinda eerie, don't you think?'

'It does,' Kate said and flicked a glance at her colleague. 'I know Lou is a pretty hard-nosed pragmatist about it. I guess you're used to it too, commander.'

'I don't think you ever get used to it, doctor, especially seeing it in the flesh.'

Lou looked up from the large colour prints. 'The *Titanic* is different,' he said. 'Don't ask me why. It's not just the scale of it.'

'It's because the ship was meant to be unsinkable. It was a symbol of man's technological prowess and it was brought down by a chunk of ice,' Kate said. 'I mean, just look here.' She pointed to an opened book close to the prints. It was an annotated collection of photographs of the interior of the gigantic liner all taken by a photographer from the Illustrations Bureau a few days before the launch. The photo on the left-hand page showed one of the First Class lounges. It was so incredibly opulent – gorgeous cornicing, ornate brass lamps, sumptuous chesterfields. Then she sifted the prints from the probe and found the one she was after. 'If I'm not mistaken, this is the same room now.'

The image showed a shattered mockery of the first picture: the cornicing had crumbled, the beautiful hardwood floorboards were entirely gone, the furniture was now no more than a pile of nails and a collection of corroded steel truss rods. A piece of brass lamp lay in the centre of the room.

'Something like 6,000 artefacts have been removed from the wreck since its location was discovered in 1985, all retrieved by robot probes,' Derham said, unrolling a schematic of the ship's interior. 'The ocean floor is strewn with wreckage, but the source of the radiation is not there. It's definitely inside the ship. Commander Milford has been concentrating on narrowing down the precise location.'

'We now think the epicentre of the radiation source is situated towards the bow of the ship beyond the forward Grand Staircase, two floors down from the boat deck.' She pointed it out on the diagram. 'Our best bet is here – a First Class cabin, C16. We've tried, but we haven't been able to get a remote probe that far into the ship.'

'Isn't that a little worrying?' Kate said, still looking at the schematic.

'Why? You mean, if a probe can't get in there, how can we?' Milford asked.

'Precisely.'

'I appreciate your concerns,' Derham responded. 'But no probe is that manoeuvrable. Also, the radiation down there interferes with the signal we use to control them.'

'Most importantly, though,' Milford interrupted, 'there's no substitute for human eyes and ears. This is the whole reason we need you both. You are world authorities in the study of marine wrecks.'

Derham pointed to the print on the table. 'The latest images we have show the best way to get into the wreck is close to the port anchor . . . here.' He then found another close-up and a computer-enhanced image of the exterior. They could make out every dent and rivet. 'You can see here the displaced sediment rises up either side of the hull almost reaching the anchor. It'll be perilous, but we should be able to reach the boat deck using some of the holes and protrusions in the hull above the anchor. It's then a question of finding an entranceway into the ship and locating cabin C16. I can't reiterate too many times just how dangerous this trip is going to be. The ocean floor nearly two and a half miles beneath the surface is as inhospitable as deep space.'

'I don't think either of us is expecting it to be a walk in the park,' Kate remarked.

'You're certainly right there,' Milford said quietly, and she glanced round at the three of them with a very serious expression. 'And, there is one more thing you probably should know. The suits. We've just had the final tests conducted on three sets at Norfolk. The technicians have emailed over the results.'

'When was this?' Derham asked, suddenly concerned.

'Just five minutes ago, sir.'

'Is there a problem?'

'No,' Milford replied emphatically. 'No problem, but the final tests show that suit integrity can only be guaranteed for up to sixty-two minutes forty-four seconds.'

Kate looked grave. 'And what happens then?'

Milford shrugged. 'Maybe nothing. The suit might be fine for a long time after that.'

'But at some point?'

'At some point, the liquid metal carbon of the suit will reconfigure.'

'Reconfigure?' It was Lou. He gave Milford a hard look.

'It changes state . . . The suit becomes a solid block of carbon.'

6

An hour later they were pulling on thermal suits – the standard uniform while they were aboard the *JV*s where the temperature and pressure levels were computer-controlled. *Jules Verne 1* was ready to power up, the final systems checks almost completed.

The interior of the sub was extremely cramped and utilitarian. Four seats were set out in two pairs of two. The front left was the pilot's seat; next to that, the co-pilot. Two passenger seats had been squeezed into the restricted space in the second row. The designers had packed the craft with the latest communications and navigational technology. There were no windows. Instead, visual displays relayed images from a set of cameras mounted on the exterior of the sub. Two large control panels were in front of the pilot and co-pilot's chairs. All the controls were digital, touch-sensitive pads set into flat plastic.

'You guys didn't waste money on soft furnishings, did you?' Lou commented dryly as the four of them buckled up.

Behind the main cabin was the airlock. Through a

pair of doors lay a tiny changing room where the crew could don the LMC suits before leaving the sub. Once the integrity of the suits had been triple-checked, the submariners could enter the airlock, and from there emerge onto the ocean floor via a short ladder that extended from the side of the sub. When they were first shown how it all worked, Lou and Kate couldn't get over how similar it seemed to the famous *Apollo* lunar modules. And, as the commander had reminded them, the environment 12,600 feet down on the ocean floor was every bit as inhospitable as the lunar surface.

Final checks complete, the main door of the sub was closed and locked from the inside. Commander Milford told the bridge of the *Armstrong* they were ready. The ship's hold began to fill with water, the pressure was equalized and the outer door of the *Armstrong* began to slide open. They all felt *JV1* move forward, and they were in open water directly beneath the ship.

Lou and Kate had been on countless dives, but neither of them had gone deeper than a few hundred feet. This was going to be an entirely new experience and one any marine archaeologist would give their eye teeth to have. Little more than twenty-four hours ago, the very concept of actually walking around the *Titanic* would have been complete fantasy to them. They could still barely believe they were here now.

Milford kept an open-mic link with the ops control room of the *Armstrong*, sharing constantly updated telemetry figures and receiving instructions to alter course where necessary. Lou and Kate sat in silence, mulling over the task ahead of them.

Lou glanced at Kate, the outline of her features dark against the background of illuminated control panels and swathes of neon. He knew he could never grow tired of that profile. When they were splitting up as a couple there had been times when a part of him had wished he had never applied for the job with Kate's team. But then he had realized that it was better to have her as a friend than not have a relationship with her at all. In fact, for him that friendship was the most precious thing in the world.

On the screens they could all see the colours change very quickly, shifting from light blue to an inky, bubbling black. By the time they reached a depth of 300 feet, sunlight had been completely absorbed. The only source of illumination came from *JV1*'s powerful lights. At the depth of the *Titanic*, they knew the water would be absolutely black, blacker than interstellar space. To cope with this, the *JV*s were equipped with four 100-million candlepower lamps, which in tests piloted by Milford had been capable of lighting up large portions of the wreck.

In this region and for many miles around, the ocean was totally devoid of all life; everything had been wiped out by the radiation still leaking from the ship.

They quickly reached a comfortable cruising speed of twenty-five knots, and at 6,000 feet, they began to slow. Derham scanned the seabed with deep-ocean sonar. Images appeared on the monitors – a poorly defined shape about 6,500 feet beneath them. Milford pulled back the speed a little more and manoeuvred the sub to descend towards a point on the ocean floor about fifty yards north of the ship's bow. The final thousand feet of the descent used the inertia of the sub, and as they approached the wreck Milford applied a quick burst from a set of retro jets that slowed the machine so it could be brought down with minimum disruption.

It really is just like bringing the lunar module in close to the landing site at the Sea of Tranquillity, Kate found herself thinking as she watched the image change on one of the monitors.

Two hundred feet above the ocean floor Derham slowly brought up the lights, and on the screens the outline of the century-old shipwreck began to appear as though a mist was slipping away to reveal a hidden tangle of rusted iron and steel.

They had all seen films of the wreck, read the many books about it and the accounts of other submariners who had travelled there and launched robot probes, but seeing it first-hand was almost overwhelming. The wreck looked utterly surreal, and as they descended and the light beams picked out more details it felt as though they had been transported to a fantasy world. The sense of isolation so far beneath the surface was all consuming. Only Milford had gone so deep before. For Kate, Lou and Derham, this was a completely alien world.

The bow section of the *Titanic*, almost 500 feet in length and the height of a twelve-storey building, lay buried in the silt and sediment at an angle of about ten degrees. Lou knew from his reading that the bow and stern had separated as the two sections had sunk. The bow dived at about ten knots and followed a descent at an approximate angle of forty-five degrees, hitting the ocean floor with phenomenal force. Pushed from behind by 30,000 tons of ship, the prow had sliced into the ocean floor and scythed the seabed like a plane ploughing through a runway made of butter. Now the hull was buried in almost sixty feet of soil at the anchors, and part of the wreck some hundred feet back from the prow had fallen backwards, distorting the original shape even more. This once glorious expression of man's ingenuity looked like a dead animal.

Kate glanced round at Lou and was stunned to see a tear slide down his cheek. She quickly turned away and made much of studying the monitor in front of her.

'This is just . . . God, I don't have the words,' Derham said. He glanced round at Kate and then at Lou, who merely shook his head slowly, looking down.

The final hundred feet of the descent took almost five minutes as Milford used the sonar to find a spot close enough to the wreck but without disturbing it. They all felt the vehicle make contact with the ocean floor, and for a few minutes the monitors showed the silt and sand being kicked up. Milford and Derham manipulated the controls on the panels in front of them, keeping their eyes glued to the monitors. Then the sound of the engines quietened and stopped.

'I think this is the weirdest moment so far,' Kate said, her voice filled with a blend of terror and excitement. 'Listen to that.'

'What?'

'Precisely. There is no sound down here. No sound whatsoever, except for the noises we make, the noises the *JV* makes.'

They fell utterly silent, holding their breath. The only sounds were non-human ones – from the computers and the engines cooling, their metal casings contracting.

Then a buzz from Derham's control panel broke the spell. '*JV1*. Come in, *JV1*. What is your status?'

'*Armstrong*,' Derham responded. 'We are on the ocean floor. All systems seem to be functioning at optimum levels.' He glanced at Milford.

'All systems check A1,' the commander confirmed.

The sound of their voices was transmitted to the surface via a fibre optic. This was encased in a narrow sheathing made from carbon nanotubes. The entire 13,000 feet of cable weighed less than twenty pounds.

'Congratulations,' came the response from the bridge of the *Armstrong*.

'We plan to get prepped and outside as soon as possible, *Armstrong*.'

'Copy that, commander.'

'We'll make regular ten-minute call-ins, as planned. Out.'

Jerry Derham turned from the control panel. 'OK, guys,' he said. 'Let's go.'

*

It took more than half an hour to run the checks and get suited up. Lou, Kate and Derham stood in the stark white interior of the lock as Commander Jane Milford ran diagnostics from the control panels on the bridge. Everything checked out: integrity for each suit was one hundred per cent, communications were functioning correctly. A radio link could be maintained over distances of up to 300 yards thanks to another DARPA innovation – a wave booster that used ultra-short wavelength signals. This had been placed on the ocean floor by a remote-controlled probe a few hours before the *JV1* was launched. Milford checked on this from the bridge as the other three inspected the systems on their suits.

'OK, commander,' Derham said through the radio link to the bridge. He glanced at Lou and Kate and they each gave him the thumbs up. 'Suited up and ready to go.'

'Copy that, captain. Your systems check one hundred per cent.'

They synchronized chronometers.

'I'm limiting the time outside the sub to exactly fifty-five minutes,' Derham said. 'That's well within the test parameters of the suits and gives us seven minutes forty-four seconds' grace.'

'Agreed. I'm calibrating pressure,' Milford said. 'Helmet cameras have been switched to "auto". We'll be recording everything in triplicate and I'm patching it through to the *Armstrong*.'

A hissing sound started overhead in the airlock. Kate took Lou's besuited hand and squeezed. He couldn't feel it through the bizarre material of the suit, but he had seen her hand move downward and lift his. He looked into her eyes and knew she was feeling the same thing as he was. They were about to enter an utterly alien world, but they had each other. Smiling, Kate released her grip.

'It'll be the most amazing experience of your life,' Lou whispered through the comms.

The outer door slid open, and a moment later, they were stepping onto the ocean floor almost 13,000 feet below the surface of the Atlantic.

7

The great beams of *JV1* lit up the front of the *Titanic*, so they didn't need their helmet lights and could save the energy for when they were inside the wreck. The port leading edge was about fifty yards in front of them, and the bow section lay at an angle, the elaborate forestay pointing away slightly.

Stepping out onto the ocean floor was just as surreal as they had expected. No one had ever been here before. Bathyspheres had descended to release remote-controlled devices that explored the outside of the ship and sent back images, but no human had ever walked on this ocean floor.

'*JV1*. We're outside,' Derham reported back. Milford, he knew, would be able to see the same view as them from tiny cameras built into the front of each helmet and projected onto a set of monitors on the bridge. This, along with a voice feed, was transmitted via the fibre optic back up to the *Armstrong*. Derham then checked the suit parameters displayed on a small screen on his lower arm. Everything was as it should be. He turned to Lou and Kate. 'You guys OK?'

'Fine,' Kate replied. Lou nodded.

It took a few minutes for them to adjust to the suits and the weird experience of walking on the ocean floor. They had trained for three hours in a simulator before leaving the naval base, but as good as the simulator software had been, the real thing felt quite different. The suits were surprisingly easy to manoeuvre in, but they were hot and the noise from the internal generators and their cooling systems was louder than they had expected.

In the light from *JV1* they could see thousands of shells, crustaceans of all shapes and sizes.

'More corpses,' Kate commented through the comms.

As they approached the wreck, they heard a grinding sound, a grating of metal on metal. 'That's the hull creaking,' Kate said. 'We've disturbed the water and the shockwave has moved the corroded infrastructure.'

'What are the radiation levels?' Lou asked Derham.

The captain glanced down at his screen where a reading was displayed in the top right corner. 'Almost thirty times the level on the surface. A touch over two times ten to the twenty curies.'

'Lovely.'

Derham led the way. In his left hand he had a small sonar device which he used to sweep the surface directly ahead of them. One of the greatest dangers they faced was falling into a giant hole or a disguised crevasse. This gadget indicated how solid the ground was beneath their feet.

'The ocean floor is composed of very pure compacted

sand and silt,' Lou said. 'It's amazingly uniform and regular.'

'That's because the water is only a little above freezing point at this depth,' Kate commented. 'Just a few inches under our feet the sand and silt will be mixed with ice crystals.'

After five minutes they reached the base of the churned-up ocean floor heaped up against the sides of the hull like giant snowdrifts. On this side of the ship the sand and silt rose up almost to the anchor and it was packed solid, as hard as rock. Looking up, they could see the hull covered with rust, a blend of coloured oxides – greens, spots of orange and yellow, smudges of ochre.

'I can't get over how huge this thing is!' Lou exclaimed, looking up at the thousands of tons of rusted steel towering over them. 'The length of a large city block.'

'Yeah, and this is just two-thirds of the original vessel,' Kate replied.

Derham had started skirting the base of the sand pile that rose up against the hull. 'This part seems to be the most stable,' he said, coming back to join them and pointing to a region of the slope a few yards to their left. He twisted round and pulled a pack from his back, opened one of the compartments at the front and withdrew a palm-sized mini-harpoon. Pressing a button on the side, a spike appeared and slithered out six inches from the base. A release switch caused the end of the spike to open up, sending out four sharp hooks. He then took a step forward and aimed the harpoon at a point close to the anchor. The projectile shot through the water and into a hole in the hull, leaving behind an ultra-thin, but extremely strong carbon nanotube cable. He tugged on it and tested his weight. The hooks seemed to be jammed fast inside the opening in the hull. 'Right,' he said, 'I'll go first.'

Lou and Kate watched as the captain scrambled up the slope. He had tucked the mini sonar into his back-pack and pulled the bag back on. The sand and silt were indeed packed solid; his boots barely produced a trail or raised sediment as he climbed. Reaching the top, he spoke into his radio. 'Lou. You next.'

Lou took up position and followed the same course up the slope. He was neither as fit nor as strong as the naval officer and took a bit longer to reach the point just below the anchor where the slope levelled off against the side of the ship. Sixty seconds later, they were joined by Kate, who was panting a little over the radio link.

'How you feeling?' Derham asked.

They nodded. 'All right,' Lou said, a little breathless.

Derham pointed to the hull above the anchor. 'We'll need to pick our way up . . . but be careful.'

'We've been out for nearly eight minutes,' Lou commented.

'That's all right,' Derham replied. 'We're still finding our feet. OK, I'll lead, then you, Kate. But watch your step. If you slip and fall, it won't be the same as falling through air, but you can still injure yourself or, worse, you might damage the suit. Follow my foot and hand-holds.'

They watched Derham get a grip on a ledge on the outside of the hull.

There was no shortage of grips and holds to get fingers and toes into because the hull was covered with gaping, rusty punctures, smashed-in portholes, and uncovered recesses. The real difficulty was coping with the fragility of the structure.

The two researchers followed the captain, keeping to the same holds and support points. Derham reached the boat deck first, then Kate clambered up. She straightened and Lou's cry reverberated in their helmets. 'Aghh!'

Kate looked down and saw him clinging to the hull with one hand. His second foothold gave and he yelled again.

'Hang on!' Derham ordered. He took two steps back, found some new footholds, and pulled up parallel to Lou. Grasping his arm, he helped him to find a new footing. Then Lou swung an arm round to get a grip.

'My God!' he exclaimed. 'Thanks, man.'

'No problem. Take hold of that ledge there.' Derham pointed to a rim of metal about two feet above Lou's head. 'That's it. Good. Now there's a footing about eighteen inches above where you're standing. See it?'

He peered down. 'Yeah.'

'Get onto that, then that window ledge – see?'

He followed the instructions and got his waist level with the top of the hull, pulled himself up and forward and hauled his body onto the boat deck. Derham clambered back up after him.

'No time to waste,' Derham said, pointing towards

the stern. 'According to the robot probes, there should be a blown-out hatch over there, about thirty yards towards the stern.'

The deck was covered with sand and a slimy substance making it difficult to maintain purchase on the rusted metal. There were wires and cables strewn randomly around the deck, along with metal rings, raised hatch doors, severed posts and bits of metal debris that had landed on the deck. All of these things offered good handholds as they made their way towards the stern.

They found two blown hatches next to each other about three feet apart. Derham crouched down at the first one and shone the beam from his helmet light into the darkness of the interior. It illuminated slimy walls of steel. Thirty feet on lay the floor of a corridor. But there was no way down into the opening. At least one of the floors beneath the deck had collapsed inwards, leaving behind it a jagged shaft three decks deep.

Derham pulled himself up and paced over to the second opening. He could see a ladder connected to the wall just inside. His helmet light lit up the nearest rungs and showed that the ladder stretched downwards on the side of a shaft extending to a point two levels beneath the boat deck.

'Good!' he said, straightening and checking his watch. 'Looks like this shaft goes down to the second level beneath the boat deck, and it has a ladder.'

'C16 is on the second deck down, yes?' Kate asked.

'It is, and about two hundred and fifty feet that way.' Derham pointed towards the stern.

He keyed in a link to *JV1*. 'Commander?'

'Sir,' came Jane Milford's response.

'We are –' and he looked at his watch again '– sixteen minutes into the mission. We've reached a hatch that leads down into the interior of the ship. We're all fine. Suit integrity one hundred per cent.' He stopped and glanced at the other two. They nodded their acknowledgement. 'We're now about to proceed into the *Titanic*. I think comms may be a little intermittent once we're inside because of the steel and the radiation level, which –' he glanced at his screen '– is now thirty-two times the level on the surface.'

'Copy that, captain,' Milford replied. 'Good luck. Out.'

*

Their helmet lamps flicked on and illuminated a world of decrepitude and sadness, everything ruined, everything slowly dissolving away to nothing.

The ladder was secured to the inside of the ship's hull by at least a dozen bolts, but many of these had corroded and three of them had crumbled to powder. To make it worse, the metal rungs were also severely corroded and covered with slime. The ladder creaked horribly as they descended with Jerry taking the lead again and Lou at the back.

They all felt relieved when they reached the second level below the boat deck. The corridor they found themselves in was one of the service passageways. Turning left, the beams of their helmet lights lit up a pair of steel doors a dozen feet away. One of them had fallen off its upper hinge and was poised at an angle to the floor. The captain had the sonar in his hand and was scanning the floor. It produced an image of the topography of the ground directly ahead, its screen displaying the configuration of the floor in different colours. Red patches indicated holes, orange areas were fragile because the floor was no more than a fraction of an inch thick, while green areas marked the safest regions.

He stopped just short of the doors and pulled on the right-hand one. It opened slowly, the sloped bottom edge scraping on the metal floor of the corridor. Then suddenly, a few inches from his body, it dropped off the remaining hinge. He jumped and hit Kate with a glancing blow that knocked her off-balance. The door just missed the outer edge of Derham's suit and dropped through the water, bouncing and coming to rest.

'You OK?' the captain asked, spinning round quickly.

Kate had grabbed a rail to break her fall, but it had come away from the wall. She pulled herself up as Lou leaned down to help her.

'I'm fine,' she said.

They stepped through the opening into a wide passageway. Directly opposite, a fire-hose reel was hooked to the wall. A metal sign above it hung by one corner. It said: 'Emergency Use Only'.

This was one of the corridors linking First Class cabins. Seeing it now, it was almost impossible to imagine how it would have once appeared when some of the wealthiest and most celebrated people of the early twentieth century had walked this way.

The metal shell of the corridor was still there, but it had been horribly disfigured. There were a dozen doors, six to a side. A single chandelier remained suspended from the ceiling; another had crashed to the floor, a tangle of brass, a carpet of crystals and glass scattered on the rusted steel. A sumptuous red carpet had once run the length of the corridor. Now almost every strand and fibre had been consumed by microbes.

They headed towards the stern. Their helmet beams lit up a wasteland of tangled metal, buckled hull sections and caved-in door frames. Twisted and rusted furniture lay in the corridor – the frame of a deckchair, half a round steel table. In the middle of the corridor they found a pile of plates and cups and beside this a row of twenty or so bowls. They were almost completely untouched and gleaming white. Each item carried the White Star Line emblem – a red flag with a white star in the centre and the company name written on a folded banner beneath the flag.

Kate, Lou and Derham stood transfixed, silent, each trying to take in the immensity of the ruin. Lou crouched down and picked up one of the bowls, turning it in his hands. 'As perfect as the day it was manufactured,' he said, placing it back carefully.

'Where now?' Kate asked.

'According to the ship schematic, C16 should be just beyond the First Class Grand Staircase and one more level down. This way.' Derham turned to their left, his helmet light scouring the corridor ahead.

The passage curved away left then turned back on

itself. Thirty yards along, they came to a sharp right turn. Derham took two steps forward and stopped abruptly. The sonar device in his hand was beeping loudly in their helmet headsets. They looked down and saw that the floor had dropped away to nothing.

'Goddammit!' Derham exclaimed.

'Ah!' Lou commented.

'Yes, "ah". OK, back we go.' Derham glanced at his chronometer. They had been gone twenty-two minutes. He squeezed past Lou and Kate and took it slowly, concentrating on the sonar screen and watching the floor at the same time.

They retraced their steps back to the last junction and took a right. 'It's a longer way round, but it should take us back to a point beyond the chasm,' Derham said. 'If there's a problem with this route, it's over.'

This corridor seemed to be less severely corroded. The walls were streaked with green slime and the tears and rips in the metal were smaller. 'The wildlife is just getting tucked in here,' Kate observed. 'Give them a few years and it'll be as decayed as the last corridor.'

'Let's hope the critters haven't been too hungry,' Lou said.

Ahead, the corridor twisted to the left and then stretched straight for some sixty yards. It was strewn with a miscellany of objects. They saw a woman's hairbrush and a shattered mirror. Against the wall leaned a rusted grille – ornate swirls of brass and steel interlinking to form the shapes of flowers and birds. About halfway along they saw what they thought was a section of bulkhead that had been thrust out into the corridor, but as they drew close they realized it was actually a large metal box about two yards square attached to the wall by clamps. The lid was heavily corroded, and as they approached chunks of rust fell away. On the floor, they could see a few tiny fragments of rope, an axe head, the wood of the handle gone entirely. Next to this, a hose reel lay on its side. Some of it had been paid out and long sections had crumbled to dust.

'An emergency equipment station,' Kate remarked. 'This stuff must have fallen from the base of the box.'

Lou noticed a crumpled metal cylinder lying against the wall. 'A fire extinguisher,' he said, excitement in his voice. 'One of the classic copper ones. It was beautiful . . . once. It must have leaked and then the pressure crushed it.'

There came a crackling sound from the box on the wall. Its corroded bottom edge gave way, and with a rush a white object slithered out of the container, fell through the water and landed on the floor with a dull thud.

Kate was the closest to the object, realized what it was and screamed.

'Christ!' Lou hissed and took a step forward, saw what had fallen from the box, and recoiled.

On the floor lay a heap of bleached bones. The legs had broken at the knees, but the spine was largely intact. The skull lay on its side. They could see one hollow eye socket. The jaw lay slack where the lower joint had fragmented. They could just make out, around the neck of the skeleton, a silver chain and a crucifix.

Lou crouched down to get a closer look. 'This is amazing,' he said.

'How've the bones survived?' Kate asked.

The box must have been sealed and only recently corroded so badly the water got inside.'

'What were they doing in there, for God's sake?'

Lou stood up and shrugged his shoulders. 'No idea. Well, actually, one. They must have locked themselves in the box thinking they would be rescued.'

'But that's ridiculous!'

'People do ridiculous things in extreme peril,' Derham said.

'Where were you?' Lou said, half to himself as he stared at the figure of Christ on the silver cross.

They turned away and carried on along the corridor. The floor was surprisingly solid; some of the metal was clear of silt and slime. The corridor opened out and the walls fell away to reveal an astonishing sight. They had reached the remains of the Grand Staircase.

It looked like a cave, a gaping hole that fell into the abject darkness of the ship's interior. The roof was supported by eight steel columns. These were covered with rust. Great stalactites hung from the ceiling. The floor sloped perilously towards the massive hole where once the magnificent staircase had stood. The view up the staircase had been considered one of the most spectacular aboard the ship. Now, nothing was left but a dark, slime-covered pit.

They edged as close as they dared to the opening, the light from their helmets swallowed up entirely in the chasm that fell away at least thirty yards into darkness.

Looking up, Lou let out a whistle. The other two followed his gaze and they could see a vast crystal chandelier hanging directly over the centre of the hole. It was mangled and twisted and at least a third of the original crystal had broken away from the structure. It looked like a postmodern sculpture awaiting the day the microbes and simple chemistry would overwhelm the metal holding it aloft. On that day, it would plunge through the total darkness unobserved, unlamented and shatter into a thousand pieces deep in the belly of the ship.

'This way,' Derham said, breaking the reverie of the two scientists. They could see another wide corridor stretching away towards the stern. 'By my calculations, it's not too far along here,' he added. 'We need to find a way down one deck.'

Lou and Kate pulled themselves away from the remains of the stairwell. The captain weaved a route left then right to avoid frail sections of floor. About twenty yards along the passage, they found a doorway to the left. Derham scanned the area to check its integrity and then signalled the others to follow close behind.

Through a doorway so encrusted with rust it had shrunk to half its original width, they emerged into a much narrower corridor. This was once another service causeway running parallel to the main passage.

Directly ahead, they found exactly what they wanted – a metal ladder bolted to the wall and descending into an opening in the floor. They took it slowly.

'*JV1*,' Jerry Derham said into his radio. 'Come in.'

They could hear a fragmented voice, but the signal was so degraded they caught only a few words: 'Captain . . . lost comm . . .' And then static.

Derham turned to Lou and Kate. 'I think we're on our own for a while. He glanced at the screen on his sleeve. 'No wonder! Radiation levels have doubled again. Let's go.'

Two doors along on the left, they came level with a brass sign that said 'C15'. The '5' had broken free from its fitting and dangled down beneath the 'C1' like an 'S'. A few more paces and they reached C16. The door was missing but a steel beam two yards long lay diagonally across the opening.

'Fantastic!' Lou said.

Derham glanced at his chronometer. They had been away for twenty-five minutes. 'OK, let's get this sucker out the way. Gotta move fast.'

Lou and the captain leaned down and grabbed the base of the metal column. It shifted a few inches and snapped in two. Kate tumbled forward and the men jerked back. She rolled to her right as the sections of beam dropped down into the corridor, just missing Lou and Derham.

'Thank Christ everything moves through water one hell of a lot slower than it does through the air!' Lou exclaimed, picking himself up.

Kate and Derham moved to the doorway in a second.

It was an elegantly proportioned room but, like the rest of the ship, it was extremely hard to imagine how it looked a century ago. The porthole had been blown out. What had once offered a fantastic view of the ocean was now a ragged gash in the wall. The bed was still there – the frame of it at least; the mattress, pillows, blankets were all long gone; so too the other furniture.

Derham took the lead again, and checked the screen on his suit. 'Radiation levels are almost off the scale,' he said and pointed to a box on the floor. It was about six inches to a side and looked to be in remarkably good condition except for a tiny patch of corrosion at one corner. 'That is definitely the source,' Derham said. 'See where it has finally been breached? It survived for a hundred years, but the elements got to it in the end. The split looks less than a quarter of an inch long, but it's enough.'

Lou was right behind him. 'Unreal!' he exclaimed.

Derham didn't waste a second. From his backpack, he removed a small metal contraption – a spindly steel framework. He pushed a button on its base. 'We had no idea what to expect,' he said. 'But reasoned the source of the radiation was something pretty small – how else could it have been brought onto the ship in the first place?' He flicked a glance at the box. 'Thankfully, we were right.'

He leaned forward, opened the metal framework and slipped it over the box. Flicking a switch on the side, the ensemble started to glow red. 'This is another thing we have to thank the eggheads for,' he added, and tapped a button on the side of the device. 'A radiation containment frame. It's more than a million times more efficient than a lead container of the same size. It'll keep the radiation levels manageable until we can get it up to the *Armstrong* and then back ashore.'

'Another product of DARPA?' Kate asked.

Jerry nodded and noticed Lou poking around inside a metal framework – a rectangle about two feet high and eight long.

'I think this must be what's left of the wardrobe,' Lou said. 'There would have been timber panels and doors attached to this metal structure.' He shifted some debris with his gloved hand. 'Looks like there's another metal box.'

In the helmet beams they could all see a steel container the shape and size of a large attaché case. It had corroded along one edge.

'What is it?' Kate asked.

'Not sure. It says "EF" on the side.'

Derham glanced at his chronometer again. 'Gotta go, people.' He placed a hand on Lou's shoulder.

'Sure . . . I'm taking this back, though.'

The captain nodded and the three of them headed for the door.

8

University of Manchester, England. January 1912.

It was absolutely freezing in the lab, both day and night. As he prepared this, the fourteenth attempt at the experiment, Fortescue happened to notice the mercury had dipped to minus three degrees inside, and it was already nine o'clock. At that moment, with his long thin fingers numb as prosthetic digits and his thoughts hazy from sleep deprivation, he felt he could just give up and return to the experiments after a good rest at home. He pulled his scarf tight about his slender neck and rubbed his hands together in an effort to get the blood flowing again.

Leaning across a bench, Fortescue helped his boss, Ernest Rutherford, set up the final pieces of apparatus ready for the next test. The lab was a bit of a jumble, but it was a jumble he and Rutherford could navigate with consummate ease. To any outsider, it would have looked as though the large, high-ceilinged room was nothing but a dumping ground for a menagerie of equipment, but every machine, every wire, every truss rod and metal lever had its place and its purpose.

Fortescue and Rutherford had spent four months putting the apparatus together. A long wooden bench took up the centre of the room. Over this had been built a steel gantry which held much of the heavier equipment clasped in strong metal brackets. To vary the many parameters of the experiment, they could move the apparatus along rails built under the arches of the gantry.

By eleven o'clock, they were almost ready. Fortescue went off for a few minutes and came back with two cups of freshly brewed tea and the pair of them gave the equipment one final inspection. At one end of the bench stood a mahogany box about a foot square. On the front of the box was a circular metal plate some quarter of an inch thick. This was called the receptor plate. At the other end of the bench, on the far side of the room, thirty-five feet from the box, stood a device that lay at the heart of this complex array of apparatus – a neutron emitter. The design of this alone had taken them almost two years to complete, and Fortescue was very proud of it.

They made a good partnership. Rutherford was the senior one of the pair, acclaimed both within the scientific community and beyond; Fortescue, twelve years younger than the professor, but still not quite thirty, had already published three important papers and was widely regarded as one of the brightest of his generation, a man set for greatness.

The idea behind the experiment was for a stream of particles called neutrons to be fired at the box at the far end of the bench. The box contained an incredibly small quantity of a substance Rutherford had christened ibnium. It was what scientists called an unstable heavy element. The objective was to smash the neutrons into this minute fragment of ibnium, causing a tiny controlled explosion inside the mahogany box. Attached to the box were wires connected to a collection of special measuring instruments, each of which had been hand-made at the university workshops in the basement of this building. These instruments could measure the size of the tiny explosion, and from this data the scientists hoped to calculate the power of the process occurring when the neutrons hit the sample of ibnium.

'I think we're ready, sir,' Fortescue said after triple-checking a set of wires connected to one of the generators close to the neutron emitter.

'Well, we could go on checking until the cows come home, old chap,' Rutherford replied. 'But at some point we have to let this beauty do its stuff.' And he patted the top of the emitter – a curved sheet of steel stretching over a large cylinder half-buried beneath a tangle of wires and metal cables.

Fortescue walked over to the windows running along one side of the room and drew closed two pairs of heavy black curtains. Rutherford switched on a low-wattage lamp close to the control box. A rectangular glass screen stood in front of the control panel. It reached seven feet into the air and was five feet wide. The two men took up position behind it and Rutherford went through the complicated process of getting the generator to maximum power and achieving the correct voltage, which he measured on a rather temperamental voltmeter to one side of the main control box. The coils inside the neutron emitter started to hum as they warmed up. Vacuum tubes in the main unit under the curved steel panel glowed an intense white, creating a ghostly halo at one end of the twilit room.

'So, Egbert. Are you ready?'

'Yes, sir,' Fortescue replied.

'Righty-ho. On three. One . . . two . . . three.' And Rutherford pulled on a lever in the centre of the control panel.

For a second, nothing happened. Then, barely audible at first, the humming of the vacuum tubes increased in pitch and a buzzing sound started up within the emitter. Rutherford and Fortescue stared through the glass, rapt, each lost in their own world of hope and anxiety. Rutherford's right hand moved to a second lever and he pulled it back slowly. The humming and the buzzing grew suddenly louder.

'So far, so good,' Fortescue said and was just turning back to the experiment when an incredibly loud squeal burst from within the neutron emitter. A bright-orange beam of light shot across the room, making the air sizzle as it went. The intense stink of ozone reached their noses and stung their eyes. The beam hit the metal dish on the front of the receptor. There was a bright flash and the two men saw a fireball expand from the heart of the device then rapidly dissolve. The mahogany box exploded with a low-pitched thudding sound, sending shards of wood and metal around the room. A section of the receptor dish slammed into the screen protecting the physicists. It cracked the glass with a piercing snap of noise. Both men ducked involuntarily.

As the boom of the explosion died away, the emitter let out a squalling sound; the noise from the vacuum tubes ebbed to nothing and their white glow faded. Rutherford and Fortescue rose from where they had crouched under the control panel, each looking a little sheepish. The younger man ran a hand through his slick black hair and a smile broke across his face.

'Well, I say, sir,' he commented quietly. 'That was . . . well . . . really quite astonishing.'

9

London. 16 February 1912.

During the weekend, the mercury had risen. In London, it was not so bitterly cold as it had been in the Manchester lab where Fortescue and Rutherford had conducted their experiments. Indeed, as the hansom cab turned into Whitehall, the sun was high in a blue unclouded sky and the trees lining the street were free of frost for the first time in two months.

Rutherford was nervous. 'You have everything straight in your mind, Egbert?' he asked, turning in the seat to face his assistant.

'I hope so,' Fortescue responded with a grin. 'Bit late now if I haven't, sir.'

'I'm being serious, man!'

Fortescue nodded, his face straight. 'I could not be better prepared, professor.'

Rutherford turned at a noise from outside and peered through the glass. The grey stone buildings and black railings were sliding past, but then out of the corner of his eye he caught something quite extraordinary. Two women had handcuffed themselves to a line of railings close to the entrance to Downing

Street. In their free hands they held placards. One declared: *VOTES FOR WOMEN*; the other proclaimed: *WOMEN BRING ALL VOTERS INTO THE WORLD*. They were yelling something he could not make out.

'Good Lord!' Rutherford declared, unable to draw his eyes away from the spectacle.

'What is it?' Fortescue asked. Rutherford did not answer, just pointed towards the women. The younger man managed to catch a glimpse of a black dress and a crisp white blouse, then he saw a police officer walking briskly towards the protesters. The hansom turned right into Downing Street and the sounds of the suffragettes dwindled to nothing.

The cab stopped outside number 10 and the door on Rutherford's side was opened by a footman who escorted the two scientists up the steps, past the police officer on duty and through the black door into the hall.

The two visitors each carried a briefcase stuffed with documents and scientific papers. The footman guided them towards the sweeping staircase and led the way up. To their left hung portraits and photographs of the thirty-two prime ministers preceding the present incumbent dating all the way back to Robert Walpole.

They reached the first-floor landing. The footman stepped to one side of a door with a brass handle, bowed and swung the door inwards.

They were the last to arrive. The four men already in the room rose together and the Prime Minister, Herbert Asquith, came round a dark oak table dominating the centre of the room, his right hand extended.

Asquith had a warm, lean, intelligent face, slightly unruly

white hair and a piercing gaze. He escorted the new arrivals to the table and began his introductions.

'Gentlemen, I'm sure these men need no introduction, but good manners demand it of me.' Asquith indicated the man to the left of the three, a rounded-faced individual wreathed in blue smoke from a fat cigar. A chubby hand was stretched out towards them. Winston Churchill, First Lord of the Admiralty. Asquith then nodded to the middle man. 'This,' he said, 'is Mr Whitelaw Reid, the United States Ambassador to the Court of St James.' The American was elderly, a little stooped with a shock of pure white hair and a neatly trimmed beard. He gave the two scientists a curt nod and shook their hands. 'And here,' added Asquith, 'is someone you may have already met: Mr Thomas Edison, who has sailed over from New York to attend this meeting.'

Rutherford and Fortescue were a little taken aback.

'My goodness!' Rutherford exclaimed. 'No, we have not met, but this is indeed a great honour, sir . . .' He stepped forward and shook hands with the American inventor, who clasped the Englishman's shoulder and produced a broad smile.

'It is my pleasure, professor,' he said in his gruff Midwest accent. 'I have read much of your work.'

They all sat and the prime minister began the discussion. 'You will, of course, realize, gentlemen, that what is exchanged in this room will not go beyond these walls. We are here to ruminate on one of the most important military and social matters humankind has ever faced. I am no scientist; although I do not understand the technicalities, I do realize the import of what the esteemed gentlemen, Professor Rutherford and Dr Fortescue, have discovered.' He smiled briefly. 'Now, I suggest that the professor explains his findings, so that we are all *at least aware of his work from the horse's mouth as it were.'*

Rutherford cleared his throat and explained to the gentlemen their discovery of ibnium . . .

'. . . and when the isotope is split open,' he concluded, '. . . it forms two smaller atoms, or isotopes, and a certain, rather large amount of energy. I believe that it would be possible for a special team with enough funding and resources to use my technique to generate a form of energy that could improve upon our steam turbines presently in use and power industry far more efficiently and with hitherto unimagined potential.'

The room was quiet for a moment. Winston Churchill leaned back in his chair appraising Rutherford and Fortescue. 'Professor,' he said, 'you offer a picture of truly inspiring development, but have you considered other applications of this new science?'

'Well, of course, for every application to benefit mankind there would be an alternative use. The potential for this advance to be used militarily has not escaped us.'

Churchill nodded and took a puff on his cigar, staring at the scientists through the haze. 'It strikes me that your work has come to fruition at a particularly auspicious juncture.'

Asquith shifted in his seat. 'What my esteemed colleague means,' he said, 'is that war is brewing in Europe. You will, of course, be aware of the arms race between the Germans and the British Empire.'

'I read The Times,' Rutherford said flatly. 'But the fact is,' and he surveyed the gathering, 'my work is nowhere near complete. When I offered you a way to greatly enhance industry, productivity and eventually the wealth of the nation with this

potential power source I was talking about a long-term commitment. I don't imagine this form of energy – what we call "atomic energy" – would be practicable for many years.'

'Professor,' Edison said, 'may I ask how far you have got with your experiments?'

Rutherford indicated that Fortescue should speak.

The younger man glanced round at the five men and cleared his throat, his bristly moustache twitching involuntarily. 'Our first conclusive result was achieved last month, in early January,' he said. He glanced at his papers. 'Since then we have repeated the experiment thirty-four times. Our average energy production is 40,185 joules from one hundredth of a gram of ibnium.'

The ambassador turned to his compatriot. 'Could you translate please, Mr Edison?'

The American scientist was startled and staring sceptically at Fortescue. 'Well,' he said after a moment, 'if these figures are to be believed, then this material has an explosive power in excess of ten thousand times the power of TNT.'

'We still have a great deal of analysis to do on these experiments,' Fortescue insisted and glanced at his boss.

'We have merely scratched the surface,' Rutherford added.

'And what is your set-up in Manchester, professor?' Edison asked. 'How many in your team? Are you funded privately?'

Rutherford allowed a smile. 'Our "team" sit before you,' he said. 'And as for private funding, that is a completely alien concept to us, sir. My research is financed solely by the University of Manchester.'

Edison raised an eyebrow and glanced first at the prime minister then at the other two men seated opposite the British scientists.

'I thought this was the crux of the reason for this meeting,' Rutherford added and turned to Asquith. 'My understanding, Mr Prime Minster, was that the government was interested in establishing a team to exploit the potential of my work, to produce a powerful new source of energy for industry.'

Asquith nodded. 'Yes, but whatever you read in The Times, professor, it is in reality a mellowing of the facts. Things in Europe are in a much worse state than many would admit. The Germans are gearing up for war, and so must we.'

'Because of this,' Churchill interrupted, 'the prime minster and myself have already concluded that the direction of your research into this amazing new science must be guided by defence principles. It must be studied as a potential weapon first, and as an enhancer of our industrial power second.'

'I see,' Rutherford commented without the slightest conviction. 'I must say,' he stated as he glanced at a nonplussed Fortescue, 'and I think I also speak for my colleague here, you have taken us completely by surprise. This would explain the presence here today of Mr Edison and the honourable ambassador.'

Asquith nodded. 'Indeed, professor. My government has decided that we should put all possible resources into the development of a weapon based on your work. We have also concluded that we do not have a second to waste.'

'But my work is still at a very early stage,' Rutherford protested.

'That may be so,' Asquith replied, but the theoretical grounding is there and you have achieved, I think I'm right in saying, quite remarkable practical results.' He held the scientist's eyes, challenging him to deny his own accomplishments.

'That is true,' Rutherford acknowledged, 'but . . .' For a second he looked a little out of his depth.

Fortescue filled the breach. 'Mr Prime Minister,' he said with an authority that surprised them all. 'One aspect of the work you may not be aware of is that it is extremely hazardous.'

Asquith considered the scientist. He nodded slowly. 'Explain.'

'As Professor Rutherford described, the power unleashed by ibnium provides a form of energy in excess of ten thousand times the equivalent release from TNT. However, in order to produce an effective weapon, researchers would need to handle much larger quantities of the material than we have done. They would need to find a source of ibnium, purify it and then manage to handle it safely.'

'The young man is probably quite correct,' Thomas Edison interrupted. 'The potential of such a device works both ways. The damage it may inflict on an enemy could also destroy those creating it!'

'We have considered this,' Asquith replied and looked around the table. 'Not withstanding the potential dangers, we plan to construct a fully functioning, adequately funded top secret research facility at the earliest possible date.'

'And, I assume,' Ambassador Whitelaw Reid said, 'you would want my government to help with the financing of the project?'

Asquith nodded to Churchill, who spoke with his cigar clamped to the side of his mouth. 'Actually, Whitelaw, we wanted a little more than that.'

The room was incredibly still. From outside, the sounds of

the main road barely filtered through the windows. A carriage drawn by a single horse passed along Downing Street, hooves clip-clopping on the cobbles.

Churchill leaned forward and eviscerated the remains of his cigar in an ashtray in front of him on the oak conference table. 'You're not going to like it, Mr Ambassador, but we request that the United States government agrees to host the site for the development of the weapon.'

'What! Are you quite . . .?'

Churchill had a hand up. He did not even glance at his superior, the prime minister. 'I did say you wouldn't like it, old chap.'

'Too damn right, I don't, and you honestly think the boss will go for it?'

'I rather imagine that when he is furnished with all the facts and all the consequences, President Taft will understand and offer his support.'

'So, let's get this straight,' said Reid. 'The British government wants to build a bomb-making plant in America. And it is not just any old bomb-making plant but a research centre to create a device with unimaginable power that could explode as it is being made, causing – presumably – massive devastation.'

Churchill afforded Asquith a glance, then said. 'Well, yes, Whitelaw, that just about sums it up.'

'You're out of your mind, man!'

'Gentlemen, gentlemen!' Asquith interceded. 'We need only look at a map to see the logic behind the suggestion. Which other country is such a close friend of ours and able to offer wide open spaces far from any habitation, great technical knowledge and the richness of resources we will need from a partner?'

Reid held the prime minister's gaze, unblinking. 'And you with your vast empire!' He shook his head.

Asquith gave the ambassador a wan smile, then turned to Rutherford and Fortescue. 'Gentlemen, what, in your opinion, would be needed in terms of infrastructure and resources?'

Rutherford was taken aback. 'Well, I can only offer an answer based upon what we were invited here today to discuss,' he replied pointedly. 'However, I was working on the assumption of a team of perhaps twenty researchers, a capital investment of around 100,000 pounds, and a five- to ten-year plan to develop a fully functioning industrial energy base that would transform manufacture.'

'Sounds about right to me,' Edison offered.

'But, of course, I had no idea you were thinking in the way you have described,' Rutherford went on. 'I assumed this research would be conducted here in England where we have scientists, electricity, laboratory equipment and other resources.'

'We will need to move far quicker than this and with a team and a budget at least ten times the size you suggest. America can provide all we need – power, isolation, expertise, materials,' Asquith asserted. 'Where does one obtain raw ibnium?'

'It is extracted in minute amounts with tin and dumped as waste by a small British concern . . . Imperial Mines in the Congo. It is extremely rare.'

'Very well. So it can be shipped across the Atlantic.'

'Now hold on!' Reid exclaimed, barely able to contain himself. 'I really cannot believe you are serious!'

'Have you not considered anything but the negatives?' Churchill said, turning in his chair to face the American.

'You've not been terribly effusive over the positives, Winston!'

Churchill grinned and waved a hand towards the prime minister.

Asquith ran a hand through his hair then interlinked his fingers on the table in front of him. 'Mr Ambassador, the knowledge this achievement will provide will be used to transform industry. Now, Whitelaw, are you telling me that the United States government would not like a piece of that?'

Perhaps for the first time in his life Whitelaw Reid was lost for words. He turned to his adviser, Thomas Edison, who had grasped the concept immediately and visualized the enormity of the potential profits involved.

'You want my personal opinion, Mr Ambassador?' he asked.

'Yes, I do.'

'Well, then, I think,' the inventor said slowly, deliberately, 'that we should grab this marvellous opportunity to become partners with our British friends with both hands.'

'Well said, sir,' Churchill commented.

Reid looked pale, but as the concept began to filter through his mind, the gradual realization of what was being proposed was almost visible in his lined face. 'I will speak to the president,' he said.

10

Institute of Marine Studies, Hampton, Virginia.
Present day.

Kate and Lou's lab in Virginia had been closed up for three months while they were in Bermuda, but a team of technicians had cleaned it and checked it over while the pair were on USS *Armstrong*.

Walking into the lab that morning felt odd. The place was much as they had left it but this facility was so different from the lab they had used while studying artefacts brought up from the wreck of the *Lavender*.

The isotope from the *Titanic* had gone straight to Norfolk Naval Base a few miles from the institute, but they had been given exclusive access to the other container Lou had retrieved.

Freezing rain beat in a steady rhythm against the lab window.

'Almost makes me wish we were still in the insect-ridden lab on Bermuda,' Lou commented as he turned from the rain-streaked window and looked over to where Kate was operating the controls of a pair of automated arms on the other side of a glass partition. 'At least the rain was warm there.'

She said nothing, lost in concentration.

Inside the radiation-proof chamber the atmosphere was almost pure nitrogen, inert and kept at a low pressure to ensure the preservation of whatever may lie inside the metal box. She had opened it to reveal a partially rotted leather briefcase.

The chamber was a standard piece of equipment for handling delicate fragments of ancient materials. The bag under the scope was relatively modern – a little over one hundred years old – but it came from the most famous wreck in history and it might just hold the secret to what the mysterious 'EF' was doing with a deadly radioactive isotope on the long-lost ship in the first place.

Guiding the robot arms and using the pincers to open the case and extract the contents was a slow and tricky business, but Kate was a veteran. Lou watched as she unclasped the latch, pulled up the flap and dipped the pincers inside.

The first thing to emerge was a sheaf of papers covered with dust. She placed it on the flat surface inside the chamber, then tilted the briefcase. There was only one other object inside. A single sheet of folded paper covered with illegible words and symbols.

She picked it up and placed it next to the pile of papers. Then, removing her hands from the controls of the robot arms, she tapped at a panel to her left. On the other side of the chamber Lou was seated at a control module. He ran his hands over a keyboard and a rectangular plastic box about a foot in diameter scooted across the inside of the chamber's roof. It moved down to a position a few inches above the papers.

As Kate set up the pages, Lou adjusted the controls and with a click of a mouse he took a photograph of each one. After they had gone through the total of twenty-two sheets, Kate slid the single separate piece of paper carrying the encoded line of text under the camera's crosshairs and Lou ran off another shot. Ten minutes later, they had finished and were seated at a table on the other side of the lab with hard copies of all the pages laid out before them.

Lou picked up a few and stared at the writing. 'What do you make of it?' He handed them to Kate and plucked the single sheet of notepaper with the line of code from near the bottom of the pile.

'Formulae. Maths was never my strong suit.'

'Nor mine.'

Lou held up a photocopy of the sheet that had been in the bottom of the briefcase. It contained a single line of numbers and letters quite different from the writing in the main sheaf.

'Looks like a coded message.'

'It's not mathematical, nor is it English.' He put it to one side. 'Pages of formulae kinda make sense. The owner, EF, must have been a scientist. Why else would he be on the *Titanic* with a radioactive substance?'

Kate was staring at the pages of symbols and equations, trying in vain to work it out. To find anything even vaguely comprehensible.

Lou's computer buzzed – a Skype video call. He swivelled in his chair and scooted it across the floor, stopping at his terminal and tapping his keyboard. 'Jerry . . . What's happenin'?' he said.

'Anything interesting?' Derham asked.

'Impossible to tell yet,' Lou replied. 'We were just looking at some papers from the briefcase inside the box we found – a collection of pages of formulae and a single sheet of fragile notepaper. We copied them in the inert gas chamber. The math in the formulae is indecipherable.'

'And the single sheet?' Derham leaned back in his chair and ran a big hand over his crew cut.

'Some sort of brief encrypted message or statement by the look of it. Hard to tell and impossible to translate without careful analysis from an expert.'

'OK, look, you'd better get over here. I have some people who can get on to it. Coffees are on me.' Derham clicked off.

*

They met up in the captain's office at the naval base ten miles north of the lab. They had been given security clearance and passes as soon as they had returned from the Exclusion Zone the day before. Derham stared at the collection of papers as Kate and Lou pulled chairs up to the far side of his desk. He had a surprisingly small office – racks of shelves along one wall; a large painting of the USS *Minerva*, an aircraft carrier he had served on, dominating a wall at a right angle to the shelves. Behind him, a window opened out to a view of the naval yard, cranes and gunmetal hulls in the distance.

He punched a button on his phone. It rang and a man answered. They heard him over the speaker. The guy sounded very young.

'Kevin. Got a job for you,' Derham said. 'Can you drop by?'

'Sure.'

The office door opened and the captain's secretary came in with two mugs of coffee.

'I did promise,' Derham said without looking up from the papers. 'Kevin Grant's one of our boffins. Works a few doors down.' He nodded towards the corridor. 'Encryption specialist. Away with the fairies most of the time, but a genius when it comes to encryption.'

There was a tap at the door and a young man appeared around the edge. He had cropped hair, big brown eyes, a large nose and acne. He looked like he was barely out of his teens.

Lou took a gulp of coffee, stood and offered the kid his chair.

'It's cool,' Kevin Grant said.

'Kevin. What do you make of this?' Derham handed him the single sheet from EF's box. 'By the way, this is Dr Kate Wetherall and Dr Lou Bates.'

Grant gave them a brief nod, barely lifting his eyes

from the paper. Kate and Lou watched as he scanned the encoded message.

'Clever shit,' he muttered.

'Sure you don't want to sit down?' Lou asked.

'Yeah, actually I will,' Kevin Grant said and lowered himself into the seat as Lou stood to one side cradling his coffee.

'It's a short message,' Derham commented. 'Should that make it easier?'

'The opposite, actually,' Grant replied, barely paying the commander any attention. 'The shorter the message, the less I have to go on to find the key. And . . .'

'And?'

'The dude who put this little baby together created such a convoluted key. It's . . .'

'You can crack it, though, right?' Kate commented.

Grant looked at her as though she were mad. 'Of course I can crack it. Might just take a bit of time, is all.'

'I can keep this, yeah?' Grant asked Derham.

The captain nodded. 'But don't flash it around.'

'What? You reckon anyone one else will be able to decipher this? No friggin' chance . . . sir.'

'Confident guy,' Lou said, returning to his seat as the kid left.

'Has every reason to be. If anyone can make sense of any code known to man, he's the one to do it. Never seen him beat yet.'

'OK,' Kate said. 'So the rest of the papers?'

'That takes a different set of skills. Come with me.'

*

Professor Max Newman, the chief scientist at the naval station, worked in a state-of-the-art facility that was all pristine metal benches and halogen lighting. Rows of slender plastic machines lined one wall, their function a mystery to all but the initiated; flat screens displayed dancing numbers and geometric shapes.

The lab was empty and Newman evidently about to leave. He was clasping shut his briefcase as Jerry Derham tapped on the door.

'Got a moment, professor?' Derham asked.

'I was about to head off, actually,' Newman replied.

He was a tall, slender man. Bald, his forehead deeply lined, he possessed an air of carefully nurtured self-containment. He headed up his department efficiently but, according to reports, clinically. He could not claim to have any friends here at the base or indeed elsewhere. He looked tired and self-absorbed.

'Just wanted a quick word. Can you spare five minutes?'

Newman checked his watch and nodded. 'Sure.'

Derham introduced Lou and Kate.

'Ah, yes, working on the *Titanic* material. Pleased to meet you.' He shook their hands. 'Too cramped in here. Let's go outside.' He led the way to a bench and they drew up stools.

'We've got some papers we'd like you to take a look at,' Derham began.

'From the *Titanic*, I assume?'

The captain laid out the collection of photocopies on the shiny metal surface of the bench. Newman pulled on a pair of glasses and picked up the top few sheets. It was quiet in the room, nothing more than a low hum from the machines and computers close by. From beyond the lab they could just discern voices, shoes on concrete floors, a lift door swishing open, then closing.

'It's a complete mess,' Newman said after a moment, picking up a second set of sheets. He scanned them then laid them back down and started to mumble to himself as he repeated the process with the rest. Finally, he tossed the last page on the bench, pulled off his glasses and looked up. 'Utter nonsense . . . Means nothing.'

'What!' Kate exclaimed and turned to Lou.

'These were taken from the wreck?' Newman asked, as though Kate had not spoken.

'Yes, but the details are classified at the moment, professor,' Derham replied.

Newman sniffed. 'Well, God knows why, it's a crock. Written by a lunatic or a child, I'd guess!'

'All of it?' Lou asked, studying Newman's face.

Newman put his glasses back on. 'Well, the math itself is standard – most of it. This section –' and Newman indicated the first three pages '– is a set of equations describing radioactive decay. Nothing odd about that. But here –' and he tapped a fingertip on one of the sheets '– it goes off at a ridiculous tangent.'

'What do you mean?'

'To be honest, I'm not sure. As I said, a lot of it is nonsense.'

'Explain,' Derham said.

Newman shrugged. 'Whoever wrote this knew some physics, but they . . . well, they seem to have had something of an overactive imagination. They make ridiculous, nonsensical leaps from a simple, acceptable premise . . . like here.' Newman pointed to the top page again. 'Straightforward, undergraduate math . . . until bang!' He pulled up the third page and then the fourth. 'Take this –' he nodded to a photocopy of densely packed formulae '– might as well be Venusian!'

'Does it pick up?' Kate asked, eyeing the scientist suspiciously.

Newman moved some of the papers to one side and clutched up a handful of the remainder. He glanced through them, adding page after page to a growing pile on the bench. Pausing, he considered one sheet. 'Here, he's gone back to some form of simple logic,' Newman commented. 'But then, Good Lord! Here . . . he's off again. Look at this . . . it's nuts!'

He placed the remaining copies on the pile, slipped off his glasses again, rubbed his eyes and looked at the three visitors. 'Sorry to disappoint.'

*

'I don't trust him,' Kate said matter-of-factly as they walked along the corridor away from the lab.

Derham gave her a surprised look. 'Why? The guy knows what he's talking about.'

'I agree with Kate,' Lou said. 'Don't believe a word of it.'

They stepped into the lift.

'Why? Why would Newman lie?'

'No idea. Well, maybe one,' Kate began. 'Perhaps he just didn't want to look stupid . . . but he is lying. We shouldn't have left the papers with him.'

Derham raised an eyebrow. 'What? So you're telling me the chief scientist of the largest naval base in the United States, Professor Max Newman – who has a very high-level security clearance indeed – is a liar and may also be grossly incompetent?'

'I guess she is,' Lou remarked.

Derham started to answer, but just shook his head.

'I'd like a second opinion,' Kate said.

'Oh would you now? Our chief scientist doesn't meet your spec?' Derham retorted.

They left the lift and walked along the corridor that led back to the captain's office. There was an uncomfortable silence between them.

'Look,' I didn't mean to insult your precious—' Kate began as they sat down, the door closing behind Derham.

He held up a hand. 'It's OK, you're entitled to your opinion.'

'Those papers are too important to ignore,' Lou began.

'I realize that. I had no intention of ignoring them.' Derham frowned at Lou. 'I've got nothing against a second opinion. Newman's a good man, but he's not the oracle of all knowledge. I know some people at

MIT. They'll have to be security-screened first and the material will have to be divided up between at least two groups who are not in communication with each other or aware they are working on linked papers . . . You still don't look happy!'

Kate held Derham's eyes. 'By all means, get your contacts to go through them, but I would also like to try someone I know.'

'They'll have to be cleared.'

'That won't be necessary. He already has one of the highest clearances possible from the work he has done for the Pentagon.'

'Who?'

'It's Professor Campion.'

Derham was stunned for a moment. 'You know George Campion? *The* George Campion?'

Kate felt Lou's eyes on her. She nodded. 'He's my godfather.'

11

Professor Max Newman placed his briefcase on the passenger seat of his white Ford Taurus and sent a text: 'Significant discovery. Would like to share.' Then he pulled out of the car park, swung the car round and out onto the carriageway leading to the security post and the exit of Norfolk Naval Base.

The clock on the dash told him it was almost six thirty. He felt hungry and tired, but fired up with barely controllable excitement. He had known within minutes of seeing the papers Derham and the other two had shown him that he had been offered the greatest opportunity to make a fortune he would ever have. He had also recognized the author of the document. It had to have been composed by a man he had admired since he was a schoolboy – Egbert Fortescue, the exceptionally talented British scientist who had died tragically young, before he could join the elite club that included Einstein, the Curies and Niels Bohr.

Out on Admiral Taussig Boulevard, Newman accelerated away and took a right. There he connected with his in-car Bluetooth and pushed a speed dial number. 'I have it,' he said simply.

'Meeting point Beta, half an hour,' said a voice at the other end of the line and hung up.

*

Professor Newman parked on East Ocean View Avenue, Norfolk, clicked the remote to lock the car and headed into the brisk wind blowing off the Atlantic Ocean.

Down a side street the view opened onto an expanse of blue-grey water tipped by breakers, white in the moonlight. Newman turned right, crossed a narrow road and stepped onto the beach. Looking behind, he could see a line of impressive waterfront homes, many of them dating back to the 1930s. Most were gabled and painted in bright nautical colours; a few had picket fences and white, freshly painted wooden gates. There was no one about and except for the waves foaming over the sand it was almost totally silent.

A short jetty stood about a hundred yards away along the beach. The professor knew it from previous visits in daylight. It was an old and neglected relic projecting out a dozen yards into the frothy ocean, the water beating about its corroding struts. Where it left the land there was a raised concrete platform a few feet above the sand. Newman strode towards it, ducking as he reached the iron platform and crouching under a wooden beam. The jetty stretched overhead with enough headroom for him to stand comfortably. He sat and waited.

'A cold evening,' a man's voice came from the blackness.

Professor Newman started to get up, but the man put a hand on the physicist's arm. 'It's OK.'

Newman unclasped his briefcase and extracted a narrow blue plastic file.

'You implied in your message that this was something pretty important,' said the new arrival who stood quite still.

'And it is,' Newman replied indignantly. He had met this man, Sterling Van Lee, on a couple of occasions and had taken an instant disliking to him. 'This –' and Newman waved the folder in front of him '– could be one of the most important discoveries in a century.'

Van Lee said nothing, just looked into Newman's face. Their eyes had adjusted to the gloom under the jetty and they could make out each other's features. He took the folder and opened it.

'A copy of the original documents written by Egbert Fortescue.'

'Who?'

Newman closed his eyes for a moment. He was a man who had dedicated his life to learning, a man who had sacrificed love, family and money to reach the pinnacle of his chosen field of study – nuclear interactions in radioactive sources. He hated ignorant people. 'Egbert Fortescue was one of the greatest physicists who ever lived,' Newman explained. 'He worked with Ernest Rutherford on an early nuclear theory. In fact, he was the real genius behind it.'

Van Lee continued to stare at him, expressionless.

'Within these pages,' Newman went on, 'Fortescue

describes an alternative form of nuclear energy, a way to enhance the power of the atom which is completely novel and totally different to the methods developed two decades after his death and which led to the creation of the atomic bomb.'

'And you can prove this?'

'I'm almost there. I've only had these documents for a couple of hours.'

Newman eased himself up from the concrete ledge. Van Lee turned and walked out in front of him onto the beach carrying the file.

'Contact me in the usual way if you need any guidance . . .' the professor called after him.

'Sorry?'

Newman started to speak again, then saw the gun Van Lee had drawn, its barrel very black in the darkness.

'Do you really think I can just let you go?'

'You're going to kill me?'

Van Lee laughed and handed back the file containing Fortescue's work. 'Now why would I kill one of our most valuable assets, professor? Your brain is much more useful to us in one very clever piece.'

12

One hour later.

Newman found himself in a comfortable room on the top floor of one of the waterfront houses. It had a large window with an expansive view over the wintery waters of the Atlantic Ocean, and it was warm and quiet. In spite of the fact that Newman seriously resented being kept a prisoner here, he realized he could do little but to acquiesce.

They had taken a short drive to the house and were met at the door by one of Van Lee's buddies, a short, flabby man with a shaved head and wearing a black suit and black tie. He had come to the door with a gun in his right hand.

'So what do you expect from me?' Newman asked the men after he had been led to the room at the top of the house.

'You're a physicist, right? Top nerd at the base? We expect you to translate this gibberish into something even my friend here could understand,' Van Lee said, flicking his colleague a humourless smile. The two men made an odd couple. Van Lee was almost the complete physical opposite of his associate: tall, very fit, square-jawed and tanned.

'Just made some soup,' the flabby guy said. 'You want some?'

Newman sighed. 'I guess.'

Van Lee pointed to the professor's briefcase. 'May I?' he said, his hand extended. It was, of course, a rhetorical question.

'Just my laptop, work papers.'

Van Lee plucked Newman's cell phone from the bag, pocketed it and handed back the briefcase.

After that they left him to his own devices. There was a Mac on a desk; next to that a scanner/printer. Professor Newman placed his bag beside the computer and pulled out his laptop, opening the lid. He then placed the blue plastic folder of photocopied notes from EF's box on the other side of the Mac.

It was no ordinary laptop. It was fitted with a modem, scrambler and long-range transmitter coded into a satellite link. Newman tapped a couple of keys and watched as the screen changed.

There was a rap at the door. Newman closed the laptop and turned to the Mac keyboard as the door opened and the flabby guy came in with a tray. He put it on a low table in the middle of the room a few yards behind Newman.

The professor spun round. 'I really don't know what you people want from me,' he said.

The guy shrugged.

'What's your name?'

'Jimmy.'

'Jimmy . . . I only just got this document today.' Newman picked up the slim file.

He shrugged again. 'Ain't nothing to do with me. I'd eat your soup, man. Reckon you're in for a long night!'

Newman watched the door close, ignored the soup and quickly turned back to the laptop. He had to get his message out fast if he was to evade Van Lee. The machine had found the satellite and was online. He tapped at the keyboard. The word 'Crosshair' appeared. It was his password of the day.

Nothing happened for twenty seconds. Then a brief message appeared – 'Betty Grable.'

The exchange was enough to trigger an encoder program using an algorithm that changed every twenty hours. It meant Newman could write his message in English. It would then be scrambled and transported via satellite to its destination: a nuclear submarine in the mid-Atlantic. There, it would be decrypted and translated into Chinese and forwarded to Beijing.

He wrote: 'Crucial discovery concerning NATO designation REZ375. Have copies of documents taken from wreck of *Titanic* that describe alternative nuclear energy process. May hold many other valuable secrets. Other parties very interested. Please make your bid.'

He stared at the screen for a few minutes listening to the waves breaking on the sand. A gull landed on the window ledge, its head swivelling to get a good look inside the room. It pecked at the brickwork and flew off.

A message appeared on the screen: 'Authorized to offer $2 million. $250,000 now, the rest upon delivery of interpretation of document and satisfaction with its value.'

Newman ran a hand through his hair. 'I assume you are attempting a joke,' he typed in reply. '$10 million. Fifty per cent in my Swiss account by –' he glanced at his watch '– 9 p.m. EST today. The remainder on acceptance of interpretation.'

There was a much longer silence. Newman pulled himself up from the desk, picked up the bowl from the table in the middle of the room and started to eat the soup as he gazed out at the ocean swelling and shifting in the darkness.

A low bleep came from the laptop. A new message. He walked over and read the response, feeling a stab of disappointment before turning towards the Mac and Fortescue's calculations. He would let the Chinese stew for a while before giving his final offer to them.

He scanned in the pages and created a password-protected file on the Mac, opened the first page and started to study the equations. There was another bleep from the laptop. The same message resent. Newman smiled to himself. 'Getting antsy, are we, guys?' he said aloud, and with remarkable self-control, he turned back to the Mac.

He gave it ten minutes, during which he was able to delve head-first into Fortescue's handwritten equations from over a century ago. Then he broke away and tapped a new message into the laptop: '$5 million – same terms as my previous offer. This is my last.'

He had barely returned to the desktop Mac when a reply came through. A single word: 'Agreed.'

13

Max Newman had always had a natural empathy with mathematics. A prodigy who had entered Yale at the age of fifteen, he obtained his degree in a year and a PhD by the age of eighteen – just as most kids were starting undergraduate courses. It was both a gift and a curse – he had always known that. He had lived and breathed mathematics to the exclusion of all else. He had no friends, no lovers, he could barely hold a conversation with his parents. Aged nineteen, he had been diagnosed with Asperger's; no one who knew him was in the slightest bit surprised.

He had gravitated towards the US Navy because he had become interested in nuclear physics and it offered him the best opportunity to research at his own pace. And Professor Newman was ambitious. Not in any normal sense. He wanted money, but not to spend on Lamborghinis and loose women. He wanted to establish his own research facility, to explore his more cutting-edge ideas without some admiral breathing down his neck.

Which was why he had agreed to spy for the Chinese

and why, when he saw the documents that had been recovered from the famous wreck of the *Titanic* and flown straight to Norfolk Naval Base, he knew he had hit pay dirt. But he also knew the Chinese were not the only people interested in this find and he had already established nefarious links with others along the way.

Sitting in this room, for all its pretty vistas and comfy furniture, he was beginning to regret this last decision, and in particular choosing Glena Buckingham's multi-trillion-dollar colossus Eurenergy as a second paymaster a few months ago. This was his first job for them. He had called them as soon as he heard of the radiation leak – even before Fortescue's notes had been retrieved. His contact at Eurenergy had got it immediately and was super-keen. So keen in fact it had landed him here, holed up against his will. Glena Buckingham, the CEO of Eurenergy, one of the two largest energy resource conglomerates on the planet, was clearly anxious to get hold of the information from the *Titanic*. Three years ago she had appeared on the cover of *Time*, and only a few months earlier she had been listed as the second most powerful woman in the world. Newman knew a little of her past. She was British by birth, a scientist by training, a former Cambridge fellow. She had started out as a biochemist before setting up a biotech firm that had made her extremely rich when it was floated. Four years ago she had assumed the helm of Eurenergy. Famed for her ruthlessness, she was nevertheless respected for her intelligence and vision.

Clearly, Eurenergy did not trust him; which was, he

had to admit, understandable. He did have every intention of giving them the information, just not on an exclusive basis.

He studied the mathematical symbols and lines of figures on the screen. To anyone other than a specialist in the field of particle physics, the equations would have been totally meaningless – sets of squiggles as indecipherable as Egyptian hieroglyphics. But to Newman, the screenful of information was as easy to interpret as a musical score in the hands of Mozart.

'But my God!' he thought, 'Fortescue's thinking had been weird, so utterly radical!' He could only wonder at the sheer genius of the man who, over a century ago, had created an atomic theory three decades ahead of its time and via an entirely different and beautifully simple route. It was staggering.

He ran through the basic history in his head. Just as the Second World War broke out in Europe scientists across the world were beginning to realize the power held within the atom. A couple of years later, Lise Meitner and Otto Frisch laid out the theory for fission – a nuclear process for creating vast amounts of energy from splitting uranium with neutrons.

But, twenty years earlier, unknown to anyone, Fortescue had envisioned a nuclear process that released even greater amounts of energy from a quite different procedure. He and Rutherford had then apparently developed experiments to test it.

It was all here in this file, all here in the twenty-odd pages of notes Fortescue had with him on the *Titanic*.

And it had almost reached the States, almost initiated a nuclear weapons development programme before the First World War.

But why, Newman wondered, hadn't Rutherford continued the research after the *Titanic* went down? Why wasn't the programme reinitiated? Was Fortescue carrying the only available sample of the enriched ibnium? Perhaps Rutherford could have refined more, but the British government had lost heart. Yeah . . . that was one possibility. Another was that without Fortescue the bomb could not be made. He was, after all, a formidable physicist, a far greater scientist than Rutherford. *That must be it*, Newman concluded. *Fortescue was the real brains behind this, and when he died the bomb died with him, only to be resurrected in a different form a generation later.*

He gazed at the screen, transfixed by the equations. A cold chill ran down his spine. 'No,' he said aloud. 'No, No . . . that can't be right!' He tapped the mouse, froze the equations and retraced his reasoning, finger to the screen.

'What the . . .?'

He pushed back his chair and started to pace, his head filled with mathematical figures, symbols, numbers. 'Fortescue had discovered cold fusion!' Cold fusion – a way to harness nuclear power at room temperature using only everyday chemicals to make it work. Even today it was the 'Holy Grail of modern physics'. He was talking to himself again, his voice quiet, incredulous. He stared around him in a daze. 'How is that possible?'

He strode back to the computer, sat, scrolled down the scanned-in pages and stopped abruptly. 'Jesus Christ!' He closed his eyes and kept them closed. A crazy part of him thought that when he opened his eyes again, the Mac would tell him something different.

He opened them, read through the clustered figures and slammed his fist down on the desk so hard it sent a tremor of pain along his arm to his shoulder. 'It's not all here! For Christ's sake! It's not all here!'

*

Newman had no conscious awareness of time passing. He existed now in a bubble of his own cerebral creation, an ocean of mathematics roiling like the real one beyond the window. Once he had spotted the enormous leap forward Fortescue had made, he could not rest. He saw that some of the work was missing, but this would not stop him. He had to at least try to fill in the gaps . . . to make it all fit together.

By the time he had fully reasoned through what was there in the short collection of papers, dawn was breaking, autumnal sun slithering over the oceanic horizon, revealing clusters of yachts in the swell.

Rubbing his eyes, he leaned back in his chair straining to hear any sounds of movement from the rooms below. Then he booted up his laptop and dialled the connection he had made the night before. As the computer found the uplink to the satellite, he checked his account. The promised deposit had been made. Excellent.

The laptop produced a series of clicks and bleeps, then a message flashed across the screen: 'Connection Green: Signal Strength 84%'. *Not great, but good enough*, Newman thought and started to type again. He wrote: 'As promised. Here is the interpretation of the work found at REZ375. It has exceeded my expectations and I'm sure it will yours. Please have your scientists confirm interpretations and authorize second payment within twenty-four hours.'

A few minutes passed and a response came. 'Receipt acknowledged. Will update you in due course.'

Newman yawned, feeling incredibly tired. A strange sound came from the desktop Mac. It took him a few moments to realize that it was an in-coming Skype call. He brought up the management screen, found the Skype icon, clicked it, then scanned the name of the caller. It simply said: 'EURENERGY'. He hovered the cursor over the green 'connect' symbol and a woman's face appeared.

Even though they had never met, Newman recognized her immediately. It was Glena Buckingham herself.

'My people picked up your encrypted call to us last night concerning the find at REZ375,' she said. 'I then had a call from Van Lee. He impressed upon me the fact that you were very excited and that you had complied with our wishes to interpret the find.'

Newman took a deep breath before replying. He felt incredibly nervous. This woman exuded an indefinable power, and it terrified him. 'Your, er . . . colleague was very insistent,' he said.

'I told him to be, professor; and he is indeed a very persuasive man.'

A sound came from behind Newman. He half turned to see Jimmy coming in through the door, another tray in his hands. Van Lee walked two paces behind him. Jimmy put the fresh tray on the table, lifted the old one and walked out, closing the door behind him. Van Lee stood close to the coffee table, arms folded across his chest. He'd changed into a tracksuit and trainers and he smelled of sweat.

Newman swung back to the screen. 'Well, you'll be pleased to hear I didn't sleep last night and I have something very, very interesting for you.'

Buckingham raised an expensively groomed eyebrow. 'I take it this line is secure?'

'Couldn't be more so.'

'Could I have some of that coffee?' Newman turned to Van Lee.

The man tilted his head and was about to make a flip response but changed his mind.

A few seconds later Newman had a mug in his hand and had taken a gulp. Then he explained what he had discovered.

Buckingham said nothing, just let him speak. When he had finished she remained silent for ten seconds, fixing Newman's eyes. 'Cold fusion. You have proof?' she said finally. 'You're able to show me your working? Clear notes explaining everything in detail?'

'I can send it all to you now.' He lifted the document from a file on the management screen and dumped it into the Skype 'send' box.

It arrived almost instantly. Newman could see Glena

Buckingham open it and start to read. It was identical to the one he had sent to the Chinese submarine.

Van Lee had poured himself a coffee and was seated in a sofa on the far side of the room from the desk, his eyes fixed on the back of the professor's head.

Newman understood that he should say nothing, nothing at all. Let the work speak for itself. There was no need for him to add anything. But as the minutes passed, his anxiety mounted. Buckingham was studying the information, her face bone hard.

She stopped, looked up, met Newman's gaze. 'This is quite extraordinary,' she said. 'Who else has the raw data?'

'Just the pair at the Marine Institute, Lou Bates and Kate Wetherall . . . and, of course, Captain Derham, the section commander.'

'I'm not so sure they are the only ones. I am concerned that this information has gone further.'

'But how? How could it . . .?'

Buckingham waved a hand in front of her face and Newman shut up immediately.

'I will ensure all parties are eliminated, all copies destroyed.'

'So, you're pleased?' Newman asked, almost child-like in his enthusiasm. 'I was staggered when I—'

'No! I can't say I'm pleased with this turn of events at all, professor. This discovery represents a terrible risk. The radiation leak from the *Titanic* is coming from some unknown energy source; that much is clear from its profile. The governments of the West will know that, the Chinese will know it from satellite surveillance, so too will the Russians . . . the whole shooting party will be alerted by now. If that energy source could be harnessed as this information will allow, within five years conventional forms of energy production will be made quite obsolete. That scenario must be prevented at all costs.'

'There is something else you need to know,' Newman said nervously. 'This material –' and he nodded towards the screen '– is incomplete.'

'Explain.'

'It is only about, oh, I'd guess, maybe seventy per cent of the total.'

'How can you possibly know that?'

'Whole chunks are missing, random sections. The math jumps; concepts are missing as though its creator has gone through the original completed work and deliberately taken out sections. It's like reading a book with thirty per cent of the pages ripped out indiscriminately.'

'And you cannot fill in the gaps?'

Newman shook his head. 'It would be like trying to put in several minutes of missing score from the music of a master composer.'

'Please,' Buckingham had a hand up. 'Spare me any more tedious analogies, Professor Newman. So this work really was written by a scientist travelling on the *Titanic*?'

'I am convinced it is the work of Egbert Fortescue.'

'Rutherford's assistant?'

'Yes. He must have been on the ill-fated ship. This work has his personality stamped all over it. It is as unique as . . .' He stopped himself. 'He must have deliberately split the work in case it fell into the wrong hands.'

'Aboard the *Titanic*?'

Newman merely shrugged.

'So then . . . this missing material could still be somewhere within the wreck, or may have been utterly destroyed.'

Newman stayed silent and Buckingham seemed lost in thought for a few moments before turning her piercing eyes on him. 'We are grateful to you, Professor Newman. Now you must return to the naval base before anyone notices you are missing. For our part we have to find the location of that missing thirty per cent – before anyone else does.'

14

But Professor Newman did not return to the Norfolk Naval Base. That had never been a part of his plans. Instead he walked back to his car where he had parked it the previous evening. He pulled onto Chesapeake Boulevard, headed south and then turned onto the 64. A very ordinary blue saloon turned onto the highway behind him. The man in the passenger seat spoke into his cell phone as he gazed out at the trees and buildings flashing past.

'Mistral here,' he said. 'We have the professor in sight. He's heading south-east on 64.'

'He must be on his way to the airport,' Sterling Van Lee replied. 'I'll alert them.'

Twenty minutes later Newman's Ford Taurus pulled into the long-term parking compound of Norfolk International Airport. The blue saloon kept a discreet distance and the two men in the car followed Newman, who had no other luggage but his briefcase and laptop.

Inside the airport, the professor headed straight for the United Airlines desk. After making a call from his cell phone, Mistral watched with satisfaction as a man in a United Airlines manager's suit walked over to the First Class check-in desk just as Newman approached with his passport in hand. The manager whispered a few words to the girl at the desk and she vacated her seat to let the manager sit in her place.

Newman smiled at the man and offered his passport and credit card.

'One return ticket for Acapulco,' the manager said, glancing at his computer screen, his words passing into a miniature contact mic under his suit lapel and along the open line to Mistral standing fifty yards away.

'Holiday?' the man asked cheerfully.

'Much needed,' the professor replied.

'Right, that will be 1,695 dollars,' the manager intoned, lifting his eyes from the screen.

Newman slid the credit card across the countertop and the man processed the fare. 'Beautiful this time of year,' he commented.

'I think it's meant to be beautiful at any time.'

The man chuckled. 'Gotta beat Virginia in the fall. Rain? Enough already!' He handed Newman his card and a ticket as a boarding pass emerged from a printer under the counter. 'No luggage, professor?'

'No. I plan to buy my bathing trunks there,' he said jauntily.

'You have a safe journey now,' the manager said.

Newman headed towards the gate, followed by the two men from the blue saloon. They held back as he presented his boarding pass and passport at the security check. He then put his bag and laptop onto the conveyor belt, strode under the metal detector arch and disappeared behind a screen.

'He's on the 11.50 United flight to Acapulco,' Mistral said into his cell. 'Lands 14.55.'

'Good work,' said Van Lee.

Passing behind the screen, Newman lowered himself onto a bench and watched the other passengers coming through security control. He waited five minutes, ten minutes. There was no sign of the two men who had been tailing him.

Standing, he pulled the plane ticket and boarding pass from the inside pocket of his jacket, ripped them into half a dozen pieces and tossed them into a metal bin beside the bench. From the left pocket of his trousers, he withdrew a different ticket, for American Airlines, and stopped at a large display listing departures. He checked the time of the flight leaving for JFK, which connected to a Thai Airways flight to Bangkok departing at 15.10 that afternoon.

15

Kate and Lou met for an early breakfast at their favourite cafe, Donovan's, close to the beach half a mile along the coast from the institute. They both had fond memories of the place. It had been their secret rendezvous when they were first romantically involved and wanted to keep their relationship to themselves.

They found a table in the back and watched despondently as the rain came down outside. Their drinks arrived.

'You're a constant surprise, Kate Wetherall,' Lou said suddenly, looking away from the rain, searching her face with his dark-blue eyes.

She gave him a puzzled look and tucked a few strands of blonde hair behind her left ear, a habit Lou had always found endearing. 'What do you mean?'

Lou shook his head. 'Oh, nothing.'

'Lou! That's not fair!' And she leaned forward, arms stretched across the table each side of her coffee mug to take his fingers as she gave him her best 'big-eyed' look.

'Well, you're only the goddaughter of the most famous scientist since Einstein, and you hadn't told me!'

'Oh, that . . . It wasn't my decision, Lou.' She let go of his fingers and pulled back into her chair. 'I was only two weeks old when I was christened.'

'And I suppose your granny is the queen of England.'

'Well, actually . . .' Kate laughed. 'Look, my father was a don – you knew that. He spent two years at Princeton. He and Uncle George became best friends.'

'Uncle George!'

'And,' she went on, ignoring Lou's sarcasm, 'although I said it wasn't my decision, I couldn't be happier about it. Professor Campion and his wife Joan are probably the nicest people I've ever met.'

'I'm sure they are. Where do they live?'

'Only an hour from here, near Franklin.'

'So we'll go see them? Talk to Uncle George about the EF docs?'

'Well, yeah. That's what I was thinking.' She was flicking through screens on her iPad. 'Oh, damn!'

'What?'

'I've got a conference call at eleven o'clock.'

'Anything important?'

'Yeah. It's the CEO of Avalon. The company in Oregon? Remember back on Bermuda I mentioned there was some interest in putting private money into our *Lavender* project?'

'I'd totally forgotten. The last few days have been a whirlwind.'

'You're telling me!'

'So OK, let's call the Campions,' Lou said. 'When could we get there by?'

'Can't do that.'

'Why?'

'They don't have a phone, no cell, no computer. They're kinda eccentric . . . in a nice way.'

Lou pulled a face.

'I'll be done by twelve. We'll go straight after the conference call with Avalon.'

*

In the end, they didn't get away until one o'clock. Lou's T-Bird was in the garage for new brake linings, which he had no time to install himself, but the garage had provided him with a little Toyota courtesy car for a couple of days.

Lou went back to the institute to pick up Kate. He was wearing his authentic Second World War USAF flying jacket which Kate had always loved seeing him in.

'Not quite the right attire for this titchy thing, is it, Lou?' she said, nodding towards his jacket as they approached the Toyota compact.

'You should have seen the second choice of car,' he laughed.

They headed south-west on the freeway, the rain driving hard against the windscreen, the wipers beating. Weekday, early afternoon, and the traffic was light. Kate had her iPad perched on her knees.

'We still know almost nothing about this character EF,' she said, tapping on the screen.

'We know he was in First Class, cabin C16; probably a scientist, although he could have simply been a courier for the isotope and the documents.'

She pulled up the *Titanic* manifest on Google. Scrolled down. 'That's interesting.'

'What?'

'There were no First Class passengers with the initials "EF".'

'Travelling under an assumed name then. Who was in cabin C16?'

Kate tapped the screen again, ran her finger across the glass. 'C16. A John Wickins.'

'John Wickins?' Lou said and glanced at Kate. She gave him a blank look. 'While Isaac Newton was at Cambridge, he shared a room with a John Wickins for almost twenty years.'

'How did you know that?'

'History of science unit at UCLA. There was a great book on the reading list – *Isaac Newton: The Last Sorcerer*. You read it?'

Kate shook her head.

You should – will change any preconceived notions you had about Sir Isaac Newton.'

'Well, using that pseudonym adds weight to the idea "EF" was a scientist, I guess; but it doesn't tell us any more about who the man was.'

'Or why he was on the *Titanic* with a radioactive sample.'

They turned off the freeway at intersection 13B taking the road to Suffolk. The rain had stopped, the trees lining the road left dripping. They passed along Main Street, through an old-fashioned city centre with low-rise brick buildings, some dating back to the early nineteenth century, and picked up the highway west towards the small town of Franklin.

They pulled off onto a narrow two-lane road. The landscape became more wooded, houses fewer and further apart. The rain started again.

'So tell me a bit about Professor Campion,' Lou said, his eyes fixed on the beating wipers and the soaked road.

'Well, you know the public figure – "science celebrity", "the cleverest man since Einstein", all that nonsense. My godfather is a great physicist, but you know what it's like – the usual stampede to make some sort of cartoon figure out of any amazing talent. The media did it with Stephen Hawking, then ten years ago they repeated the trick with Uncle George.'

'After he proved that the speed of light was not the upper limit for the universe.'

'Yes; refuting Einstein is one thing, proving him wrong is quite another.'

'The myth is all true then? Campion couldn't stand the limelight and retreated to . . .' Lou lifted a hand from the wheel and swept across the view through the windscreen.

'That's pretty much it. He was never one for drawing attention to himself. He hated the constant trivializing of his work, the film crews barging into his rooms in Princeton. And then to cap it all, he attracted the opprobrium of some of his colleagues.'

'With his radical ideas.'

'Now he's seen as existing on the fringe. It's almost as though the scientific community have ostracized him for being right and Einstein wrong. They have to accept it, of course. Science is all about progress – absorbing a concept if it is proven to be right, adapting one's vision of the way the universe works – but scientists are human too . . .' She pointed to a sign indicating a track off to their left: 'It's there.'

A hundred yards along the track Lou pulled the car up outside a stone cottage.

'Wait here a second,' Kate said, getting out of the passenger seat. 'I'll see if anyone's home.'

She walked quickly through a low arch on to a cobbled path running between two stretches of wet lawn girded by rose beds, the flowerless bushes looking a little bedraggled in the rain.

The white painted door had an old-fashioned bell pull. Kate tugged on it and heard sounds from inside the house. The door opened slowly and an elderly lady with greying auburn hair and a round, rosy-cheeked face stood at the opening. She was dressed in a flowery dress covered with a flour-stained apron. The smell of baking wafted along the hall.

'Kate!' the woman exclaimed, breaking into a rapturous smile. 'Sweetheart, it's been so long!'

Before she could reply, Kate saw a figure appear from the shadows at the end of the hallway. The elderly lady stepped forward and hugged Kate as George Campion arrived at the door, a big smile on his face. He was wearing worn-out corduroys, a brown sleeveless sweater over a shirt and an ineptly knotted tie. He held a pipe in his left hand. Tufts of white hair either side of his bald head softened his weathered face.

'My dear girl,' Campion said and held her tight. 'What on earth brings you here? It's not my birthday, is it, Joan?' he added, turning to his wife.

She rolled her eyes and was starting to usher in her guest when Kate said, 'I have a colleague with me, in the car. I wanted to check you were home first.'

'Oh, we're always home,' Joan Campion remarked, leaning out and seeing Lou in the car. He gave her a brief wave, opened the driver's door and approached along the path.

The Campions' house was a modest but cozy home that suited them perfectly. Their two sons, Nick and Simon, had left some twenty years ago, but their presence remained in plentiful photographs on the living-room wall and atop a grand piano that took pride of place in a small conservatory looking out onto a lush rear garden.

Joan fussed over the young pair, fetching tea and freshly baked cake as the professor led them to his study. This was a room perfectly appropriate for a world-famous academic. There was an intense odour of tobacco in the study, ancient and ripe, a smell that came from smoke ingrained in the fibre of the place, and the room itself seemed anchored by the sheer weight of books filling floor-to-ceiling shelves. A cluttered desk stood in the bay of a large window offering a view onto trees and a grey cloudy sky. Books had spilled over into precarious piles close to the shelves. A Brahms piano sonata played softly.

Campion found two battered chairs, offered them to Kate and Lou and paced around his desk. Moving some papers, he tugged out an ancient-looking cassette player, switched off the Brahms and pulled up his chair.

'So, my dear, although it is always a delight to see you, to what do we owe the pleasure?'

'Lou and I have been commissioned to work on a project for the navy at Norfolk Base,' Kate began.

'The last I heard you were off to some exotic place. Where was it . . . Fiji?'

'Bermuda.'

'Ah, yes.' Campion was suddenly distracted, moving books and papers in search of something. He had his pipe clenched between his teeth. A moment later he extricated a box of matches, struck one and brought it to the bowl of his pipe. 'So, young man,' he said, turning to Lou. 'You are a marine archaeologist too?'

'Yes, sir,' he replied. 'Kate and I were working together on the wreck of a pilgrim ship.'

'Fascinating, fascinating. But how on earth did that lead you into the clutches of the US Navy?' Campion sucked on his pipe.

'It was Marine Phenomenon REZ375. The *Titanic* site.'

'The what?'

'You may not have heard,' Kate said, 'there's a serious radiation leak from the wreck of the *Titanic*.'

'Radiation leak?'

At that moment, Joan Campion appeared in the doorway with a tray. She came in and searched for a place to put it. 'George, you really must try to sort this room out,' she declared. Lou got up to help clear a space and found a small table, carefully transferring a pile of papers to the floor. He took the tray.

'Thank you, young man.'

'Shall I pour?' Lou asked.

'No, no, thank you . . . you sit down.' Joan served the tea and cake, taking a slice and a cup round the desk to her husband before leaving them to it.

Kate and Lou took turns to explain what had happened and went on to describe the descent to the *Titanic*. Campion grew animated at this, interrupting them to ask how the suits worked, how Derham's sonar device functioned. They did their best to explain. When Kate started to describe the mathematical text and the initials EF, Campion looked startled. Lou finished by detailing what little they had learned from the box of papers.

For several moments Campion said nothing. Getting up from his chair, he puffed on his pipe and turned to look out at the wet trees and the grass. Kate studied the man's profile, his strong nose and high forehead wreathed with bluish pipe smoke.

'So, you have copies of the papers?' the professor said suddenly, turning back to face his guests.

Kate leaned down to a small attaché case she had brought. Unzipping it, she handed a sheaf of papers to the old man.

'These are photocopies, of course,' Lou said. 'They are taken from the original twenty-two pages of notes and mathematical formulae we found.'

'And the navy people haven't studied them?'

'We showed them to a guy at Norfolk – Professor Max Newman.'

'Ah, yes, I know Max well. A fine scientist.'

'I have no doubt,' Kate replied. 'But he wasn't very helpful.'

'I see. Let's go through to the dining room,' Campion said. 'Less clutter there. We can have a proper look at these.'

They could hear Joan in the kitchen as George Campion spread out the sheets on the dining table. He fell silent as he studied the lines of equations.

'Ah, yes, now this is interesting,' the scientist said half to himself while running a finger across the second page of symbols. 'Clearly a very sophisticated line of research. Yes,' he added and peered down at the pages. 'Remarkable, quite remarkable.'

Lou wanted to ask what was so remarkable but a look from Kate warned him to hold back. After some time concentrating on the papers, Campion looked up, removed his spectacles and stared at his young guests.

'You say these came from the *Titanic*?'

'Yes. From the same cabin where the radiation source was found.'

The old man shook his head slowly. 'And you said the box these came in was marked with the initials "EF"?'

'Yes, sir.'

Campion put his glasses back on and gave the equations another look. 'If I had been given these by anyone else,' he said and looked up again, 'I would not have believed it. Even so, I find it hard to conceive.'

'Why?'

'Because these equations describe a way of harnessing the power of the atom – a theory describing how to make an atomic bomb.'

Kate felt a tingle pass down her spine. 'How? The *Titanic* sank decades before scientists developed the theories that led to Los Alamos and the bombs used in 1945.'

'Yes.'

'So you're saying that this EF went down on the *Titanic* and he had the secret of how to build an atomic weapon before the First World War!' Lou leaned back in his chair, arms folded across his chest. 'That's ridiculous!'

'Well, I would have said exactly the same thing five minutes ago.'

'But how?' Lou went on, staring at Campion then at Kate.

'Well, EF was a remarkable man.'

'Who was—?'

'Who was EF?' Campion said, a faint smile playing across his lips. 'Egbert Fortescue.'

'Never heard of him.'

'That's because he died before he could really make his mark on the world. He was Ernest Rutherford's assistant at Manchester University. According to the history books, he was the victim of a drowning accident in Manchester in 1912. His body was never found. Some have speculated that he was the real genius behind some of his boss's discoveries.'

'So you're saying,' Lou replied, 'that Rutherford and this Fortescue guy discovered a way to harness atomic power a generation before the accepted version of history? And that Fortescue then died on the *Titanic*, taking his secrets with him?'

'It seems to be the only explanation.'

'He was probably being secretive on the ship, travelling under the pseudonym John Wickins,' Kate added. 'But how could he and Rutherford have done it? The process to harness the power of the atom, I mean.'

'Both men were profoundly brilliant. It's clear from this –' the professor tapped the nearest page '– they were decades ahead of their time. But it's also startling that Rutherford and Fortescue's method was entirely different from the process Lise Meitner and Otto Hahn developed in the 1930s which led to the Allies building the first atomic weapon at Los Alamos.'

'Different?' Lou said.

'Rutherford and Fortescue have come at it from left of field, but it looks very effective.'

'But,' Kate said, 'what was Fortescue doing on the *Titanic*?'

Professor Campion seemed to have lost interest and was looking down at the pages again, running a finger across the equations, his spectacles perched on the end of his nose. 'Good Lord!' he exclaimed suddenly and straightened.

'What?' Kate and Lou said in unison.

Campion ignored them, plucking up the last page he had been reading.

'Uncle George?'

He turned to Kate, a lost look on his face. 'It's hard to believe! I don't know if this is work that Rutherford was doing with Fortescue or if it was something the young man was developing on board the *Titanic*, but it's truly remarkable.'

'Uncle, you're talking in riddles!'

The old man ignored Kate and focused on the pages. Then he put them back down carefully on the table. 'Astonishing!' he said and looked at his young guests. 'These later equations describe a means to develop cold fusion.'

'But I thought—'

'That we can't do that today?' the professor interrupted.

'Well, yes,' Lou said.

'We can't,' Campion said. 'You probably know there have been many attempts, but Rutherford and Fortescue were almost . . .'

They all fell silent for a few moments, taking in the enormity of what the professor had just said. Kate and Lou each knew enough physics to realize this work had the potential to solve all the world's power demands with clean, almost limitless resources.

'It must have been Fortescue doing this work on his

own, when he was on the ship during the first days of the voyage leading up to the night the *Titanic* hit the iceberg,' said Campion.

'How can you possibly know that?' Kate asked.

'There's a faint imprint at the top of the paper . . . see?'

Kate and Lou leaned over and saw the words: 'White Star'.

'The company insignia,' Kate said. 'How did we miss that?'

'Fortescue's reasoning, though . . . it seems to jump,' the professor went on. 'Hang on . . .'

The room fell silent except for sounds from the kitchen.

'There's a dramatic leap in the math . . . but Fortescue must have reasoned through the missing section. He couldn't have gone straight from here to here.' Campion tapped at the paper.

'What do you mean, sir?' Lou asked.

'This isn't all of it,' the elderly man said. 'It's clear Fortescue was working away on this stuff solo, developing these ideas about cold fusion while he was crossing the Atlantic. Problem is . . . there's a chunk missing. There must be another set of documents somewhere that fills in the gaps. And I guess they can only be in one place, can't they?'

16

It had grown dark and storm clouds had brought with them a fretful, squally evening.

Lou and Kate had agreed to stay for dinner and George Campion built a fire from logs that had been stacked in an old brass bucket beside the grate. He had just managed to get a roaring blaze going as Joan Campion came through from the kitchen pushing a trolley carrying a huge casserole dish. Lou lifted it into place on the table and Joan started serving the piping-hot food into heavily patterned bowls.

The guests made appropriately appreciative noises as they sampled the casserole.

'Joan is an exceptional cook,' George commented. 'You can see it wasn't just her looks that attracted me to her.'

Kate and Lou laughed.

'And it wasn't his sense of humour that hooked me!' Joan retorted with a grin.

'So, professor, you believe Fortescue's notes are just chunks of the last work he did?' Lou asked. 'You're sure it's not all there in the documents?'

'Sadly, it's not. There are gaps. In the papers are a few conclusions, but they could not have been reached just from the equations in the rest of the material.'

'But there are some important results on the way to realizing cold fusion?'

'I didn't say that. There are no final solutions in the papers you've recovered, just partial solutions. If you can get the missing sections, then I think . . . we might just be able to piece together what the man was thinking and see if it was indeed a practical solution.'

'So, who's for coffee?' Joan asked.

Kate and Lou helped clear the plates, but Joan insisted only Kate and she should take them to the kitchen while Lou and George refuelled the fire.

Joan put the kettle on and ensured the door was closed. 'So, Kate, is Lou your young man?'

She shook her head, smiling. 'We work together.'

'Come on,' the older woman coaxed. 'He is a sweetheart and very handsome; those blue eyes!'

'Joan!' Kate exclaimed and set some cups and saucers on a tray. 'Look, we were romantically involved a while back, but . . .'

'But?'

'It got too complicated. We agreed to just stay friends.'

Joan gave Kate a sceptical look.

'That's how it is, Joan.'

'I can sense a lot more going on between you.'

'Can you now!' Kate placed the milk jug on the tray and her godmother made the coffees. 'You're an incorrigible romantic, aunt.'

Joan led the way back into the dining room and Kate helped her distribute the cups.

'So what happens next?' George asked.

Lou shrugged. 'To be honest, professor, we're playing it by ear.'

'I don't really know that we can be much help to the military,' Kate said. 'It'll be up to their science guys to make anything of what we brought up. I imagine studying the isotope will be their first priority.'

'They'll try to reverse engineer,' George offered. 'But, really, the important thing is not so much the ibnium isotope, it's Fortescue's documents.'

'But as you said, uncle, if he had the rest of the work with him on the ship, it has almost certainly been destroyed.'

Lou glanced at his watch and turned to Kate. 'I think maybe we ought to head back.'

'You're most welcome to stay the night,' Joan offered. 'It's pretty foul out there.'

'That's very kind of you, aunt,' Kate replied. 'But we've got an awful lot of work to catch up on.'

'That was absolutely delicious, Mrs Campion,' Lou said. 'I wish we could stay longer.' He turned to George. 'And thank you, sir, for sparing the time . . .'

George waved his comment away. 'Don't be silly, young man. It's not every day I get to see Fortescue's handwritten work . . . It's a marvel.'

*

They ran for the car parked in the narrow lane just past the hedge. The Campions stood arm in arm at the door to the cottage, the warm glow from inside surrounding them. The rain was coming down in sheets. Lou got into the driver's side and brought the car to life and the wipers began to swish away the water from the windscreen. Giving a final wave, they set off into the darkness, the twin beams of the car headlights the only illumination.

The trees skirting the lane flashed past like spectres in the night. After a few minutes they reached the main road, and the lights of civilization. They turned onto the highway heading east back towards the institute.

'Do you really think there's another set of notes somewhere down in the wreck?' Lou asked.

'George seemed pretty certain about it. God knows if they have survived, though. And what are the chances of finding them now, a hundred years after the *Titanic* sank?'

'Couldn't the work have been done in Manchester? Maybe Fortescue hid the stuff there.'

'I don't think so. One thing I've learned from my godfather is that mathematical physics is an organic mental process. One physicist can see the mental processes at work when they study another's equations. It's a bit like when we peel away the debris from a relic and can see what has happened to the object over intervening centuries.'

Lou was distracted by headlights in the rearview mirror. 'God! They're driving fast!'

'Who?'

The lights grew brighter as a car drove up close behind.

'Them.' Lou flicked his head back. 'I'm doing a steady sixty, they must—'

Kate was just starting to turn when they felt a jolt.

'Christ!' Lou exclaimed.

There was loud crunch from the rear of the Toyota as the car rammed them again.

'What the hell's going on?' Kate exclaimed.

They could see almost nothing behind except for the outline of a vehicle and the dazzle of its powerful head-lights.

Lou gripped the wheel. 'I'm going to pull over.'

'You sure that's the right thing to do?'

'Well, I can't outrun them in this tin can.'

He put his headlights on full beam, lighting up a larger patch of road ahead. Fields lay each side skirted by wire fence. He was about to yank the wheel round when the car hit them again, much harder this time. They heard the grating of metal, the smash of glass. Something broke away from the car and clanked along the road behind them.

Kate screamed as Lou lost control. The Toyota spun a hundred and eighty degrees, and for a second they were travelling backwards along the highway, the other car, a white Cadillac, bearing down on them. They skidded to the left and ploughed through the wire fence and into a field, the car's suspension grating. The drive shaft disengaged and the engine squealed like a pig. Two airbags inflated and the Toyota rolled once, twice, then stuttered to a stop a hundred feet from the highway.

17

Lou opened his eyes. Everything was a blur of colour. Then he smelled petrol.

He turned and saw Kate's face partially concealed by an airbag. He did a mental check. He could feel pain, but it wasn't intense – a stabbing in his left wrist. He could move, so he found the seat-belt buckle and released it. He felt around for the door handle, pulled and then pushed and the door fell away. He crawled out and around the car to the passenger side.

Kate's door was stuck fast. But he wrenched it and it swung out. Leaning in, he saw that Kate was regaining consciousness. She opened her eyes as he reached around her and unclasped the belt.

The smell of petrol was growing stronger. Lou heard a hissing sound coming from the front offside tyre. Gripping Kate's lapels, he pulled her away from the airbag, helping her out of the car. She groaned and mumbled something unintelligible.

He saw a light. It came from about fifty feet away, up towards the road and the ripped-open fence. The light bobbed about. Then he saw another. Torches. The beams swept the wreck of the car. Lou ducked and pulled Kate to the hard ground beside him. Looking down, he could see her face, eyes half-closed. She winced. Lou put a finger to his lips and Kate realized what was happening, gripped Lou's arm, and together they scrambled away from the Toyota.

They headed towards an oak tree fifty yards into the field. Lou stopped. 'The documents,' he said and started to turn.

'Lou . . . No!' Kate grasped his arm.

The car exploded in a great ball of yellow flame. The heat hit them and they shielded their eyes from the burst of light. Lou glimpsed two dark figures running back towards the highway.

Gripping Kate by the shoulders, he looked into her eyes. 'You all right?'

Her face was smeared with grease and mud and a line of blood trailed from her nose to her mouth. She was clutching her side with her right hand. 'I think I've cracked a rib,' she rasped. 'It's agony to breathe.'

Lou helped her up and went for his mobile. 'Damn, I left my phone in the car.'

Kate searched for hers, pulled it from her pocket. The screen was shattered. She tapped it. It was dead.

'Can you walk?'

She nodded then noticed blood running down Lou's cheek. 'You're hurt.'

He touched a spot above his ear and gasped. 'Ow!' He lifted his left hand. 'I think I've damaged my wrist too.'

They looked back to the devastated car, fire engulfing the chassis. A second explosion ripped through the night, followed by a roar of flame. They lurched back from the intense heat. A sound came from up on the highway: a car accelerating away, its tyres screeching on the tarmac. They saw a flash of white then red rear lights disappear into the darkness.

Lou supported Kate under her shoulder and helped her up a gentle slope leading away from the wreck. Keeping a safe distance from the Toyota, they picked their way through the damp undergrowth, brambles scratching at them in the dark. The ground was stodgy and wet; mud clung to their shoes.

They reached the highway, looked back and saw the red and yellow flames still feeding off the petrol spilled from the Toyota, the burning rubber and the plastic turned to stinking black smoke. They sat beside the road. Lou put his arm around Kate. She was shaking. He took off his ripped flying jacket and wrapped it about her shoulders.

Lou had no idea how long they sat there. Both of them felt too traumatized to speak, and when he saw the lights of a car approaching his first emotion was fear. He got up and was about to help Kate into the shadows when he realized the car was not the Cadillac that had followed them but an SUV. It started to slow. They could see a man and a woman in the front, two kids in the back.

The car stopped and the driver, a middle-aged man in a windcheater, jumped out and ran over to them.

'You folks OK?' he said.

Kate was clutching her side and looked very pale.

'I'm all right,' Lou said. 'But my friend . . .'

'I'm fine,' Kate said – and fainted.

*

'Wake up, sleeping beauty.'

Kate recognized the voice immediately, opened her eyes and saw Captain Jerry Derham staring down at her.

It took her a few moments to comprehend where she was and what was happening. She made to get up.

'Easy, Kate. You've got a nasty concussion.'

She brought a hand to her head. 'Lou?'

'I'm here.'

She turned and saw him sitting on the other side of the bed. He lifted his left arm to show her a bandage about his wrist. 'Nothing broken. We both got off pretty light.'

'How long have I been out?'

'A couple of hours. Doctors checked you over. Two cracked ribs, cuts and bruises. Lou's filled me in on what you learned from Professor Campion.'

Kate began to get out of bed.

'Hey, hey . . . where do you think you're going?' Derham began.

She glared at him. 'I'm not hanging around here.'

'Just—' Lou began and stepped forward.

'I'm perfectly OK!' Kate pushed Lou's hand away.

'Hasn't it occurred to either of you that the Campions might be in danger?'

Lou turned to Derham. The captain sighed.

'The bastards who ran us off the road knew who we were. It wasn't an accident. They must have tailed us from the base.' Kate's expression hardened. 'Someone has betrayed us.'

Lou stared at her. 'Newman,' he said. 'Professor Newman.'

Derham strode towards the door and out into the corridor beyond, pulling out his cell phone as he went.

Lou left Kate to get dressed. A nurse stopped him at the door. 'What the hell is—'

'We're leaving,' he said matter-of-factly.

'We'll see about that—'

'No, we won't,' Lou snapped, blocking the door.

Kate appeared, looking pale.

The nurse turned and left. 'I'm fetching the consultant.'

Derham appeared around a corner close to Kate's room. They could tell from his expression that something was very wrong.

'Newman has vanished,' he said. 'My people are searching the base. I've sent men to his home. Another team is checking security footage at the base and from cameras on the roads around it. No one's seen the man since he left the base twenty-four hours ago, soon after we talked to him.'

Kate turned on her heel and walked away towards the exit. 'Get me to my godparents,' she said without looking back.

18

Outside, the rain was still heavy. It seemed to have set in for the night. After the accident Lou and Kate had been taken to Sentara Obici Hospital, a five-minute drive north of Suffolk and about twenty miles from the Campions' place.

Jerry Derham was driving a navy pool car, an unassuming silver Ford, and a young uniformed naval officer, Lieutenant Niels Goldman, sat next to him. Lou and Kate were in the back. They couldn't see much through the windows other than the black shapes of passing trees and occasional lights, the rain hammering out a tribal beat on the roof. Kate was dosed up with painkillers, but her anxiety more than counteracted them; she felt jumpy, anxious.

The traffic was light, the town of Suffolk almost deserted, and soon they were back on the highway heading out into the wooded windswept countryside, retracing the journey Kate and Lou had made a few hours earlier. They turned left off the highway onto the same country lane they had driven down, the street lights falling away behind them, the wheels of the Ford crunching over the uneven and rutted surface.

Lights were on at the Campions' house, and for a few moments Kate held on to the image of her godfather burning the midnight oil in his study, poring over his books and papers.

The car had barely stopped when Kate reached for the door handle and started to push her way out.

'Kate . . . please,' Derham snapped.

She kept going.

The captain was out, heading her off. 'Kate!'

'I'm going in there.' She went to push him back, ignoring the sharp pain in her side.

'Not yet! We don't know the situation. Just wait . . . please!'

He pulled out his pistol and turned towards the house. Lou eased out the other side of the car and Lieutenant Goldman came up on Derham's right side, his weapon raised in both hands. The younger officer shifted the gate inwards and was first onto the path, Derham close behind.

The front door was ajar. Kate saw it in the half light and felt a stab of fear in the pit of her stomach. The two officers stood either side of the front door and beckoned to Lou and Kate to fall back into the shadows. Derham slithered into the hall.

It took all Kate's willpower to stay still and quiet but it was not enough; she made for the path. Lou gripped her arm, hard. She whirled on him, furious, but he kept hold of her and met her gaze, jaw set.

Goldman emerged from the house, his gun lowered. Kate pulled free from Lou and ran.

The hall was empty, but through a gap between the frame and the door to the living room Kate caught a flicker of movement. She went to push on the door just as Derham was emerging.

'Kate . . . I don't think you should . . .'

She shoved at the man's shoulder. He resisted but then saw the resolve in her eyes and reluctantly let her through.

The scene was instantly etched into her brain. A vision she would never forget, one that would haunt her at night and tear into her dreams. George and Joan Campion were slumped in a pair of chairs against the far wall of the living room. They had been gagged, their hands tied to the chair backs behind them. They had been tortured, disfigured, then dispatched with a bullet to the temple, execution style. Great fans of blood and brain tissue covered the rear wall. It had sprayed in an arc across the ceiling and the light fixture in the centre of a plaster rose.

Kate could not move. Then slowly she brought her right hand to her mouth as vomit swept between her fingers and down her front. She stepped towards the dead couple. Derham moved to hold her back but she knocked his hand away with surprising force and let out an almost inaudible cry as she knelt down between the two pathetic, mutilated figures. 'What have they done?' she whispered and ran a finger along her god-father's knee. She pulled up, turned to the three men behind her, her face ashen. 'Why?' she said. 'Why?'

Lou gazed at her, stricken, barely able to take it in.

Kate went to him and fell into his arms, the tears exploding from her, her body heaving as he guided her back to the hall.

19

The place had been completely trashed. The door to George Campion's study hung open. Kate could see the edge of the devastation before she reached the opening into the room. The shelves had been emptied, the chairs upturned, the upholstery shredded. The contents of her godfather's desk were scattered around randomly.

Kneeling down behind the desk, she plucked the professor's ancient cassette player from the wreckage, brushed away some crumbs of sandwich from the top and placed it back where it had sat earlier under a pile of papers. Tears streamed down her cheeks.

Back in the hall, Jerry Derham had emerged from the living room. He was tucking away his cell phone. 'This is now a crime scene for military investigators, and it won't be made public just yet,' he said. 'The police have been notified. The FBI are on their way.' He gave Kate a sympathetic look. 'Shall we get you and Lou home?'

Kate wiped away a tear from her chin. 'Need to get cleaned up,' she said and turned towards a downstairs bathroom.

Closing the door, for a second she could almost believe

she was shutting off reality, but the thought was as fleeting as melting ice. If only life were that simple. She stepped over to the washbasin and peered at her reflection in the mirror.

She could see her younger self there, the little girl who had stood on this very spot years before when she visited the Campions with her parents. Then she recalled the afternoon of her mother's funeral. They had buried her in a church not far from here, and her father, Nicholas Wetherall, George Campion's closest friend, had accepted the Campions' kind offer to act as hosts for a small gathering after the service. She was ten, dressed in a dark-blue dress, pigtails tied with black silk ribbon. She had cried before this same mirror that day too. But then she could leave the room and feel the embrace of her father and the love of her godparents. Now, all of them were gone.

Derham led them back to the car. It had stopped raining, but it was cold with an insipid dampness in the air. Before they could pull away, a Chevrolet compact drew up in front of the navy pool car. Derham got out again and spoke to a couple of men in black suits. Kate and Lou sat in the back of the car immersed in silence, lost in their own thoughts.

'It's the Feds,' Derham said, leaning in through the back window of the navy car, '. . . insist on talking to both of you.'

Lou went off to the house with one of the FBI agents, the other came around the car and opened the back door.

'You mind if I talk to you here, Dr Wetherall?' the agent asked. He looked at Goldman who was in the driver's seat. He got the message immediately and stepped out. Kate watched him and Derham walk back to the house. The agent slipped into the car and sat down where Lou had been.

'I'm sorry for your loss,' the man said, extending a hand. 'Special Agent Mike Colm.'

Kate took his hand limply and met his eye.

'How were you related to the deceased?' Colm asked, pulling a notebook and pen from his wet jacket.

'I'm not. They are . . . were my godparents.'

'Can you talk me through what you know of what happened here.'

Kate was silent for a moment, turned to her right to look at the house lit up from inside. 'Lou and I visited this morning . . .'

'What time?'

'We got here about two o'clock.'

'So not strictly this morning,' Colm said, gazing down at the notebook.

Kate looked at him and the man lifted his head. 'Go on.'

'We drove over from our lab in Norfolk. I wanted to show my godfather a document we had been studying.'

'A document?'

'Yes.'

'What sort of document?'

'I'm afraid I'm not at liberty . . .'

'This is a double murder investigation, Dr Wetherall.'

'I'm aware of that,' Kate replied acerbically. 'That doesn't change the fact . . .'

'Why were you consulting Professor Campion?'

'Because my uncle's area of expertise was pertinent to our research. George is . . . was . . . one of the most respected physicists on earth.'

'And you and Dr Bates talked at length with the professor?'

'We did. Then we had dinner.'

'And you left . . . when?'

'About eight thirty . . . nine.'

'Which?'

Kate took a deep breath. And chose not to answer.

'I realize this must be a difficult time for you Dr—'

'Do you?' Kate snapped.

It was Colm's turn to fall silent.

'I apologize,' Kate said. 'You're just trying to do your job. OK . . . I remember we were pulling onto the highway and the clock read eight forty, so I guess we must have left about eight thirty-five.'

'Captain Derham reported that you were then driven off the road and ended up in the ER at Sentara Obici.'

'That is correct. We were pursued by a white Cadillac. It rammed us. We were in a rented Toyota. Neither of us got the licence plate of the Cadillac.'

'You then discharged yourself and came here with Dr Bates and Captain Derham.'

Kate nodded and looked away to see Derham approaching the car. Goldman and Lou behind him. Lou had the collar of his flying jacket turned up.

The captain tapped on the glass and indicated to the agent that he should open the window. It lowered and Derham leaned in. 'That's it for now, Agent Colm,' he said, a hard edge to his voice. 'These people have been through quite enough . . .'

'This is an FBI matter now, captain.'

'No, it's not,' Derham snapped. 'I've just had a call from the commander of the base, Admiral Davis. Right now he is in a conference with the Joint Chiefs of Staff at the Pentagon. He has given me explicit instructions to terminate this little chat immediately.' He glanced at Kate, who stared back hollow-eyed. Derham stepped back and held the door open.

Colm did not move for a moment. 'You can verify this officially?'

'I don't need to, Agent Colm. You either get out and let us be on our way or I have instructions to take you into custody at Norfolk Naval Base.'

Colm still refused to move and glanced at his colleague who had just approached the car behind the naval officers and Lou. Sighing, he slowly closed his notebook, returned it with the pen to an inside pocket and stepped out. 'Very well. I will have to contact my superiors also.'

'You do that,' Derham replied evenly.

Lou slid into the back of the car beside Kate, Goldman got into the driving seat as Derham lowered himself into the passenger side and the car pulled away.

They were soon out on the main highway, heading east back to the naval base. No one spoke for several minutes before Lou broke the silence. 'Anything on Newman?'

Derham half-turned towards the back of the car and shook his head. 'I have a dozen men on it. We've seized his office computer. The technician guy you met, Kevin Grant? He's going through the hard drive with a fine-toothed comb. Newman's team are all being questioned. We'll get to the bottom of it.'

'Whoever killed the Campions must have been trailing us from the start,' Kate commented.

'They have been dead for at least three hours. I think whoever is responsible attacked the house immediately after you left.'

'Which means there are at least three men involved.'

'Four, minimum,' Derham replied. 'Lou . . . you told me you saw two figures near the crash. They couldn't have been the same people who killed the Campions. There wouldn't have been time.'

'Unless they went back to the Campions' home after our car exploded.'

'It's possible. But I reckon a more likely scenario is that two of them followed your Toyota, two stayed back at the cottage. They wanted to cover all bases. Someone – Newman, I guess – tipped somebody off about the papers from the *Titanic*. They realized you either handed them over to the professor to study or took them away with you. I take it you didn't leave them?'

'They were in the car when it went up,' Kate said. 'I led my godparents to their deaths and they never did have the damn documents anyway.'

'Kate, you can't . . .' Lou began.

'I'm OK,' she said gently as he went to put an arm about her shoulder. 'I didn't do it intentionally. But I'll have to live with what happened for the rest of my life.'

He took a deep breath and looked to Derham. 'So, what now?'

'I think both of you should get some rest. I'll assign a couple of my men to your apartments.'

'No, thanks,' Kate responded. 'Last thing I need. Can you take me back to the lab?'

'You sure about that?'

Kate's expression was hard. 'I've always found that work is the best therapy.'

'Very well, but I still want you two under guard, OK?'

'Would it make any difference if I said no to that?'

*

The Institute of Marine Studies was an open campus, with no security gates, no armed guards – a fact that did not please Derham. He stopped the car close to the building where Kate and Lou worked and stepped out with them. To their left, ten yards away, stood a multi-storey car park. The whole place was very quiet.

'You're certain about this?' He turned to Kate then Lou. 'It's past one o'clock. Place is deserted.'

'The car hasn't turned into a pumpkin,' Lou quipped.

'All right,' Derham shrugged. 'I want you at the base at 08.00, no matter what time you quit work tonight.

And my guys should be here within the hour. They'll take up a spot around here, I guess,' and he indicated a space in the car park. 'You'll be able to wave to them from the lab window.'

'How nice,' Kate retorted.

He took a step towards her and squeezed her shoulder gently. 'I'm so sorry,' he said softly, turned and shook Lou's hand. '08.00.'

They watched the captain drive away, the car's brake lights flicking on, then off. The car park lay silent.

'So what are we working on?' Lou asked and yawned.

Kate produced a faint smile, the first since she had woken up in Sentara Obici Hospital. 'I love you, Dr Lou Bates . . .' she said, shaking her head.

Lou looked at her askance. She gazed back at him.

A loud sound broke through the silence. A car with its lights off screeched around the corner of the car park and accelerated towards them.

It took Kate and Lou a few moments to realize what was happening and to react. Car doors swung open, three figures leapt from the car and charged towards them.

Lou grabbed Kate's arm and they took off towards the multi-storey directly ahead. It was an ugly cube of concrete four floors high. Lights inside cast a faint lemon glow above the parapets skirting each floor. A pair of blue doors faced the narrow road. Kate and Lou reached them in seconds, not daring to look back.

Praying the doors were unlocked, Lou pushed on the bar with his good arm. They flew inwards. Ignoring the pain in her side, Kate took the lead, sprinting into the ground level of the car park. They heard voices, then a loud crack like a whip shooting through the night.

'Christ!' Lou exclaimed, 'they're shooting at us!'

They ran towards another door twenty yards to the left.

The men were through the main doors now. Kate and Lou could hear the echo of boots on concrete growing louder . . . Another crunch cut through the air, then a burst of gunfire from an automatic weapon. Shards of wall flew into the air inches in front of Kate. She felt a stab of pain on the left side of her face, ignored it and produced an extra burst of speed.

They crashed through the door onto a stairwell and heard shouts from the first level of the car park as they tore up the stairs. The entry door on the floor below slammed against the wall.

Kate risked a glance back and saw three men in black balaclavas rush through the doorway and into the stair-well. Two of them were carrying assault rifles, the third a pistol.

'Stop!' the leader hollered.

Kate and Lou ignored them, yanked on the handrail and tore up two more flights of stairs. Reaching another door directly above the ground floor opening, Lou tore at the handle and they tumbled out into a level of the car park.

A cloying voice in Kate's head was telling her it was all futile. She shoved it aside. They had to keep going. There was no plan, but there was also no alternative but to run and run until they could run no further.

There were only a few cars on this level . . . not many places to hide. They darted across the concrete, gasping for air, sweat running into their eyes.

The men emerged from the stairwell and fanned out. 'Stop!' The man leading the group yelled again. 'This is your last warning.'

Lou pulled Kate down behind a car and a spray of bullets stuttered along the parapet, the sound reverberating across the cavernous space.

They heard the men come closer.

Kate touched her face and saw blood on her fingertips and felt a sharp sting run along her cheek. Her damaged rib was screaming at her. She and Lou rose together slowly, hands raised. They stepped back unsteadily until they reached the parapet. The three men regrouped, guns poised. Through the gaps in the balaclavas, Kate and Lou could make out their eyes, their mouths.

'So what was the point of that?' the leader said.

They stared back like startled rabbits in the headlights of an approaching car, knowing there was nowhere left to run.

'I want the papers.'

'What papers?' Lou stuttered.

The leader took a step forward. 'Don't be fucking cute.'

'If you mean the photocopies, they were destroyed in the car,' Kate said shakily. 'Search us if you don't—'

The shattering noise came a second before Kate and

Lou expected it and the vibration of the air reached them a second later. Bullets exploded around them and they heard a series of dull thuds as they found flesh.

20

The three men lay in a broken heap on the floor of the multi-storey car park, their blood rippling out across the concrete, black in the dim fluorescence.

Kate heard Lou gasp and they both glimpsed Jerry Derham slipping between two cars, a US Navy-issue M110 semi-automatic rifle in his hands. He ran forward, checked the men were dead, plucked his cell phone from his pocket and snapped an order into it. Flicking it off, he reached Kate and Lou. Lou had his arm around Kate's shoulder. A line of blood ran down her neck; it had stained her blouse.

'You both OK?' Derham asked as he checked Kate's wound and pulled back. 'A scratch.'

Kate couldn't take her eyes from the three corpses. When she did speak, her voice came as a rasp. 'How . . . How did you know?'

'I circled the block; wanted to make sure you got to the lab in one piece. I've learned I can't let you out of my sight without something terrible happening,' Derham retorted.

'Who were . . .?' Lou nodded towards the dead men.

'I would guess they're the men who killed the Campions or drove you off the road. They obviously have a problem with anyone knowing about the contents of Egbert Fortescue's papers.'

Kate closed her eyes for a second and brought a hand to her forehead.

'Come on,' Derham said, reaching for her elbow. 'You've had enough for one evening.'

'But . . .'

'No more "buts" . . . and that's an order.'

'I'm not under your command.'

'As far as I'm concerned, you are.'

Kate gently pulled her arm back. 'OK, OK, but I need to get some papers from the lab. I know I won't sleep a wink – but whatever you command!'

Jerry glanced at Lou, who shrugged his shoulders.

They took the stairs down to ground level. Derham's cell phone rang.

'Yeah . . . OK.' He looked up. 'Clean-up team should be here in a couple of minutes.'

'Makes it sound so horribly clinical,' Kate responded.

They heard the rumble of heavy vehicles approaching. Two navy trucks and a military police car were heading along the road to the institute.

Derham indicated the door to the lab building. 'I'll come up with you.'

They took the lift to the fourth floor. It opened onto a silent, dimly lit corridor. Kate led the way, right, then left. The door to the lab stood ajar, lights ablaze. They ran towards it and stopped in the doorway looking on in disbelief.

'Fuck . . .' Kate said resignedly.

The place was a wreck. It looked like nothing remained where it should have been. The floor was covered with broken glassware, papers had been scattered randomly, their desks upturned, chairs smashed. Two Macs lay shattered on the floor.

'The scanner has been destroyed,' Lou said, pointing up to a metal box about the size of a desktop printer dangling from the ceiling by a few wires. Its front screen was smashed in.

He looked over to the sealed analysis chamber in the far corner. This was where they had studied and photocopied the delicate papers from Fortescue's briefcase. He ran over to it, Kate close behind. The front panel had been staved in; glass pellets lay scattered across the floor. The briefcase and the papers had gone.

'Oh, God . . . No!' Lou yelled, the pain of the past few hours finally getting to him.

They picked their way around the vandalized glass unit. Lou leaned in and using a length of metal he gingerly pushed aside piles of glass inside the box.

'What was in there?' Derham asked, pointing to the chamber.

'The original documents from Fortescue's briefcase.'

Derham closed his eyes for a second, tipped his head back, and took a deep breath. 'Please tell me there are copies.'

'There were. We gave one set to Newman, remember? The other is now ash.'

21

Southampton Docks. Wednesday, 10 April 1912.

Dr Egbert Fortescue turned up the collar of his overcoat. At 6.45 a.m., the sky was a fresh and radiant blue, casting the cranes and dock winches into sharp relief.

Last night he had stayed at the South Western Hotel in Southampton. The place had been packed with other passengers ready to embark on the Titanic and there was an atmosphere of excitement in the smoking room after dinner.

The porter had come at six o'clock to take his luggage and he had been free to make his way over to the nearby docks with plenty of time before the ship was due to depart at noon.

Two pieces of luggage he would not hand over, but kept close by him: a pair of metal cases, one about the size of a Gladstone bag contained his briefcase of papers; the other, approximately six inches square, carried the ibnium isotope. Both were latched and locked and he kept a firm grip on their leather handles. On the train down to Southampton he had shut himself away in a private compartment and worked on his papers, trying to perfect and extend the work he and

Rutherford had forged ahead with after the success of the experiment three months earlier.

He was excited. He had been chosen to make what the small cadre of insiders in their project knew would be a historic voyage across the Atlantic. He knew, Rutherford knew, and a select few within the British and American governments knew that time was running out, that war with Germany could not be far away. Diplomats persisted in denying the possibility, but war was inevitable, and with the contents of his boxes, Fortescue had the key to victory.

The fact that he was the only man for the job gave him a huge confidence boost. Rutherford was too old and he had a professorship and a family to keep him in England. But, more importantly, even though he was officially just Rutherford's assistant and nothing was ever said between the two scientists, they both knew that he, Fortescue, was the real genius of the pair. It was he, not Rutherford, who had come up with the concept of atomic fission, and it was he who had derived most of the theoretical basis behind their experimental successes.

With just an hour to go before the huge ship was due to cast off and begin its six-day transatlantic voyage, many of the passengers were already aboard, and relatives and friends of those about to set sail had gathered on the quayside. Fortescue turned the corner close to the end of the western dock and there it was, RMS Titanic, the largest man-made moving object in creation.

He had been prepared for it, of course. He had read the statistics, analysed the plans; he was a scientist, not easily impressed by engineering feats, but even he was staggered by it.

Fortescue had approached the vessel head-on, the bow soaring up into the clear blue sky, the paintwork and the chrome glistening, deck upon deck; smooth, elegant lines; blue, black and white shining metal sweeping the length of three football pitches.

He stopped and stared, transfixed, following the graceful curves, admiring the symmetry, and he felt a burst of excitement deep inside. Hundreds of passengers stood leaning on the railings surveying the people on dry land below. Some of them were waving; others simply admired the grandstand view across the quays to the outskirts of Southampton, where chimneys spewed smoke and terraced houses stretched in long curving rows that seemed to dissolve into fog and low cloud.

There was a palpable sense of excitement to which Fortescue was not immune. He walked along a wood-panelled corridor that opened out into a large circular space, the floor covered with a sumptuous red and black patterned Worcester carpet. And there, directly ahead, he caught his first sight of perhaps the most beautiful and impressive part of the ship: the aft Grand Staircase, one of two elegantly sweeping stairways that looked as though they had been lifted from a massive hotel or stately home and inserted into this floating palace.

Fortescue had read about the staircase and some of the other wonders of the ship, such as its many restaurants, including the Ritz à la carte fine dining restaurant, the Café Parisien, which included an outdoor section called the Verandah Café, and the Palm Court for the use of First and Second Class passengers. Then there was the gymnasium with its full-time exercise instructor and, on the Middle F Deck, the indoor heated swimming pool with its accompanying hot showers and Turkish baths.

He strode over to a framed plan of the ship hanging on a wall close to one of the corridors leading away from the staircase. A couple turned and walked away, disagreeing about the best way to get to their room. Fortescue put his metal boxes on the carpet between his feet, and with one finger tracing the route on the glass he quickly worked out the way to his cabin, C16. Turning, he almost collided with a young couple standing just behind him. The woman was tall and slender, wearing an elegant powder-blue dress with matching bonnet and gloves. Blonde curls trailed to her shoulders beneath the hat. She had a strikingly beautiful face, high cheekbones and large brown eyes. The man had a neatly groomed moustache styled according to the French fashion, dark, very short hair, and a handsome face that was only ruined by his current stern expression. He looked a little older than the woman.

'I beg your pardon,' Fortescue said formally and lifted his hat a fraction of an inch. He stepped aside and the woman gave him a bright smile, the man a frown, and he was then striding towards the main corridor leading on to the First Class cabins on C-Deck.

After it had been decided that Fortescue would be the one to carry the documents and isotope sample to America, there had been some considerable debate about the details of the voyage. In the original government plans, Fortescue was to be assigned a Second Class ticket. It was believed to be the best compromise. Third would have been insulting and perhaps even unsafe; First was seen as extravagant; Second was about right. Fortescue, though, was not happy about it. He had been born into money. His father, Sir Clive Fortescue, was a millionaire businessman; his mother, Cymbeline, had come from a noble family who could trace their ancestry back to Henry VII. Egbert himself had attended Harrow before going up to Cambridge. He was a practical, hard-working and unfailingly dedicated scientist but he was also used to the finer things in life and he saw no reason to ignore comfort simply because he had chosen a career in science.

He had forsaken much of his birthright by becoming an academic. His family, in particular his father, had not approved initially and it had taken Egbert several years to thaw the frosty attitude his father had towards his middle son. But the old man had gradually relented when he realized Egbert was serious about what he was doing in Manchester and took heed of those who spoke up for the young man's brilliance.

At the university, Fortescue had mucked in with his sleeves rolled up. He had a decent enough flat in the city, which he had furnished nicely and he still liked to dress well, even in the lab, but many of the harder edges of his upper-class upbringing had been worn down and he was a far better man for it.

Fortescue's sense of style had always amused Rutherford, who was himself a stoic, nuts-and-bolts, no-nonsense type who lived in a comfortable home with his family, wore modestly tailored suits and had no taste for fine food, strong liquor or luxury of any sort. He viewed Fortescue as something of a dandy, but he would never have considered his assistant spoilt. To be spoilt meant precisely that – to have been ruined by mollycoddling or overindulgence and privilege. Fortescue was that rare and noble figure, a man born of privilege who had been guided by a desire to understand and to learn. Rutherford respected the young man even more because he was from a wealthy family.

Even so, the British government had refused to cover the extra cost of a First Class cabin, a difference of some eighteen pounds. Rutherford would not even contemplate asking the university for the money and so Egbert had dipped into his own pocket.

He walked into C16. It was actually a little larger than he had expected. One of the advertising slogans for the Titanic trumpeted in The Times was that Second Class on this ship was like First on any other liner, so First was extra luxurious. And it seemed to be true. He knew from what he had read that the First Class cabins, the parlours and massive suites were decorated in a variety of styles. Some were done out in what was called Empire Style – plenty of gold leaf and red velvet; another design was called Adams – a little simpler, but frilly. His room was decorated in what was known as Dutch Traditional – dark wood, curtains and a heavily patterned carpet. It was pleasing to Fortescue's eye.

Glancing round, he saw the ample bed, a nice sofa and a small table with four chairs, all very good quality and customized specially for this room. The pillows were fulsome and the coverlet nicely embroidered in gold and red. The sink to the left of the room was marble and came with gold-plated taps. Above these was a beautifully framed mirror. He caught his reflection: a rather gaunt face, his black hair slicked back with Roland's Macassar Oil accentuating his prominent cheekbones and large, dark eyes.

Turning back to the room, he noted that his suitcases had been brought from the hotel. 'Well, I think this is going to be worth every penny,' he said aloud.

Crouching down, he found the safe under the bed. Recalling

the private combination he had been given with his ticket, he opened the safe and stowed away his precious boxes with their priceless contents – the ibnium isotope in its protective case and his leather briefcase holding his latest research documents secured inside the second locked box. He then spun the dial on the front of the safe and stood up.

With his brief perusal of the plan near the Grand Staircase he had memorized the layout of the entire ship. It was one of his gifts – an almost perfect analytical memory, a natural ability that had served him extremely well in his chosen career. He stepped out of his cabin, locked the door and headed along a carpeted corridor feeling elated.

He emerged onto the boat deck, a promenade that was used by both First and Second Class passengers, and as he approached the railing he heard a whistle sound. This was followed by a loud blast from the ship's klaxon. The Titanic juddered as it pulled away from the quayside.

22

Two days out of Southampton. Friday, 12 April 1912.

The ocean was calm and the Titanic as steady as a dart. But even so, the majority of passengers in First Class were confined to their cabins afraid to move too far from their marble wash-basins.

Fortescue was not one of them. He had been a member of the Harrow sailing club and then a leading light in the Cambridge rowing team that had gone on to win the 1900 boat race by a staggering twenty lengths. He loved the water.

The ship had sailed from Southampton to Cherbourg, a five-hour voyage across the English Channel, to pick up 274 more passengers. From there, steaming through the night, the Titanic headed north-west bound for Queenstown near Cobh on the south coast of Ireland. The ship had dropped anchor at 11.30 the following morning, taken on the final 120 passengers and raised the Stars and Stripes above her deck, signifying the next port of call was New York harbour. By early afternoon the giant liner had slipped out into the Atlantic Ocean.

It was now Friday evening and Fortescue felt more relaxed than he had done for a long time. He had been both inspired and weighed down by the responsibility placed upon him; now the heaviness on his shoulders was lifting and he was beginning to enjoy himself. And as his mind quietened, he felt energized. Alone in his cabin with a very good claret, he sat at a compact mahogany desk with a sheaf of paper from the drawer and his favourite fountain pen. He had brought his notes from Manchester and found that his mind was wonderfully receptive to picking up the theoretical threads where he had left them before leaving the university.

From the early days of the work on atomic energy he had felt that he and Rutherford were merely scratching at the surface of a vast, barely imagined world of knowledge. At times he visualized them as children unlocking a Pandora's box or stepping into some vast spectral land yet still only glimpsing one tiny corner of it. However, during the past few weeks he had sensed that he really was onto something tangible, something he could grasp.

But then, alone in the quiet cold of his flat in Manchester, the doubts had begun. Clouded by nervous tension over the task ahead of him, he had retreated intellectually, the self-questioning becoming more intrusive. Was he deluding himself? Was he chasing phantoms? Had he fooled himself into believing in a theory a better man would have instantly realized as wrong? His equations felt correct instinctively and that was half the battle, and the early experimental successes were irrefutable. The equations were also very beautiful and that proved to him that he was on the right path, but something was holding him back. There was still something missing.

He ran the equations through his mind again. They did not quite tally.

Then he saw it, or thought he saw it. Juggling half a dozen different expressions in his mind simultaneously, he changed a negative to a positive and rearranged a set of symbols in the next row. But no, it still eluded him. He took a sip of wine, letting it roll around his mouth sensuously. He closed his eyes and tried to visualize the extra terms and the three or four other equations he would need to bring into the picture.

After a moment he managed to assemble them on the page in front of him and trawl through them one at a time, checking each term, every mathematical symbol. Then, he had it. The fifth equation was wrong – the power was squared instead of cubed and he needed a new term on the right. He made the changes and appraised the outcome. It worked. He pressed on, applying the new result in the next row of equations and they too all fell into place like pieces of a jigsaw puzzle.

What he had visualized was, he knew, the essence of an incredibly powerful and totally original way of thinking about energy. It was simple, pure, complete and irrefutably true.

But there was more, so much more. He knew it instinctively, but as he reached to grab it, it slipped away. Fortescue let out a sigh. He had experienced this before. A thought, a stray strand of an idea, a tiny thread that could be unravelled into something immense . . . it was there, but not there. He could see it, yet it was invisible.

He couldn't give up, not now. He tried to pull the ideas back. They moved further away. He tried harder to ensnare the elusive concept, pull it to him, but no, it was dissolving, melting to nothing.

He took a deep breath and slumped in the chair. 'You will

return to me,' he whispered. He stood up and changed for dinner.

*

He did not see another soul until he reached the main hallway leading to the First Class Dining Saloon on D-Deck and a group of passengers heading towards him. They made a stylish foursome: the women wore similar formal dresses, one black, the other white; the men had dressed just as he had done in black bow tie and dinner suit, hair slicked back. The older of the two men had a cane. Fortescue nodded to them politely and made his way to the reception area

It was a large room, white pillars breaking up the space, the ceiling heavily patterned with elegant white reliefs. The spotless carpet was a pleasing red, subtly patterned to reflect the shapes embossed into the ceiling. Wicker chairs and chaises longues had been placed in clusters around the room with little drinks tables between them. There were perhaps a score of passengers seated drinking and chatting animatedly in pairs and small groups.

Fortescue found an unoccupied table some way from the nearest party and almost before he had taken his seat a liveried waiter appeared at his elbow. The man was wearing a brilliant white uniform with highly polished brass buttons, the emblem of the cruise company over his left breast. Fortescue ordered a gin and tonic and sat back to admire the surroundings and noticed at a table a few yards away the attractive young couple he had seen when he had boarded the ship. The woman stole a glance his way.

From the pocket of his dinner jacket, he withdrew a slender

volume, Milton's Areopagitica. *He lit a cigarette then, taking a sip of his drink, he began to read the book. A few moments later he lowered it and stretched out his arm to place his glass on a delicate drinks mat. The two strangers were standing in front of him. He quickly lifted himself out of his seat.*

'I do beg your pardon,' the woman said with a friendly smile. She had a lace-gloved hand extended.

Fortescue looked from the woman to her companion and then took the lady's hand, turned and shook the man's hand.

'My brother and I were discussing you,' the woman went on.

'Oh?'

She produced a small laugh. 'That came out badly.' She had a faint accent.

'That's a relief.'

'What my sister means, sir, is that we spend an inordinate amount of time trying to ascertain who our fellow travellers might be and why they are aboard. You may tell we do not have enough to occupy us!' He had a deep, musical voice with a similar accent to his sister but slightly more pronounced.

'I apologize again,' the woman said. 'Allow me to introduce ourselves. My name is Frieda Schiel and this is my brother Marcus. We are from Switzerland.'

'It's a great pleasure,' Fortescue replied. 'My name is Wickins, John Wickins. Please do take a seat.' He indicated two chairs the other side of the table and called over a waiter.

They each ordered drinks.

'So, please,' Marcus began as the waiter retreated, 'if you do not mind, may we give you our judgement?'

Fortescue looked puzzled.

'As to who we think you are and why you are aboard?' Frieda added.

'Ah, yes . . . please do.'

'We concluded you are either a writer or a painter; definitely a man with artistic proclivities,' Frieda said earnestly. 'And we believe you are travelling to America because a close relative has died and you need to organize the estate.'

Fortescue nodded sagely. 'Well,' he replied. 'I'm afraid you are wrong on both counts.'

'Oh dear,' Marcus responded and looked forlornly at his sister.

'The truth is desperately prosaic,' Fortescue added. 'I'm simply visiting my father, a businessman in New York whom I have not seen for five years. I'm actually a barrister. Now it is your turn. What do you do and why are you aboard?'

Frieda took a sip of her wine. 'I am an actress,' she said.

Fortescue raised an eyebrow. 'My goodness. You are the first actress I have ever met. I'm most impressed.'

'My brother is a writer and film director. We are travelling to Hollywood.'

Fortescue was shaking his head. 'I'm overwhelmed! I have read about the nickel theatres.'

'Nickelodeons.'

'Yes, that is right. I thought I might visit one when I reach New York. Now I definitely shall. And you plan to emigrate?'

Frieda glanced at her brother and they both nodded. 'We have become famous and successful in Switzerland,' Marcus said. 'But it is not exactly the centre of the moving-picture world. If we are to grow artistically, we need to be where the action is, as our American cousins would say.'

Fortescue laughed. 'How jolly exciting.'

They finished their drinks and found a table in the Main Dining Saloon. This was said to be the largest room afloat, *and it was indeed impressive, stretching the entire width of the ship across D-Deck. In fact, it was too big – its few dozen diners sat lost amidst the splendid array of white-linen-topped tables and green velvet upholstered chairs that together could accommodate five hundred. A team of waiters wafted around, decidedly under-employed.*

The meal itself certainly lived up to the glowing reviews Fortescue had read in the newspapers. He ordered oysters followed by filet mignon Lili with chateau potatoes, while the young pair ordered lamb with mint sauce, creamed carrots, topped off with Waldorf pudding for dessert.

After the meal the men drank port and brandy and smoked cigars while Frieda sipped a black coffee; then Marcus suggested he turn in, leaving Egbert alone with the actress. They saw the young man off to the lifts that would take him to B-Deck where they had neighbouring rooms.

'You two are very close,' Fortescue said as he and Frieda returned to the reception area.

'We always have been. We are only a year apart. I'm the elder one.'

'And your parents?'

'They died when I was eighteen – a boating accident.'

'I am sorry.'

She waved a hand between them. 'It was almost six years ago. It drew Marcus and me closer.'

'And now you work together and have planned a career in the New World.'

'Yes.'

Fortescue raised his brandy glass. 'To your future.'

'Thank you, Mr Wickins. And now, I really must retire too.'

They rose unsteadily just as the ship pitched a little more than normal. Frieda started to fall and Fortescue just managed to find her arm to steady her. She came up close to him and he caught her aroma: a heady, expensive perfume.

'Goodness!' Frieda exclaimed, turning to face Fortescue only inches from him. 'I thought I had my sea legs. I blame it on the champers!'

Fortescue smiled and the woman stepped back. 'Perhaps we should clear our heads with a stroll on deck,' Egbert suggested. 'What do you say?'

'I would like that very much.'

They took the Grand Staircase up to the First Class promenade on A-Deck. An attendant at the exit placed a merino wool shawl about Frieda's shoulders and she pulled it tight over her flimsy cocktail dress. Fortescue joked that after Manchester in winter, the Atlantic wind held no horrors for him and they stepped out together into the night, the wooden deck illuminated by the lights of the ship, man-made brightness set against the star-filled expanse overhead.

They did not see another passenger as they walked slowly towards the bow. Barely visible in the dark stood the great funnels churning out smoke into the Atlantic air. The boilermen never stopped working; the engines kept going night and day. From beyond the railings they could hear the sweeping, splashing water against the steel hull.

Soon they were passing close to the wheelhouse and the bridge which stood one level above them on what was called the boat deck. Not far ahead stood the bow mast with the crow's nest perched halfway up. They could just discern the white cage and a flicker of a blue uniform.

'I still can't quite take in the magnificence of this ship,' Frieda said as they reached the forward railing and looked out to the dark vista, a wall of blackness in which the precise line of the horizon could only be guessed at.

'Yes,' Fortescue replied. 'It is something very special indeed.'

'Do you ever feel scared by it?'

Fortescue gave her a puzzled look and tilted his head slightly. 'What do you mean?'

'Do you not feel it is rather conceited? An act that is rather presumptuous?'

'Presumption towards whom? Neptune?' Fortescue retorted with a grin.

But Frieda looked at him seriously. 'I think it is arrogant of us tiny human beings to build this Leviathan.'

Fortescue was startled for a moment. He was used to miracles. He had performed some himself. But then again, he could understand what Frieda was saying. He knew that some people questioned the right of scientists such as himself to probe what they considered 'God's domain', but he could not now talk of such things – it was hardly the preserve of a barrister.

'What an extraordinary notion!' he said. 'Are you sure it should be referred to as a Leviathan, Fräulein Schiel? That would imply the Titanic is a monster. I see it as entirely benign, our servant; a beast of burden perhaps, but a truly magnificent one.'

'Possibly,' Frieda replied and shivered.

'You're cold.'

'It's nothing. Manchester may be cold, but Switzerland is colder.' They both laughed.

'So, when you arrive in New York you still have a very long journey ahead of you,' Fortescue said.

'A week by train to the west coast.'

'Even so, I envy you.'

She turned and surveyed his face with her brown eyes. 'I don't think for a moment that it will be easy. Being a star in Switzerland is one thing but, well, I was a big fish in a very small pond. The film studios in Hollywood make many films, but there are also many starlets and hopefuls. I've been told that the vast majority of aspiring actresses end up waiting tables. But my brother and I will try our best.'

'I'm sure you will,' Fortescue commented. 'And now I think we ought to get you inside before you freeze to death.'

They walked back at a faster pace. Fortescue was chilled to the bone. They dived inside at the first opportunity and followed a wide corridor down to the landing around the forward Grand Staircase. From there they descended one flight to B-Deck and stopped at the foot of the stairs.

'Well, thank you,' Frieda said.

'For what?'

'For saving me when I almost injured myself earlier, Mr Wickins.' Then she produced a faintly mischievous smile.

'And thank you for an enchanting evening,' Fortescue replied. He shook Frieda's hand and watched as she turned towards the corridor leading away to her cabin.

23

Fortescue opened his eyes to see a beam of bright white light coming through the porthole, dust motes floating in their thousands. He felt a sharp stab of a headache and remembered how much he had drunk with Frieda and her brother, then turned over and went back to sleep.

By afternoon, he felt a little better and ordered room service – a fulsome meal of egg, sausage, bacon and pints of strong coffee which served to sweep away the last vestiges of his hangover and tiredness, allowing his mind to wander where it should: into the realms of theory and mathematical abstraction. So, at his desk alone with coffee and brandy as well as a pair of fine cigars, he pushed forward his thinking on the new atomic theory he had begun in Manchester.

He knew he had to note down everything, write out everything and keep meticulous records of his reasoning because he planned to have them couriered to Rutherford as soon as Titanic docked in New York. Out here in the middle of the Atlantic he felt cut off from his usual academic network, but also sure of himself and aware that what he was developing was beautiful and true. Even so, it would be good to have a second pair of eyes, a fresh mind such as Ernest Rutherford's, to offer a different perspective. He always valued the older man's opinions and contributions. With this work there could be no room for error – the fate of nations depended upon it.

RMS Titanic had been at sea for two and a half days. They were now over 1,200 miles west of Queenstown and, according to the daily bulletins posted on the First Class promenade, averaging an impressive twenty-one knots. So far, everything had been smooth sailing: the weather superb, the giant ship domed by clear blue sky and surrounded by calm ocean.

Fortescue checked his watch. It was 6.05 p.m., an hour before dinner. He made a snap decision, called up the butler in charge of his corridor, ordered dinner in his room, pulled on his overcoat and walked towards the promenade.

He could not get the equations out of his mind. At his desk he had been concentrating on the page of notation in front of him so long the figures had started to distort. He had reached a dead end in his thinking.

Out on the promenade the mathematics would not fade away; the numbers kept tumbling through his mind. He sat down on a bench, his back against cold metal. There was a porthole a few feet away and he could hear music spilling from the room behind it. He guessed he was outside one of the First Class drawing rooms and then remembered there was a Mozart quartet booked to play between six and seven o'clock. He recognized the piece: the Allegretto from 'Klavierkonzerte No. 25'.

He pulled out a pencil from the top pocket of his coat and began to search for a piece of paper. Checking his jacket and finding nothing, he rummaged through his trouser pockets and in his back pocket was a folded page from the desk drawer in his cabin. Leaning forward, paper on knee, he licked the tip of the pencil and began to scribble.

Instantly the outside world dissolved. He could no longer hear the waves lapping against the hull of the ship. The almost subliminal throb of the engines was stilled. He wrote a single line, then stopped, the pencil poised over the paper. Another line came, followed by a third. He started to feel the familiar buzz of expectation, a thrill running along his spine as he jotted down a fourth line, a fifth, and the equations began to intermesh. 'Yes,' he said under his breath. 'Yes . . .'

The gust of wind was totally unexpected and Fortescue was so absent from the real world he had no chance of stopping the paper slipping from his knee. It was caught in a vortex of air and flew away over the deck.

Jumping up, he tried to grab the paper, but grasped nothing but ocean breeze. The scrap of notes slipped further away, towards the deck and then up again. Fortescue swung left then right and tried again to catch the paper. He was so lost in concentration he did not see a young boy leap out from behind a bulkhead, dash across the promenade and snatch up the paper. Almost colliding with the child, he tripped and fell to the deck.

'You all right, mister?' the kid asked, helping Fortescue to his feet.

Egbert peered at the boy holding the paper out towards him.

'Just caught it,' the kid said proudly and gazed at the symbols for a second.

The boy was small and pale. Fortescue guessed he could have been twelve or thirteen, but looked younger because of his size. He had an intelligent, pleasing face, but his clothes were too big for him, the baggy trousers worn through at the knees and the tatty jacket stained. The boy gave Fortescue an uncertain gappy smile.

Egbert took the paper from him. 'Thank you,' he said. 'What's your name?'

The boy looked around. The promenade was empty. 'Billy. Billy O'Donnell.' He had a strong Irish accent.

'Well, Billy, I am extremely grateful.' He pulled a thrupenny piece from his trouser pocket and handed it to him. 'My name is John Wickins.'

Billy took it. 'Thanking you, sir. Looked like some strange mathematics,' he added and flicked a hand towards the paper.

Fortescue produced a small laugh. 'It is indeed, Billy.'

'Don't look like no maths I ever saw. I love numbers and stuff.'

'Do you?' Fortescue said. 'Well, there are far worse things to study. I'm very keen on maths myself. I teach it.'

'You're in First Class and you're a teacher!' Billy exclaimed, then stopped himself. 'Meaning no disrespect, but . . .'

Fortescue was grinning. He liked this boy – he had character. Touching the side of his nose, he said: 'Rich daddy.' And he gave Billy an indulgent wink. 'So you're good at school then?'

Billy exhaled loudly through his nose. 'Ain't been to school for over a year. Nah. I taught meself to read and write and I found a book of mathematics. I brought it with me on the ship. Actually, I nicked it from the library.' He pulled a face.

Fortescue shook his head slowly. 'I wouldn't go announcing that to the world, my lad. So, what are you doing here?'

Billy looked around again nervously. 'Exploring,' he said in a conspiratorial whisper.

Fortescue raised an eyebrow. 'Well, your secret is safe with me. One good turn, deserves . . .'

The boy had heard a sound and shot a sideways look along the deck. He held a finger to his lips. Fortescue glanced down the promenade and saw a man in a blue uniform. The officer was lifting a tarpaulin and flashing a torch beneath it. He recognized him as Herbert Pitman, the ship's Third Officer, a short, muscular fellow with a finely chiselled jaw and full moustache.

Billy scrambled away behind the same bulkhead from which he had appeared a few minutes earlier. At that moment, Pitman looked up, lowered his torch and flicked it off. Then he strode along the deck towards Fortescue.

'Good evening, sir,' he said as he came close.

'Lost something, Mr Pitman?'

The officer flicked his head back and rolled his eyes. 'Some little brat from Third is sneaking around First. I've already had complaints from two of the lady passengers. You haven't seen anything?'

Fortescue shook his head and caught a glimpse of Billy peeking around the bulkhead immediately behind Pitman and pulling a comical face to try to impersonate the rather starchy officer.

'No, I haven't,' the scientist said. 'But I'll be sure to let you know if I do.'

'Well, you have a very pleasant evening, sir,' Pitman replied. He touched the brim of his hat and proceeded along the deck. Fortescue looked up to the bulkhead but Billy had gone.

He suddenly felt cold, checked his watch and realized he ought to get back to the cabin before the food arrived. Fortescue smiled and doffed his hat to a pair of middle-aged ladies as he passed through the doors into the reception area. They were wrapped up with hats and scarves and walking along the corridor leading towards the bow. He began to feel hungry.

An exquisitely attired gentleman approached; a much younger woman had her arm interlocked with his. Fortescue recognized them from the newspapers. It was the American business mogul Benjamin Guggenheim, heir to one of the world's largest fortunes. The woman was an actress named Léontine Aubart. They had created quite a stir on board due to the fact that Guggenheim, a married man of almost fifty, was accompanied by a woman half his age and known to be his mistress.

Fortescue hadn't cared a jot about the gossip, but it was unavoidable, the talk of the ship. He stood to one side to let the couple pass. They had just drawn parallel when Guggenheim stopped, turned, and to Fortescue's utter astonishment, extended a hand. 'Mr Wickins, is it not?'

'Er, yes,' Fortescue responded. He could not disguise his surprise. 'Mr Guggenheim.'

The American dipped his head ever so slightly. 'This is my friend, Miss Aubart.' The lady offered her hand.

'Delighted to make your acquaintance,' Fortescue said politely.

'I've heard a great deal about you, Mr Wickins,' Guggenheim said.

'You have?'

'Indeed. That wonderful Swiss brother and sister team, the Schiels, could not have praised you more!'

'Oh, well . . . that is nice to hear.'

'You would have had your invitation by now . . . no?'

'Invitation?'

'To the soirée tonight?'

'Ah, yes . . . sorry,' he lied. 'Indeed, I'm greatly looking forward to it.'

Guggenheim smiled. 'See you there, my friend.'

Fortescue nodded and strode on, bemused.

*

What looked like the invitation to the soirée had been slipped under the door, but there was something else; he sensed immediately that someone had been in his cabin while he was out. It was not the steward with the food. If he had received no reply, he would have either left the tray outside or taken it back to the kitchen.

The cabin looked almost exactly as he had left it, but there were some subliminal changes that had triggered his suspicions. He checked the safe under his bed, flicked through the combination and opened the door. The boxes were there. Using a letter opener from the desk, he gingerly unlatched the smaller container holding the isotope. It was untouched and he quickly flicked back the latch and locked it. Then he checked that his precious briefcase was there too. Everything was in order. There was no copy of the combination number anywhere – and there was no way to open the safe without it.

He had left nothing else of value in the room and taken his latest notes with him. He locked the safe again and straightened up. Glancing at his desk, he could tell his fountain pen had been moved a fraction of an inch and a piece of blank paper shifted slightly from where it had been when he left the cabin half an hour earlier.

He stood rigid looking around the comfortable room. He was pretty sure nothing else had been moved. But what did this mean? His instincts told him someone had intruded upon his privacy. Furthermore, they must have either been a skilled burglar or else they had obtained a copy of his key. Most importantly, there had to be a reason for it. Someone must know who he was and why he was aboard. They must have been watching him, studying his movements. He would have the locks changed first thing the following morning.

A knock at the door jolted Fortescue from his darkening thoughts. He turned, swung open the door and saw a young steward he had noticed last night at the restaurant.

'Your dinner order, sir,' the steward said. He had an earnest face, warm brown eyes, a continental accent. Fortescue guessed he was Italian or perhaps Spanish.

'Thank you. On the table, please.' He slipped the young man a sixpenny piece as he left.

Leaving the food for a moment, Fortescue glanced down at the invitation he had picked up and placed on his desk. It came in an elegant cream envelope with his name in green ink and written in a feminine hand. He sliced it open, took out a single piece of paper and read:

Dear Mr Wickins,

Please do come to our little gathering at the Verandah Café at nine o'clock this evening. We will be offering drinks and providing entertainment for our new friends aboard ship.

Cordially yours,

Frieda and Marcus Schiel.

24

The Verandah Café was usually a communal area for all First Class passengers, but on the first afternoon of the voyage, the beautiful and charming Frieda had befriended the Captain, Edward Smith, and persuaded him to have it put aside as a private function room for her planned event on Saturday evening.

The cafe was an elegant place to eat and to meet fellow First Class passengers. Long and narrow with windows looking out to the port side of the Titanic, the opposite wall was lined with large mirrors and doorways leading to another set of rooms and the kitchens. It was perhaps the least formal public area, one of the few places where children could play, but during Saturday afternoon a great deal of work had been done. The tables and chairs had been stored away, the doors out to the deck were closed and someone with a modern eye for decoration had decked out the room with great swathes of coloured silk that draped from the ceiling to produce an effect reminiscent of a Bedouin tent. Oil lamps covered with brightly painted shades hung suspended from wires traversing the low ceiling and the wooden floor was covered with small pieces of coloured paper shaped as flower petals.

Fortescue was one of the last to arrive and was immediately taken aback by the scene. A young waiter in White Star Line uniform approached with a tray of champagne glasses. Fortescue selected one and brought it to his lips just as loud music burst across the room. He had not noticed the ship's band grouped together at the far end close to the deck exit and the music they were making was like nothing he had ever heard before. To his ears it sounded absolutely cacophonous. One of the band was singing. The words made little sense to him.

'What do you think, Mr Wickins?' It was Frieda at Fortescue's right elbow.

'Wonderful,' he replied. 'Your people have a done a fantastic job with the decor, Fräulein Schiel.'

'Please, I think we have moved beyond surnames. Unless you address me as Frieda I shall be most offended.'

Fortescue smiled and sipped his champagne. 'Then it must also be John.'

She nodded. 'What do you think of the band?'

'Extraordinary.'

She detected his tone and laughed out loud. 'It is the very latest thing. I brought the sheet music on board especially. It's called "Alexander's Ragtime Band" by a man named Irving Berlin. I've given the musicians a whole ream of ragtime music; they were a little bemused, I must admit . . . But it's so dilly.'

'And what does "dilly" mean?'

She rolled her eyes. 'Jazz lingo, John . . .'

He nodded. 'I guess it's part of your job to teach yourself "Californian".'

'I'll get you dancing to Mr Berlin before the night is out.'

He raised his glass and she tugged his arm, pulling him over to a small gathering close by. Frieda made the introductions.

'Lucy, Lady Duff Gordon and her husband, Sir Cosmo Duff Gordon.' She waved a hand towards a middle-aged couple. The husband looked very formal in a stiff evening suit, but his wife had a lightness about her and a sparkle in her eyes. 'Lady Duff Gordon owns the most wonderful shop in the world,' Frieda went on volubly. 'I went there last year on a visit to London, Mr Wickins. It is Maison Lucile of Mayfair.' Fortescue gave her a blank look. 'Lingerie,' she added with a cheeky grin.

Next in line were a shy couple, newly-weds from Rome who seemed completely overwhelmed by the evening. They said 'hello', in heavily accented English.

'This is a man you may already know, Mr Wickins,' Frieda said. 'Mr William Stead. Mr Stead . . . Mr Wickins.'

'Good evening,' the man said stiffly and looked Fortescue up and down.

'Mr Stead is a famous journalist. And I only learned from him this evening that he is a very serious spiritualist.'

Fortescue nodded, keeping his thoughts to himself. He wanted to question the oxymoron of 'serious spiritualist', but kept quiet on the subject, merely nodding and producing a polite smile. 'A pleasure . . .'

'Finally, this is Mrs Helen Candee, a most accomplished author.'

Fortescue took the lady's hand. 'Delighted to make your acquaintance,' he said. 'I'm an admirer. I followed your series of short stories published last year in The Times.*'*

'Well, I shall leave you all to chat. I must circulate,' Frieda announced and was soon engrossed in more introductions.

They formed an awkward group; people who would not normally associate informally but were now thrown together in this most unusual environment.

Stead was ebullient. 'Fine young lady,' he said, looking over towards where Frieda had vanished amongst her guests. 'Terribly louche career choice, though, acting, wouldn't you agree . . . er, sorry, I forgot your . . .'

'Wickins, John Wickins,' Fortescue replied and studied the man's face. He was a showman, Fortescue realized immediately, and a big-mouth. Surely he could not be so poor with his memory as to forget a name offered only a minute earlier. It was a deliberate display of one-upmanship!

'I imagine that would depend on how good one is as an actor,' Fortescue commented. 'She has the advantage that her brother Marcus is a writer and cinematographer.'

Stead exhaled through his nose. 'Writer? Well, I suppose he could be called that.'

'I spoke to him earlier,' Mrs Candee interjected. 'He seems to have a firm understanding of what he is planning to do . . . and he is an extremely well-read young gentleman with a penchant for Proust.'

'Good old Frog literature, what?' Stead glanced around at the others. Lady Duff Gordon frowned; the Italian couple had no idea what Stead was talking about. Only Sir Cosmo seemed to concur, nodding seriously.

Fortescue turned to Helen Candee, a broad-shouldered and well-upholstered woman in her early fifties, her thick wavy hair greying. She had dark, probing eyes and a rather severe face. Fortescue knew the woman possessed a sound intellect, and was a rabid feminist who supported the suffragette movement. He could sense that she was not well liked by the Englishmen in the group.

'Will you be writing a piece about this voyage?' he asked, turning away slightly from the others as Stead began to hold forth on something Fortescue suspected would be both boring and self-aggrandizing.

'Oh, no!' Helen Candee said, shaking her head. 'Purely a pleasure trip. I do not mind confessing that I'm quite exhausted. I have just completed the first draft of a novel.'

'Indeed? How wonderful,' Fortescue replied and was about to ask what the subject matter might be when he heard a commotion from the other end of the room. He saw Marcus Schiel getting on a chair.

'Ladies and gentlemen, most welcome guests,' he announced. His accent seemed a little more defined than on the only other occasion Fortescue had heard him speak, the previous night at dinner. 'My sister Frieda and I have prepared a little entertainment for you. Many of you would have heard of the great filmmaker Georges Méliès who works from his astonishing studio in Montreuil near Paris. My sister Frieda and I have had the extraordinary good fortune and privilege to work with the great man since Christmas, and tonight we would like to show you a short segment of a film I helped direct and in which my sister acted. Ladies and gentlemen, would you please follow me through to the adjoining room where we have set up some of the equipment we have brought with us.'

Fortescue could tell the gathered elite were a little taken aback. He heard a woman say, 'Well, goodness me!' He turned to Helen Candee who had also sensed the bemusement. She beamed at him as he ushered her forward and they fell in behind Stead and the Duff Gordons. They all shuffled towards a darkened room off the side of the cafe.

It took a while for his eyes to adjust and he felt a little uncomfortable being squashed into a blacked-out confined space; but the sensation did not last long. He heard murmurs and someone trod on his left foot, but then a light burst across the room illuminating the faces of all those gathered around a central table that held a monstrous-looking contraption. A couple of the more nervous women exclaimed loudly and one of the gentlemen growled, 'Good Lord!'

Fortescue had heard of film projectors and had read about their workings, but he had no concept of how big and ugly they were. The machine on the table was the size of a large dog crouched ready to pounce. The light was intensely bright; a dazzling beam shone on the far wall forming a rectangle about six feet by four.

'Ladies and gentlemen.' It was Marcus Schiel again. 'Please don't be alarmed!' He laughed nervously. 'We would like to present to you a full five-minute excerpt from Georges Méliès' latest motion-picture masterpiece Conquest of the Pole, starring Frieda Schiel.'

Fortescue had in fact seen a movie once before. A year ago he had spent a very pleasant week in Brighton. One afternoon he had been caught in a deluge and had dashed for the closest building. It happened to be a venue called the Duke of York's Picture House. There he had paid tuppence, been escorted to a rather uncomfortable chair in a small half-empty theatre and watched amazed as two films were shown, both recently acquired from America: Frankenstein and The Abyss. He had left the cinema reeling and thrilled. But that had not prepared him for the onslaught on the senses he now experienced. For in this confined space, and aboard a ship in the mid-Atlantic of all places, he was watching the most extraordinarily clever piece of art unfold on the makeshift screen.

He could sense the excitement of the others all around him, even a reverberation of fear, surprise, enchantment. It all added to the experience, making it almost surreal, so that after five minutes in the blaze of light and scintillating images, he found he was short of breath.

In the motion picture Frieda looked like a creature from a fantasy; she was dressed in an exotic headdress and played the Queen of Ice repelling the advances of prospective explorers determined to reach the North Pole. There was no doubting her talent and Fortescue could immediately understand why she and her brother had taken the chance of trying to find success in America. The camera loved Frieda – she was a natural.

The lights came up, and for a moment no one could speak, no one could move, then someone started to clap. Fortescue quickly picked up on it and joined in. Suddenly the room was echoing with the applause of the gathered guests. Frieda appeared on one side of the room with perfect theatrical timing. The gathering parted to form a path for her to walk through. Then Marcus joined her and they both took a bow, the applause still going strong.

'My new friends, honoured guests,' Frieda said and raised her hands to quieten the gathering. They hushed and she went on. 'It is wonderful of you to give my brother and myself such a fulsome reception. We –' and she glanced at Marcus '– are *so thrilled that you have enjoyed our little distraction. Now, I urge you all to indulge in the champagne and canapés – indulge!' And with that she swept through the room and back into the main part of the cafe.*

*

'A champagne haze is a wonderful thing,' Fortescue thought as he glided slowly across the polished wooden floor of the Verandah Café. The band were still playing, a quiet, slow number dominated by a subdued piano motif, a low trombone and a single viola. He was alone with Frieda. The other guests had trickled away, Marcus, the last to go, his face filled with pleasure, eyes bright, proud and humbled at the same time. Fortescue had decided that Marcus was a jolly decent sort and had told him so at least twice a short while before the young man had retreated across the room swaying slightly.

Then suddenly the music was over, and the musicians were standing up and beginning to pack away their instruments. Frieda went over to thank them warmly and to give each a sovereign. Fortescue saw the bandmaster bow slightly and smile, then she was back in his arms even though there was no music playing.

After the silence fell the room seemed a little forlorn. The corridors back to the First Class cabins and suites were quiet, the lights dimmed. Frieda and Marcus had small suites on B-Deck. Fortescue stood at the door to Frieda's and looked into her eyes. In that moment, he believed he was the happiest he had ever been in his life. All the anxieties that had hung over him seemed now to be of little importance. The coming war, if such a monstrous thing should happen, seemed a distant shadow. His work he loved, but at this moment he could no more focus on that than walk to the moon, so why bother? 'Float,' he told himself, 'just float.' And then Frieda was opening the door and pulling him into the room.

Her lips tasted of candyfloss. It was the most wonderful flavour in the universe and he knew something of the universe.

Frieda's hands were on his face, her tongue searching inside his mouth. He felt her narrow waist under his palms and she leaned into him provocatively, the swell of her breasts against his shirt.

They seemed to melt, to merge together as if they were a single being. He was between her naked thighs, her hand reaching down, pulling him out of his dinner-suit trousers, ripping buttons and cloth. Then she had him in her hand and he had never felt so aroused in his life. Her warmth hit him, and the scent of her. He thought he would come straight away, but he managed to rein himself in and to move inside her, hearing her moan in his ear, urging him on. She wanted it quickly and he let himself go.

25

The merest tease of orange had appeared above the eastern horizon. Fortescue walked along the poop deck towards the stern. He could hear the churning of water as it slewed through the propellers, and with it a deeper sound – the throb of the massive engines producing the 50,000 horsepower that propelled the ship through the ocean.

There was a bite to the air, a predawn chill and something extra, the first tendrils of cold from the ice fields to the north. But wrapped up in a thick greatcoat over his dinner suit, a woollen scarf about his neck and good-quality leather gloves, Fortescue was feeling warm.

He had left Frieda in her room, her blonde curls decorous on her pillow, shadow and light cast across her face as she slept. She looked utterly exquisite, an angel in repose.

Alone now in the predawn, his mind was awash, a clash of intellect and emotion he had never felt before. Less than a week ago he had been in Manchester with Rutherford. The meeting with the prime minister lay behind him, the plans set in motion, his destiny decided for him by the great men – Asquith, Churchill, American politicians. Now, he was at sea . . . all at sea! He was in love, he was sure of that. But at the same time *he was on fire . . .* In love and on fire, what a combination, he mused. His mind was racing: formulae, Frieda's thighs, numbers, her breasts, powers of ten, the power of her scent, exponentials and flawless skin. It was intoxicating.

He took a deep breath. The salt and the oxygen, the spray of the ocean foam and he was imbued with – what would he call it – power? Yes, power; a strange power . . . It made him believe there was little he could not do.

Sitting down, he withdrew his pen and sheets of headed notepaper, glanced for a moment at the water as it was sucked down by the ship's giant propellers, churned and tossed around, and he started to write his formulae, emptying his mind.

The symbols flowed, a torrent of numbers, letters, expressions. Swept up in the commotion of mathematics, he could barely breathe. He paused, looked at what he had written and felt a wave of excitement. 'This is special,' he whispered, the sound caught in the air. 'This is really special.' He began to cover page after page until he felt drained.

He heard a shuffling sound from behind him and turned to see the young kid, Billy O'Donnell.

'Well, hello there,' Fortescue said, tucking his papers into his jacket pocket. 'What are you doing up so early?' He looked at his fob watch. 'It's barely six o'clock.'

'Can't sleep,' Billy replied. 'I'm sharing a bunk with another kid. Three families in the room and the men all snore like hogs.'

Fortescue laughed, but then saw Billy's serious expression and nodded. 'Can't be very nice.'

'So what brings you here, Mr Wickins?'

'I couldn't sleep either, Billy. Wanted to get some air. What's the book?' He noticed a tatty volume under Billy's arm; the cover was half off and the front scuffed and oil-streaked.

'I was tellin' you about me maths. This is me prized possession.' He lifted up the book. 'I've read other maths books in the library but this is me favourite; I take it with me everywhere I go.'

'May I?'

It was a copy of Euclid's Elements. Fortescue opened the front cover and glanced through the book that was so familiar to him from his own teenage years. The margins were covered with untidy scrawl, question marks, comments and calculations. 'You understand any of this?' he asked.

The boy looked affronted. 'Yes!'

'Who wrote in it? Your schoolteacher?'

Billy laughed. It was the first time Fortescue had seen him produce more than a brief smile. He had three teeth missing. 'Told you yesterday, ain't been to school for a long time. It's my writing. I have lots of questions, see.'

Fortescue turned back to the book and read a comment. 'This Euclid fella knows a thing or two.' He smiled and turned the page. 'Don't get this . . . oh, yes, right . . . correspondences.' Fortescue was staggered and looked up to see Billy staring at him earnestly. 'So how far through are you?' There was an edge of scepticism to his voice.

Billy took back the book. 'Well, I've been through it all three, four times, but I always find Book IX, Number Theory the best.' He flicked forward to find the appropriate section.

Fortescue considered the boy. 'How old are you, Billy?'

'Twelve, Mr Wickins.'

The scientist took the book again and found the section on number theory. 'OK.' He ran a finger down the right-hand page. 'Let's see how much you know.' He took a breath. 'If *a number multiplied by itself makes a cubic number, what can you say about that number?'*

Billy looked into Fortescue's eyes. 'I can see why you wouldn't believe me, mister.'

Fortescue held the boy's intense look. He could read so much pain there, years of neglect and filth. He could imagine how Billy had been treated all his life. He had probably been kicked from pillar to post, physically and mentally abused, and yet there was a light in those eyes, a light that was markedly absent from so many wealthy and celebrated people Fortescue had met. It was the light of a self-respect that had been hard won, battled for, squeezed from the dry sponge of the shabby life Billy O'Donnell had been allotted.

'I'm sorry,' Fortescue said and handed back the book.

'That number would itself be cubic,' Billy said, finally answering Fortescue's question.

Fortescue bit his lip and tilted his head to one side. 'Sit down.'

The kid glanced around nervously but did as he was told and Fortescue withdrew his papers, found a blank page and removed the top of his pen. On the paper he wrote out a simple equation, the meaning of which a clever fifteen-year-old at a decent private school should have grasped. 'What does that tell you?'

Billy considered the expression. 'It says that y is equal to three x squared minus five.'

'All right, so, in your head, work out what y would be if x was two.'

'Seven,' Billy said immediately.

Fortescue took a deep breath. 'Good.' He wrote out a much more complex equation involving higher powers of x and square roots and handed the pen and paper to Billy. 'What is z when x is four?'

Billy merely glanced at the paper. 'Three.'

Fortescue was stunned, took back the piece of paper, wrote out an elaborate piece of calculus and handed it to Billy. 'There's nothing like this in Elements,' the scientist commented. 'What do you make of it?'

Billy studied the symbols and the figures. 'It's a quadratic equation that has to be integrated. I think it's to work out the volume of rotation between the two points.' He paused and ran a finger along the line of mathematical symbols. 'The answer is 3.24 cubic inches.'

Fortescue was shaking his head and staring at the boy's serious expression. 'Well,' he said excitedly, 'that is truly remarkable. Come with me.'

'Where to?'

'My cabin. I want to see how much you know . . . I won't bite!'

They saw no one on the way and when Fortescue found half a jug of barley water left over from the previous evening, poured a large glass and handed it to Billy, the boy relaxed a little.

'Let's see how far this talent of yours goes,' the scientist said. 'Is that OK with you?'

Billy shrugged. 'What do I get out of it?'

Fortescue gave him a surprised look and went to reach into his pocket.

Billy was shaking his head and wore his affronted look again. 'I didn't mean money, Mr Wickins.'

'What do you mean then?'

'Just that you teach me something new that I can take away with me.'

Fortescue nodded. 'Yes, yes, of course, Billy.'

Fortescue completely lost track of the time. This young boy was an astonishing prodigy. It had taken him an hour of questions, pushing further and further into advanced mathematics, before Billy hit a wall and could not solve a problem, and that was simply because he had never learned the technique. When Fortescue had then taught him how to unravel the question, the boy had the answer in a few seconds and was ready to move on.

The rap on the door came as a surprise. Fortescue glanced at his watch to see that it was nine o'clock and his breakfast must have arrived. He got up from the desk and walked to the door, opening it only a little. The steward was there with a tray.

'I'll take that,' Fortescue said.

The steward looked puzzled for a second and then he understood his passenger must have a lady friend with him. He accepted the generous tip Fortescue gave him and retreated.

Billy was starving and Fortescue took great pleasure in watching the boy eat.

'What is that?' Billy asked.

'Raspberry jam.' Fortescue dipped a silver jam spoon into the basin and plucked a croissant from a basket, ran the jam over it and handed it to the boy.

'And that?' Billy pointed to the croissant.

'A croissant. It's French. Absolutely delicious.'

'I'll take your word for it, Mr Wickins,' Billy retorted and took a big bite. 'Um,' he said, eyes wide, mouth full . . . 'Good.'

'You have an incredible talent, Billy. Has no one else ever realized?'

The kid shook his head. 'Never told no one.'

'Your parents?'

Billy looked down between his worn leather boots and ripped trouser bottoms. 'Both dead.'

'Oh, I'm sorry.'

'No need, it was a long time ago. I live with me aunt. She don't care two figs about me, though.'

'So, how did you end up here?'

'Me aunt – Mary's her name – married a man called Bert, Bert Spindle. Me Uncle Tom, he died two years ago . . . bad lungs. He used to cough so loud we couldn't sleep. Then one morning, the coughing suddenly stopped. My new uncle is all right, I s'pose, a bit rough sometimes. Don't think he likes me much, but Mary made a promise to me mum and dad to look after me.'

'Your uncle and aunt are hoping for a fresh new start in America.'

Billy nodded. 'Uncle Bert's a strong man. Been working on the roads in East London. He reckons there'll be a lot of road building going on in New York and there'll be jobs for the both of us.'

'Well, you shall not be joining him, Billy.'

The boy gave Fortescue a puzzled look.

'You have a talent so prodigious, it would be a scandal to squander it and I shall do everything I can to make sure that does not happen. No, Billy, when we reach New York, I shall have a word with your uncle and aunt and we'll see what we can do about getting you a decent education.'

Billy looked at Fortescue and the man could see that there was not the merest hint of hope in the boy's eyes.

26

Billy did not return to Third Class; he still had plenty of zest for what he liked to call 'exploring'. Fortescue saw him out onto the deck, and from there he snuck into a 'crew only' corridor. He was an expert at dodging out of sight. It was a skill he had acquired in Belfast where he had spent the first ten years of his life before moving to Hackney. Where he came from such skills kept you alive. He had known nothing but thievery and grubbing for food, so stealth and 'exploring' came naturally.

He slunk into the kitchen. It was a large room crammed with brand-new ovens and steel counters. Pipes ran across the ceiling; the floor was spotless and buffed to a high polish. From his vantage point behind a cupboard Billy could see the staff rushing around, each dedicated to their own particular task, cogs in a well-oiled machine that produced hundreds of meals each day for the First Class passengers.

Billy watched a young lad, perhaps no more than a couple of years older than him, cutting thin slices of meat from a heavy pink ham on a thick oak chopping board. A row of deli-cate porcelain plates lay on the counter to the young cook's right. As a sliver of meat slipped from the ham onto the chopping board he lifted it and placed it decorously on the closest plate.

A gruff voice from across the kitchen called out. The boy looked up and dashed over to one of the senior chefs. Checking it was safe, Billy slipped from behind the cupboard, crouched low and shuffled over to the counter where the boy had stood. In one swift movement he peeked over the edge of the counter, grabbed a fistful of meat and swung back round. He was back behind the cupboard, stuffing his face with the luscious lean ham before the young man had even reached the senior chef.

Two minutes later Billy had slipped from the kitchen unobserved and was creeping along a little-used corridor leading from a set of storerooms to the boat deck. He heard voices – two people – a man and a woman. It sounded as though they were approaching from just beyond a bend a few yards ahead.

He felt a tingle of excitement. He could not keep going, nor could he turn and head back. Whoever was coming along the corridor would realize immediately that he was an intruder in First Class; one glance at his filthy shirt and torn clothes would give him away.

There was nowhere to hide in the corridor. He spun on his heel, then changed his mind. The excitement turned to panic just as he glimpsed a door standing ajar a short way along the passage in the direction of the two people approaching the bend. He dashed through the doorway.

It was a small, grey room; dark, the only light coming from a single porthole half blocked by one of several crates that took up most of the floor space. It smelled of damp rope, grease and rubber. Billy guessed it was a storeroom for spare parts.

He expected the two people to pass the door and for their voices to fade away, but he ducked behind one of the crates just in case.

The couple stopped outside the storeroom door. Billy held his breath, listening intently.

'Let's pull in here,' the man said.

'Good God!' the woman replied.

'The cleaners will be in our rooms now. Can you suggest anywhere more salubrious?'

Billy heard the woman huff as they entered the room. The door squeaked as it was pulled inwards and clunked closed.

'I still can't get anything,' the man said. He had a refined English voice.

'But you had at least three hours last night and then all the time he was with the boy on deck,' the woman replied. She had a distinctive foreign accent that Billy couldn't quite identify. He thought it was probably German.

'After my last attempt he had the lock changed so I couldn't get in. He obviously suspected something. It took me almost two hours to get a new key, by which time he was back in the room.'

The woman huffed again. 'You said you left no traces.'

'I didn't. The man must have a sixth sense. Did you gather anything from him? You were together long enough.' There was a raw edge to the man's voice.

'We were busy with other things. But you have seen photographs of Fortescue, the same as I have. Wickins is definitely the same man.'

'And his cover story is pure fabrication?'

'Of course . . . it's just as we were told in Berlin, Charles.

You did well to gather the information on the man and his mission. The surveillance of the scientists in Manchester was worth you suffering the cold for.'

'That's easy for you to say. You didn't have to put up with it!'

'Oh, do stop moaning,' the woman snapped. 'You turn a compliment into a chance to whinge. I thought English public schools were meant to harden you chaps, make men of you.' She laughed mirthlessly.

'I need another try in his cabin. I'm certain he has the material in the safe. We need a second diversion, get him out of there for a while.'

The woman sighed. 'And then what? If you get the stuff, we still have almost three days before we reach New York.'

'Well, obviously Mr Wickins has to be dealt with, doesn't he? It's a big ocean to lose a body in.'

Behind the crate Billy was itching to see the faces of the two people, but he could not tell precisely where they were standing, and for all he knew one of them could be looking his way. He slowly shuffled along the ground, inching his way towards a narrow gap between two crates. He slid along the cold metal floor, eased upright a little and pulled close to the crack between the boxes. With one eye to the opening, he could see the two grown-ups in profile. They stood just a few feet away.

The gasp was completely involuntary. It just seemed to escape from Billy's throat.

The couple instantly stopped talking and he saw the dark outline of a person's face peering over the top of the crate beside him. The boy yanked himself up and sprang away into the room, charging straight into the woman. She produced a low growl as they collided and fell back against a bulkhead behind her.

Billy was at the door, tugging on the handle. He felt a hand grab his oily jacket, pulled on the door and heard the fabric rip. He slipped into the corridor, head down, and sped along the hard floor. Looking up, he saw a steward in a white uniform, silver tray aloft. Billy crashed into him; the man staggered backwards, and the tray flew several feet along the passage, smashing into the wall. Remnants of a late breakfast scattered, milk splashed up the wall and a silver pot of tea fell to the floor clanging across the metal, its contents slopping all around.

Billy didn't pause for breath. He heard the steward yell but he was at the end of the corridor and out along another passageway headed for the deck.

A maintenance man repairing an electric light on the wall close to the Grand Staircase saw the boy rushing towards him. He quickly downed his screwdriver and made to block Billy's path. The boy swung to his left, then to his right like a footballer taking on a defender, slipped under the man's outstretched arm and straight into a gentleman who had at that moment emerged from a corridor diagonally opposite.

Billy protested loudly and tried to wriggle free – then he looked up into the eyes of Egbert Fortescue.

27

Colin Edwards had only been in the job for a month and he was filled with excitement and pride that he had made it to Satellite Interpretational and Correlation Directive Assistant (a SICDA). He had emailed his parents about his promotion as soon as he heard back in September, but he was a professional and had remembered to be absolutely circumspect when it came to how much information he could pass on to them, which was actually very little. Even so, unknown to Colin, his email had been intercepted and given a light censorial dusting by a colleague called Martin Fillmore, an Internet Interpretational and Correlation Directive Assistant (an IICDA) who Colin had chatted to in the canteen once or twice.

Colin was monitoring signals originating in the northeast of the United States and passing through NATO satellites with UKUSAJMA, or British-American Joint Military Assets designations, when he noticed a tiny abnormality in the signal. It was something trivial – a one per cent difference between the bandwidth of the input and output signals from a single satellite, RANOS-132, currently in geosynchronous orbit over the mid-Atlantic.

Anyone less keen than Colin, or with fewer hours at the monitoring console, would almost certainly have failed to notice the discrepancy. But Colin did notice it and he acted upon it. Isolating the part of the output signal that was different to the inputted one for satellite RANOS-132, he 'snipped it' – that is, he cut the digital impulses from the rest of the signal and isolated it in a file on his computer.

This stage, Colin knew, was almost always the easiest. He'd done it before in training when he had isolated and snipped a rogue emission from a fictitious orbiter in a simulator. It was one thing to capture information, quite another to read it and far more difficult to interpret it.

He tried to open the snatched file, but it resisted his efforts. He then ran a program to decipher regular satellite emission files, but that also came up empty. At this point Colin decided to call upon the help of his supervisor, Gordon Manners, who worked at a slightly larger console to his left.

Gordon surveyed Colin's screen. 'That's not one of ours,' he said matter-of-factly.

'But how could that happen? It's from a NATO satellite.'

'Show me the positions and telemetries of all the orbiters within a hundred miles of RANOS-132.'

Colin ran his fingers over the keyboard of his console. A series of dots appeared on his screen. Each had a serial number attached that appeared as a red alphanumeric immediately beneath it.

'There,' Gordon said, his finger indicating a point on the screen. 'A Chinese satellite within ten miles of RANOS. Must have leaked a signal. Ranos picked it up and it became embedded in the output signal from the NATO orbiter.'

'Shit!'

'Pass it on to Decryption. Could be useful.'

'Hang on, sir, I think I can get it out,' Colin said, filled with enthusiasm.

Gordon Manners sighed quietly. He didn't really like this kid, thought he was a little too full of himself, but he had been taught that good managers give their staff enough oxygen to breathe. He stood beside Colin Edwards's terminal, arms folded, as the young operator tapped away, shuffled the mouse, thought for a few moments, wrote in something fresh, had it knocked back, waited, typed again and pushed himself back in his chair.

'Gotcha,' Colin Edwards declared.

On the screen a set of equations appeared. The Satellite Interpretational and Correlation Directive Assistant scrolled down and whistled.

Gordon Manners leaned in to study the screen. 'What in God's name is that?'

28

Five miles outside Lyon, France. Present day.

Hans Secker only ever appeared contrite in the presence of one person. He dined regularly with presidents and argued with prime ministers, none of whom fazed him; but now, with the onerous task of breaking bad news to his boss, Glena Buckingham, contrition slithered across his face automatically.

They were seated on opposite sides of a Louis XVI table that the Sultan of Brunei had given Buckingham for her fortieth birthday. Secker had a MacBook in front of him.

'If your face is anything to go by, I don't think I'm going to like what you have to tell me, Hans,' Buckingham said and studied her fingernails.

'We still have no idea where Newman is.'

Buckingham looked at the table for a few seconds and when she raised her eyes to meet Secker's her expression was surprisingly neutral. 'I find it hard to believe that Professor Newman could have evaded Van Lee and two of his best men at JFK after you were tipped off that he was switching planes there.'

'He is a clever man, Glena.'

She slammed the table with the palm of her right hand, making Secker jolt. 'We are cleverer,' she hissed. 'Well, at least you and Van Lee had better be.' She took a deep breath. 'Alert every foreign agent. I want that man found. He cannot be allowed to disappear, not with the precious cargo he carries. Now, what of the other copies of the EF material?'

Secker brightened. 'I thought I would give you the bad news first.' He risked the faintest of smiles. 'Copies in the hands of the navy and the two marine archaeologists Kate Wetherall and Lou Bates have been retrieved or destroyed and we have the originals.'

'And you got them cleanly?'

He paused. 'Successfully, Glena.'

She glared at him. 'Explain.'

'Van Lee's men stole the originals from the lab at the Institute of Marine Studies and they destroyed the hard drive that had been used to store the copies Wetherall and Bates made. Van Lee lost three men in the effort. He had ordered them to stay behind at the institute so they could check that the marine archaeologists didn't have a copy.'

Buckingham frowned. 'I don't follow.'

'Yesterday morning, the two archaeologists went to the house of George Campion. Apparently the woman, Dr Wetherall, is a family friend. Van Lee assumed they had left a copy at the scientist's house. They searched the place but came up empty.'

'Hold on,' Buckingham snapped. 'He raided the home of Professor George Campion?'

'Yes. But . . .'

'But what, Hans?' she asked menacingly.

'Van Lee's men were a little heavy-handed.'

'Jesus!' Buckingham exploded and pushed herself up from the table. 'How fucking heavy-handed? Don't tell me they . . .'

'They murdered Professor Campion and his wife.'

'What! You . . . That man was one of the few human beings I ever respected. Dammit!' She returned to the table leaning forward, palms flat on the precious wood. Secker could hear her breathing. 'Well . . . what's done . . .' she said, fixing her assistant with a truly terrifying stare. 'Go on.'

'A pair of Van Lee's men followed Wetherall and Bates and drove their car off the road. They survived, but the car was . . .' He flicked his fingers in the air to signify the vehicle going up in smoke. Van Lee's men then cornered them when they returned to the Marine Institute late last night. They got nothing from them and were themselves ambushed by a navy team led by Captain Jerry Derham.'

'Sounds like an utter shambles.'

'Not at all. We have all the copies or they have been destroyed.'

'How do you know the copy in the car was not retrieved by the navy?'

'Van Lee informs me that would not have been possible. Glena, we have effectively stopped NATO in its tracks. I would suspect that we shall see the ships returning to port and the Exclusion Zone—'

'Don't be a bloody fool, Secker!' Buckingham's eyes were ablaze. 'Even if we have the original documents and all the copies have been destroyed, you're forgetting Newman.'

'But he's—'

'He's out there with a copy of the document from the *Titanic* and the scientific knowledge to know what it means. As you pointed out, he is a clever man. He was certainly not foolish enough to trust us, now, was he?'

'No, but—'

'And he must have known Van Lee's men were tailing him from the house in Plymouth. He owes us no favours, does he?'

'No,' Hans Secker agreed again, sighed and looked at the table.

'You may – I repeat, may – have snatched the Egbert Fortescue materials from NATO, but there are other forces railed against us now. I want Professor Max Newman, preferably alive, here in this building so that I may pick his very ample brain. But if that isn't possible, I want that brain . . . deactivated.'

29

Norfolk, Virginia. Present day.

The morning after the lab was wrecked, Kate was stuck in early morning traffic on Interstate 264 just outside Norfolk when her cell phone trilled. A pain shot through her side and she winced as she leaned forward to punch the 'receive' button.

'Jerry. What's happened?'

'Hi, Kate. Looks like Newman's completely vanished. Can we meet up this morning for a briefing?'

'Sure. I'm on my way to the institute. Lou's already there. You want to hook up at the cafeteria?' She glanced at the dash, then the traffic. 'Half an hour?'

*

There were a few people at the tables closest to the counter. Kate ordered and spotted Lou at a table near the back wall. Derham appeared as she walked over. A few minutes later he joined them with a large cappuccino in his hand.

'Better bring us up to speed,' Lou said, taking a sip of coffee.

'We've searched Newman's place in Plymouth. Someone had already gone over it.'

'No clue as to where he's gone?'

'We've checked. He's left the States; been skipping through airlines and continents. We lost him after he flew out of Bangkok.'

'To where?'

'Damascus. Syrians wouldn't help us.'

'So obviously Newman has been working for someone,' Kate said.

'And he either fell out with them or he's double-dealing,' Lou added.

Kate shuddered. 'This is all getting a bit . . .'

'Out of hand?' Derham offered.

'I was thinking "crazy" actually. A few days ago we were in Bermuda working on a pilgrim shipwreck. It's all a bit much to take, to be honest.'

'I hear you. But that's just the way it is. And, although I hate to upset you even more, you have to accept that you two are in the greatest danger.'

'And I guess we're no closer to retrieving a copy of the Fortescue document?' Lou said, placing his mug on the table.

'No. My tech guys will be working today on the smashed-up scanner from your lab. They may be able to recover something useful.'

The scientists did not look encouraged. 'We're pretty much left with nothing,' Kate said without meeting

Derham's eyes. 'We had Egbert Fortescue's papers and lost them. We've learned that Newman is a spy and he has a copy of the material. And, even if we were to retrieve the equations, my godfather was convinced not all the calculations were there and that Fortescue must have developed the work on the *Titanic* before it went down, so that's all gone too!'

They were quiet for a moment, the sounds of the espresso machine and the chat of the other customers a backdrop to their thoughts. Lou started to fiddle with a packet of sugar in his bandaged hand, tossed it down and took a sip from his coffee.

'Newman realized straight away that there was more to the Fortescue document than a bunch of jumbled equations,' Kate remarked.

'George Campion did say the man was a fine scientist.'

'But it even took George a while to see the cold fusion material. Newman wouldn't have seen that immediately.'

'I think that's not really the point,' Derham said. 'That document is inflammatory enough without the work that Fortescue was doing immediately before his death. It includes an alternative way to create atomic energy that could be cheaper, cleaner, safer, easier to produce than the methods we use today. The cold fusion stuff is the icing on the cake.'

'Some icing!' Lou exclaimed.

'But we don't know that it is at all practicable,' Kate said.

'Sure,' Derham replied. 'But if we put cold fusion

aside, the basic work Rutherford and Fortescue were doing could itself lead to some really significant advances in energy production. There are agencies out there that cannot be too careful. They are always on the lookout for anything that could threaten the conventional energy supply lines they control.'

'What?'

'Well, think about it, guys,' Derham said. 'The mere suggestion of an efficient powerful new form of harness-able energy would make some people very unhappy. On the one hand you have governments spending vast fortunes building conventional power stations, while on the other, private corporations earn hundreds of billions from oil, petrol, gas.'

'And Newman has had the EF document for what . . . thirty-six hours? He would have got to the cold fusion stuff,' Lou said.

'Which is incomplete,' Kate reminded them.

'Yes, but it could be enough. It could be reverse-engineered, couldn't it?' Jerry Derham asked.

'Search me. I'm just a marine archaeologist!' Kate spat. 'A very pissed-off one.'

'All right.' Derham put his hands up. 'Let's calm down.'

'Easy for you to say,' Kate persisted. 'This is the sort of thing you're used to. You're military. I'm not . . . we're not.'

'Understood.'

'I just want to get on with my work.' She flicked her hair behind her ear.

'But there's nothing to work on here now, is there, Kate?' Lou interjected wearily.

Kate looked round at him seriously. 'No, you're right. There isn't.'

30

It took Lou and Kate two hours to clear up the lab. They went through the motions mostly in miserable silence, exchanging the odd word despondently. It seemed as though every single item in the room had been moved, every piece of paper displaced, every piece of glassware smashed.

Kate slapped a soaked cleaning cloth onto a work-bench, let out a small cry and slumped into a chair. 'Hell, I've had it with this!'

Lou came over, pulled a chair up close to hers and took her hand.

'It's almost done,' he said softly.

'It's not that!' Kate snapped. 'Oh, God! I'm sorry, Lou.' She squeezed his hand and gave him a weak smile. 'It's this whole bloody thing. I've lost my godparents . . . You saw the horror . . .' She burst into tears.

Lou held her tight and let her cry on his shoulder. After a moment she pulled back and forced herself to calm down, wiped away the tears, her stoicism kicking in.

'I feel like walking out that door and getting on a

plane back to Bermuda,' she declared. 'In fact, why shouldn't I? I'm not a bloody conscript!'

'There's nothing to stop you, Kate. Except . . .'

She raised an eyebrow. 'Except what?'

'I think that you want to get to the bottom of all this just as much as I do.'

'There are limits!'

The phone rang. It took Lou a moment to find it under a pile of files.

'I've got some news.' It was Jerry Derham.

'Good news, I hope.'

'Bit of each actually.'

'OK.'

'Can you and Kate come over?'

Lou covered the receiver. 'Jerry. Has some news. Wants us to go see him. You still fighting or flying back to the sunshine?'

Kate rolled her eyes and wiped her nose. 'What do you think, wise guy?'

'We'll be there in an hour.'

*

A uniformed officer had been posted outside their lab. He drove them to the naval base, escorted them through security, on to Captain Derham's office, and then waited outside. Lou and Kate walked in to see Kevin Grant in a chair facing the captain's desk.

'You remember Kevin?' Derham said and indicated that Kate and Lou should sit. The young guy nodded and lifted from his lap a metal box about the size of a paperback book. 'The hard drive,' he said. 'Damaged beyond repair, I'm afraid. Couldn't get a thing from it.'

'Fantastic!' Lou said and turned to Kate. She had a glazed expression on her face. 'Jerry, you said you had good and bad news. Not seeing much good so far!'

'Ah, well, Kevin here can enlighten you on that too. He's decoded the message that Fortescue had with the documents.'

'You're kidding!' Lou said. 'You said it would be really difficult to crack because it was so short.'

Grant beamed. 'It did take a long time . . . by my standards!'

'For God's sake!' Kate exclaimed. 'What did it say?'

'Security Box 19AS. Cargo hold 4.'

Lou whistled. 'He must have hidden the other part of his work there. But why?'

'Who knows?' Derham answered. 'But my suspicion would be that he believed someone, an enemy agent, for example, was also travelling on the *Titanic*. Why else would he be so careful?'

'But what are the chances of the security box still being in one piece, or traceable among the wreckage?' Kate asked.

'Quite good actually,' Derham replied. He turned his computer screen to face them and walked round the desk. 'As soon as Kevin decoded the message I had my people scour all the footage of the wreck taken recently by Commander Milford and her team aboard the *Armstrong*. They've developed a program that matches up the entire wreck with the original schematic of the ship used by the men who built it at the Harland & Wolff yards in Belfast. They've found cargo hold 4, just there.' He tapped the screen then reached for the mouse and shuffled it. The image on the screen expanded and closed in on a section of wreckage about twenty yards by ten.

'That's amazing!' Kate exclaimed. 'And it's intact?'

Derham returned to his seat, rotated the screen back into place and picked up a sheet of glossy photo paper. He handed it to Kate. Lou looked over her shoulder.

'A computer-enhanced image from the lab guys,' Derham said.

The picture showed a close-up of the chunk of ship-wreck. The ends were ragged, but a long section in the middle had remained relatively unscathed. They could see two doors. There was a figure painted on each. The one on the right was illegible; on the left-hand door, the writing had been worn away and was faded in patches but it was just about discernible. A big number '4'.

'That's cool,' Lou said. 'But we don't have the first document, so whatever Fortescue put in this hold is not going to be much use to us, is it?'

Derham sighed. 'I can't argue with that.'

'I'd love to get my hands on the bastards who trashed the lab,' Kate said. There was real venom in her voice.

'I think you may have met some of them,' Derham replied.

'In the car park.'

Derham nodded. 'The three dead men were clean, no

ID, nothing. We still don't know who they are or who they were working for.'

'Professionals,' Kate said. 'They knew the layout of our lab, the function of the digital copier, and they disabled the security cameras along the corridor as well as the one in our lab.'

Kate looked to Lou and saw he was deep in thought, staring into space.

'Say that again,' he said, turning to Kate.

'What? The men were pros – they knew the layout.'

'No, after that.'

'The digital copier . . .'

'No . . . no.' Lou paused. 'The security camera in our lab. I forgot we even had one.'

'So?'

'Where is it positioned?'

'Towards the back of the room, but it covers the whole lab . . . Lou, what is it?'

'Where does the feed go? From the camera?'

'There's a hard drive in one of the lab cupboards. Records in forty-eight-hour cycles and automatically wipes. One of the technicians looks after it. Why?'

Lou was up and out of his chair, heading towards the door.

*

Kate fished out the hard drive from its cradle in a cupboard at one end of a row high up above the coun-ters that lined the back of the lab. It had an HDMI cable dangling from the back. She handed it to Lou. It took him only a few moments to hook it up to a laptop at his workstation. He pulled in his chair and Derham and Kate stood behind him leaning in towards the screen.

He tapped at the keyboard and a management screen appeared. He input a security code and the monitor lit up with a view of the lab. In the bottom-right corner of the screen they could see: '10.05, 10 October'. The lab was empty, rain beating on the windows.

'Two mornings ago,' Lou said and clicked a couple of keys on his laptop. The image fast-forwarded. They could see the lab door open and Lou coming in. He sat at a counter to study the box of papers they had retrieved from the wreck of the *Titanic*. Kate entered and they talked for a while before setting up the digital copier above the glass chamber. Then Kate placed Fortescue's papers carefully under the crosshairs of the scanner copier using the robot arms.

'It's too far from the security camera,' Derham said.

Lou did not answer, just manipulated the image from his laptop. The view expanded, zooming in on the pages of equations inside the glass chamber.

'You can almost read it!' Kate exclaimed. 'Can you get any closer, Lou?'

'I'll try.' He tapped at the keyboard and the image became distorted. 'Any closer and we lose resolution. Damn!'

'Hang on,' Kate said excitedly. 'We've got an image-enhancer. Remember we used it for the German U-Boat wreck last year?'

Lou got up, almost knocking Derham aside, paced over to a counter, opened a cupboard door, closed it again, swore. 'Kate, any ideas where it was put?'

She was searching through another cupboard the other side of the lab. 'Yes!' she said.

Derham helped Kate carry the machine over to Lou's workstation and sixty seconds later they had the enhancer hooked up to the laptop and the hard drive. Kate checked the cables. 'Ready.'

Lou opened the file, sped forward to the point where they began to copy Fortescue's papers two mornings ago. On the screen, they could see Kate poised with the robot arms. The first page lay under the copier.

Lou lined up the enhancer on the laptop and set it to 'Resolution 200%'. The image grew and kept its resolution, but the writing was still little more than a series of undecipherable squiggles.

Lou paused the film and tapped the arrow keys on the laptop. The enhancement level increased . . . '250%' . . . '300%'.

'Come on!' Lou exclaimed. 'Trouble is, this has its limits too. Tip over the edge and we'll lose resolution again.' He keyed in some parameters. A counter at the bottom of the screen read: '320%'. And as they watched, the image cleared.

Kate gasped.

'Yes!' Derham said.

On the monitor they could see the words written by Egbert Fortescue over a century ago – as clear as the day they were penned.

31

Albert Embankment, London. Present day.

'A cup of tea, Arthur?'

The man sitting across the desk from Christian Halley – the head of MI6, Arthur Bevington – had either not heard him or had chosen to ignore the question.

'Arthur?'

'Yes?' The man looked up from his papers a little startled.

'Tea? Would you like tea?'

'Er . . . yes, that would be splendid, thank you.'

Halley tapped a button on his phone. Both men could hear the secretary's call tone from the adjoining room. 'A pot of tea please, Estelle.'

Christian Halley got up from his chair and turned towards the vast window behind his desk. He had his hands clenched behind his back as he studied the view in silence. To his right lay Lambeth Bridge and a glimpse of Lambeth Palace. Turning to his left, he could see how the river took a gentle turn north-west. No more than a few dozen yards from the base of the Secret Intelligence

Service building stretched Vauxhall Bridge packed with rush-hour traffic. In the west the last wisps of daylight slipped behind the buildings, lighting up the Thames like a river of fire.

He swung back to the room as the tea arrived. Estelle poured, retreated and closed the door softly behind her.

'You sounded pretty excited on the phone, Arthur,' Christian Halley said, taking a sip of his tea. 'So let's have it.'

Bevington was a tall spindly man with thinning white hair and bushy eyebrows. He had been in the service for thirty-five years and was now number three. He would go no higher; indeed, he planned to retire within two years. He was seen as the reliable Old Man of the service, a bit of an anachronism for sure, but almost universally liked.

'Well, to be honest, it *is* exciting. We've intercepted an encoded message sent from the east coast of the United States that was en route to Beijing.'

'Not that unusual, Arthur.'

'No. But it is unusual to stumble upon it when we're not actively looking for it. This message was only picked up by chance by one of the juniors at GCHQ.'

'How?'

'It leaked from a Chinese satellite and one of ours, RANOS-132 to be precise, was within range and detected it.'

'I see. And what was the message about?'

'One of my teams has been working on it for the past sixteen hours. They finally cracked it – it's a set of mathematical expressions. A lot of it doesn't seem to make sense . . . at least that's what the chaps on the third floor tell me.'

Halley took another sip of his tea and eyed Bevington over the rim of his bone-china cup.

'The really startling thing is the non-mathematical parts of the message. Whoever sent it is somehow involved with REZ375.'

'The Exclusion Zone in the Atlantic?'

'They seem to be selling something to the Chinese, something linked to the wreck of the *Titanic*.'

Halley caught his breath, lowered his cup and inter-linked his fingers in an arch in front of his face. 'We learned only this morning that something has been brought up from the wreck. We have an aircraft carrier in the Exclusion Zone, HMS *Ipswich*, but the Yanks insisted that they use their own gear to get down there. Turned down our help. It's sent alarm bells ringing at the MOD.'

'Not ruddy surprised!' Bevington said.

'So, what's this all about?' Halley was almost talking to himself, then turned to the older man.

'The transmission to the Chinese satellite originated about ten miles from Norfolk Naval Base,' Bevington explained. 'It seems pretty clear that the Americans have a spy in their midst who has somehow gained access to whatever it was the United States Navy brought up from the wreck of the *Titanic*.'

'But mathematical expressions?'

Bevington shrugged. 'The radiation levels in the

Exclusion Zone have been dropping fast since they went down there. Clearly they brought to the surface whatever was causing it, as well as this maths stuff.'

'And you think these equations are some sort of analysis of the retrieved source passed on to the Chinese by someone from the US Navy?'

'That is one possibility.'

'Have your boys made any headway working out what the maths describes?'

'No,' Bevington said. Then he seemed to notice his tea for the first time and drank the whole lot in one go. Replacing the cup on the saucer, he held Halley's intense stare. 'But I do think we ought to get a Special Forces unit into the Exclusion Zone right away. We've been far too relaxed about all this. The Americans have retrieved something important and I wouldn't be at all surprised if they make several more trips down to the wreck. They're not willing to share intel on this, and they have refused any joint missions to the ocean floor.'

Halley looked at Bevington in silence, his mind running through the ramifications. Then he leaned back in his chair and folded his arms. 'We don't want to upset anyone,' he said cautiously.

'There is actually a further complication.'

'Oh?'

'Glena Buckingham.'

Halley blanched. 'Don't tell me that cow is involved already?'

Bevington simply nodded. 'It would make sense, Christian. Energy is her game – her bread and butter, if you will.'

'Yes,' Halley responded. 'Anything concrete on her?'

'Well, you know as much as I do – she is under constant surveillance. There's a file a mile thick on the woman. Her home, her office, her cars – they're all bugged using the latest microdot microphones. Her people have never succeeded in deactivating them even if they know the equipment is there.'

'But have you recorded her saying anything that is specifically linked to REZ375?'

'Yes . . . we think she has a copy of the mathematical material that was sent to the Chinese.'

'Good God! Now you tell me! It seems everyone has something from the bloody *Titanic* except us.' Halley jumped up, his large face pink. 'First the bloody Yanks, then the Chinese and now you tell me that arch-bitch Glena Fucking Buckingham has a lead on Her Majesty's Government. How long has this—?'

'Christian, take a deep breath, old boy.' Bevington stayed remarkably calm. 'It's all very new. We are on top of things, you know . . .'

Halley walked back to his desk, lowered himself slowly into the plush leather upholstery of his chair. 'Yes,' he said. 'Yes, of course. Apologies, it's been a long day.'

Then he lifted the receiver of his phone.

'Estelle,' he said to his secretary. 'Get me the PM, please . . . immediately.'

32

Ministry of State Security of the People's Republic of China, Beijing. Present day.

Ling Chi, Minister of State Security, stood at the window of his modest fourth-floor office looking out at the view. He had his hands clasped behind his ramrod-straight back and turned his head slowly left then right watching the world beyond the glass. At the foot of the monstrously oversized Ministry building beyond the patrolled security cordon lay a ribbon of neon-splashed tarmac crammed with cars. Across from this ten-lane highway stretched mile upon mile of concrete buildings lit up in the night and intercut with more tarmac.

Ling turned to face his visitor, Zhu Lo, Minister for Scientific and Technological Information, a grossly fat man in a tight suit, tie digging into the ample flesh around his neck. He had small black eyes and seemed never to blink. Ling had worked with him for seven years and he knew that Zhu had hated him for at least three of those . . . dating from the day he had snatched the job of Minister of State Security from under the fat man's nose.

'You can definitely rely on your source, minister?' Ling asked softly and pulled himself into his chair, his back to the view. He rested his hands on the old wooden desk.

'He comes highly recommended,' Zhu replied.

'And you have approved –' Ling glanced at his iPad '– five million dollars?'

Zhu stared at the minister, his face totally without expression. He said nothing, forcing Ling to speak.

'It seems rather a lot.'

'It is not excessive if one considers what we have obtained,' Zhu said.

Ling studied his interlinked fingers. 'Let us assume then that this material is genuine . . .'

'It is genuine, minister.'

'Let us assume this is the case,' Ling repeated. 'Your people have managed to decode it and they claim it is a description of some –' he glanced at his iPad again '– alternative source of atomic energy.'

'There is more to it than that.'

'Enlighten me.'

'The technicalities are complex,' Zhu commented.

'I'm sure they are, Zhu. I'll try to keep up.'

'The implication is that it points the way to cold fusion.'

Ling did well to hide his surprise. 'But that has been discredited time and time again. The British, the French, the Japanese, they have spent billions on the concept and got precisely nowhere. I've seen the reports from the field.'

'It seems, minister, that this work offers an entirely different approach.'

'And this breakthrough, as your man calls it, comes from the wreck of the *Titanic*?' Ling looked incredulously at the minister. 'You'll have to forgive me, but this all seems rather fanciful.'

'I understand,' Zhu replied. 'I will confess that my team and I have had the same doubts, but the lineage of the find is incontrovertible.'

Ling nodded and waved his iPad a few inches above his desk. 'I know the Americans have developed the technology to walk on the ocean floor and have been down to the wreck.'

'Yes, it is indeed hard to imagine how the radiation source and any documents detailing such advanced theoretical physics could have ended up in a century-old shipwreck, but it is . . . it was there. That much is not open to conjecture. We have looked into the possible author of the work. My contact Professor Newman in Virginia is a physicist. He recognized the mathematical reasoning as being that of Ernest Rutherford's assistant, one Egbert Fortescue, who, we have learned, was travelling on the *Titanic* under the assumed name of John Wickins. And, as you would know, minister, the material from the wreck was taken to Norfolk Naval Base in Virginia. It included a radiation source . . .'

'The source that started the whole affair, yes. I have a report that says the radiation levels have dropped off markedly since whatever was down there was retrieved.' He looked at Zhu. 'I have to admit, I am extremely displeased that we were not quicker off the mark. The boss is fuming.' He spun his chair round and returned his gaze to the world of light and dark beyond the glass.

'Minister?' Zhu said.

Ling turned back to face the Minister for Scientific and Technological Information, reading a flash of superiority in his tiny black eyes. 'There's more, isn't there?'

'The material from my contact in Virginia is incomplete.' Zhu saw Ling glare at him. 'That was, of course, made clear to us right from the start. My contact is as frustrated and confused by it as you would expect. The point is, the rest of the mathematical material, theoretical work of Egbert Fortescue and perhaps other wonders might still be down there on the ocean floor.'

'After a century?'

'The radioactive isotope and the first batch of theoretical materials survived.'

Ling took a deep breath. 'Go on.'

'It is not beyond reasonable doubt that there is more to be found down there.'

'And the Americans will be going down again . . . perhaps many times. Yes, I see.' Ling fixed his colleague with a hard, unflinching look. 'We must act,' he said.

33

Richmond, Virginia. Present day.

The team of six had been trained personally by Van Lee himself. They were professional mercenaries unhappy with their former employers and covetous of some serious cash. Two were ex-SEALs; two others former SAS; a fifth had been a KGB operative; the sixth had served as a commander in the Israeli army.

Now entering their twenty-fourth hour of confinement holed up in a disused one-bed flat on the edge of Richmond, they had learned everything there was to know about their target. At the same time they had got to know each other pretty well too. That's what happens when you keep seven guys in a space the size of a truck.

They shared a mutual respect based on experience, and each of the men had proved themselves on successful jobs. They were Van Lee's best men and they each knew the number one lesson for any clandestine operation was that you had to watch each other's backs or else you all failed . . . you all wound up dead.

Through his network, Van Lee had obtained plans,

operational details and codes for every aspect of the NATO mission to maintain the Exclusion Zone around REZ375. He also had encryption matrices and hundreds of hacked comms between the vessels and Operations HQ in Virginia.

After five stretches of four-hour intensive research programmes and protocol simulations, with an hour break between each one, the team knew every nut and bolt of the target, every name linked with the target, every procedure and routine undertaken inside the target. They were ready to move.

They drove away separately from the tiny one-bedder five minutes apart and took slightly different routes south-east, seventy-five miles to the prearranged meeting point close to the west-bound intersection of the 64 and Highway 17 near Hampton. Along a quiet track they found uniforms, kit bags, weapons, comms and official photo-IDs. They then boarded a registered naval bus, reference number 2989 Omega.

Van Lee took the wheel of the bus and pulled on to the freeway that took them to Interstate 64, the Hampton Roads Beltway across to Willoughby Bay. Reaching the north shore, they followed the curved five-mile stretch to Norfolk Naval Base.

The bus stopped at the main gate. The uniformed guard left his cabin and walked over. The hydraulics of the bus door hissed as it concertinaed. The guard stepped up.

'Small team over from Annapolis,' Van Lee said confidently. 'Seconded for Operation Northerner.' He showed his ID.

'Where're you headed?' the guard asked, flicking a glance through the window.

'I wanna park this tank,' Van Lee laughed. 'Then I want a shower, and a meal. Then I'm off duty and you'll see me go thata way –' he jerked his thumb towards the road behind the bus '– and the nearest bar. Been in this fucking crate all day.'

The guard chuckled, saluted, stepped down to the road and paced back to his cabin. Van Lee drove on.

Two and half minutes later, the bus was drawing up on the dock. Six men jumped out; Van Lee parked then ran back to join the others. No one paid any of them the slightest attention as they ascended the stern boarding ramp onto a small ship.

They knew the layout of the vessel down to the last rivet. Fanning out in pairs, they followed three separate routes along the corridors and down through the decks, converging with precision timing at the end of Corridor F, Deck 3C, close to the bow. Van Lee stood at a locked door, 'Storage Area 45' written at head height. Using a forged magnetic pass card, he opened it and they piled in, the last man pulling the door shut.

The space was smaller than the tiny apartment in Richmond and they each knew that now they were here, they would have to sit quietly in the ship's hold for twenty-six hours, give or take five minutes. Soon Derham and the marine biologists would be walking the decks above them, unaware of the danger beneath their feet.

34

The eastern sky had only just begun to lighten as USS *Armstrong* left Norfolk Naval Base and slipped out into the open waters of the eastern seaboard.

The ship was abuzz with activity, the crew of twelve working together like a well-oiled machine. Lou and Kate had nothing to do but prepare mentally for their second trip down to the wreck of the *Titanic*.

At 16.00 hours the mess hall was empty except for the ship's cook, a stocky man with a white apron over his naval uniform. Kate and Lou pulled up a couple of chairs at a table. The chef brought over two cups of strong coffee and was about to start chatting to them when Captain Derham appeared, asked for a coffee for himself and settled at the same table as the two scientists.

'You seen the news?' he said, nodding towards a TV on a shelf high up on the opposite wall. Neither of them had noticed it. It was switched on but the sound was muted. Derham picked up a remote lying on a neighbouring table and flicked on the sound.

'What's up?' Lou asked.

'Watch.'

They could see a blue band stretched across the bottom of the monitor and the words 'CHINESE FURY: EMERGENCY UN SECURITY MEETING'. It was CNN; a reporter was standing in a studio. Behind her a vast image of Chinese warships cutting through fierce waves was projected onto the wall. Along the side of the picture ran a set of stats.

'. . . but the position of the People's Republic of China is clear,' the presenter said. 'In its statement to the UN, it demanded the immediate withdrawal of NATO forces and the removal of the Exclusion Zone at REZ375. This has been categorically refused, thus prompting this extraordinary Security Council meeting.' She turned to the image behind her and the ships started to move. 'The Chinese navy, known as the People's Liberation Army Navy, or PLAN, is a formidable force which includes ten nuclear subs armed with ballistic missiles. It also has a newly built aircraft carrier, *Qu Yuan*, currently in the South China Sea.'

'It was inevitable, I guess,' Kate said as Derham pushed the mute button.

'What they didn't say, though,' the captain replied, 'was something no one outside the military knows. There are already two Chinese subs heading at top speed towards the Exclusion Zone. They will reach it within sixteen hours.'

'Oh . . .' Lou grimaced.

'And NATO has launched three nuclear subs that should get there about the same time.'

'And this UN meeting?'

'Typical panic diplomacy,' Derham said. 'They're in session right now.'

'And it will probably reach a typical Security Council stalemate.' Kate looked from Lou to Derham, her jaw set hard. 'The Brits and Americans on one side, the Russians and the Chinese on the other and the French sitting on the fence.'

'Possibly.' Derham nodded towards the silent TV. 'Whatever happens, I want us to be in and out of there before the shooting starts.'

'You really think it'll come to that?' Lou looked startled.

'I would like to think it won't, Lou. But you can understand why the Chinese are annoyed, can't you? It's quite possible the Russians are on their way too. There'll also be a lot of satellite activity. The latest spy probes can be moved out of their orbits to get a better view.'

'We're due at the edge of the Exclusion Zone at 19.00 hours, is that right?' Kate asked.

'All being well. I suggest you get some rest. There's nothing for you to do aboard ship and you'll be starting a very tough shift from 21.30 when we run final checks on *JV1*. Meanwhile, we have a meeting at 17.00.'

At 16.58 they found the *JV1* pilot, Commander Jane Milford, already seated with notebooks and her iPad in front of her on a small conference table. She was dressed in a submarine pilot's jumpsuit and navy cap, wisps of short auburn hair just visible beneath the edge. She rose and saluted Derham before shaking hands with Kate and Lou.

The captain seated himself next to Milford and across from the two scientists.

'So, sir, we have your resident geek to thank for this second trip down,' Milford said, turning to Derham.

'Kevin Grant? An arrogant sonofabitch, but a smart kid.'

'Sure is . . . And you guys.' She looked from Kate to Lou. 'You OK about going down again?'

'You kidding?' Lou responded immediately. 'Just get me in the fat suit and I'm there!'

'OK then . . . down to business,' Derham said seriously. 'This trip is a little different to your first. As you know, of course, the *Titanic* snapped in two as it sank. The two chunks dropped in opposite directions, which resulted in them ending up some 700 yards apart on the ocean floor. The bow section is at coordinates 49° 56' 49" W, 41° 43' 57" N; the stern is at 49° 56' 54" W, 41° 43' 35" N. The tangled piece of ship that contains cargo hold 4 lies to the north-east of the bow section at 49° 56' 47" W, 41° 43' 66" N, about 300 yards from where we landed on our earlier trip.'

'It should actually be easier to get to than Fortescue's cabin, though, right?' Kate asked. 'We won't have to get into the ship and negotiate the hazards.'

'You'd have thought so,' Milford replied. 'Trouble is, the ocean floor around where the cargo hold is positioned is pretty unstable. You won't have the problems you had before with the risk of the ship crumbling around you, but the seabed itself is a mess. Annoyingly, cargo hold 4 landed on a nasty cracked-up patch.'

'That's bad luck,' Lou commented.

'The job is still doable, though,' Derham responded. 'But it will be a very dangerous mission, especially because of the suits.'

'What about the suits?' Lou asked.

'We haven't been able to get the integrity up,' Milford said. 'And because of seismic instability, we can't land the *JV* as close to the hold as we would like. That means the timeline for an EVA will be tight. We'll have to park the *JV* some distance from the target and walk at least a couple of hundred yards, get into the hold, find the materials, and get back to the *JV* within sixty-two minutes plus small change.'

'Well, that's what we have to do then, isn't it?' Lou said and swept his gaze around the table.

Milford stood up and walked over to a Smart Board at the end of the room close to a porthole. She clicked a remote and a detailed image of the ocean floor appeared. It showed an area of about three square miles. In the centre lay the two main chunks of the wrecked ship. The larger piece, the bow section, which they had entered on the last mission, was positioned north-east of the stern portion.

'Hold 4 is here,' Jane Milford said and tapped the Smart Board with a pointer. Using the remote, she expanded the image on the screen, closing in so that the two major parts of the massive ship slipped away over the edge. About three hundred feet south-west of the hold, a narrow line snaked west then turned sharply north. It was a fissure in the ocean floor.

'We can't put down anywhere within a mile west of this crevasse. If we do, we run the risk of the hold going through the ocean floor, and if that doesn't happen, the fissure could fracture and send out smaller cracks in all directions. That, as you appreciate, would be cata-strophic.'

'Like being close to a magnitude seven earthquake, I reckon,' Lou commented, staring fixedly at the image on the screen.

'Correct,' Milford replied.

'OK,' Kate said, shifting in her seat. 'We obviously have to land to the east of the fissure, but as close to the hold as possible.'

'That's right. However, that presents us with two further problems. First, we estimate we can set down no closer than 300 yards east of the crack. Second, we have to cross the fissure to get to the hold.'

'How on earth do we do that?' Kate asked, turning to Derham, then back to the commander.

'We have to thank the science guys back at Norfolk Base,' Derham replied. 'The team who devised the LMC suits have made a super lightweight telescopic bridge.'

'How wide is that?' Lou pointed to the crack in the ocean floor.

'About a hundred feet.'

'What!'

'The bridge is made from nano-carbon,' Milford explained. 'It's about a thousand times stronger than steel but it weighs less than ten thousandths of a steel equivalent. The bridge collapses down into a unit that can fit into a rucksack-sized container one of us will carry on our back.'

'But the time factor is still a problem,' Kate responded.

'Yes, it is,' Derham replied. 'A serious problem.'

'What about the hold itself?' Lou asked. 'It strikes me we could lose precious time if we have problems getting into it.'

'That's also correct.' Milford pressed the remote and a schematic appeared. 'This was lifted from the original plans and remodelled into a 3-D graphic.' They watched as the CGI rotated slowly showing the hold from every direction.

'The lock is a very simple mechanism, as you'd expect. There's an outer door, an airlock and an inner door. The lock itself looks pretty heavy-duty; again, you'd expect that.'

'Too right. There were plenty of valuable items on the *Titanic*,' Kate commented. 'Some of the wealthiest people of the day went down with her; they had cash, bonds, jewels.'

'And a lot of it would have been locked away for safe keeping in security boxes in holds like this,' Lou added.

'It's a miracle that this one has survived intact,' Derham said, looking to Milford.

The commander nodded. 'It's bound to be fragile, though. Which, of course, presents us with yet another potential danger. Once we get inside the hold, the change in pressure and the disturbance to what is, after all, a century-old rusted metal box is impossible to predict. OK . . .' she added and glanced at her watch, 'it's 17.25; just over four hours until launch. I suggest we get some sleep. It's going to be a long trip and I don't see us getting much rest once we're underway.'

'I wish I was coming with you,' Derham said.

'You're not?' Kate asked, surprised.

'My orders are to stay up here to liaise with the group commander, Rear Admiral Stockton, on the *Brooklyn*. The three of you will go out to the cargo hold.'

'I'll be there to hold your hand,' Milford quipped.

35

Four hours later.

Commander Milford had been in the sub going through system checks for an hour before Kate and Lou arrived.

The two scientists were kitted out in their thermal suits in an antechamber aboard the ship. This was hooked up to *JV1* by a concertinaed walkway a little like the movable bridges used to connect airliners to airport gates.

They then entered the sub, the door sealing behind them with a hiss. Milford nodded to them without breaking her stream of chat with the control room on the *Armstrong*. They could hear Captain Derham's voice over the comms finishing up the checklist with the commander.

Buckling themselves in, they watching the screens as the displays shifted and listened in as Milford severed the cables to the ship and turned the submarine through 180 degrees close to the keel.

Descending one hundred feet beneath the ship, the commander turned the nose of the sub downward.

'Engaging main thrusters,' she said through the comms.

'Copy that, *JV1*.'

They felt a slight nudge as the submarine began to accelerate and watched the water darkening rapidly on the monitors. Within a few moments the view of the ocean had become a featureless black.

'Accelerating to fifteen knots,' Milford reported. 'Depth 4,500 feet.'

Kate and Lou had become acquainted with some of the controls and displays during their first trip to the *Titanic*, so they were able to identify speed and depth figures on the main displays close to the pilot and duplicated on the smaller screens in front of them. They watched as the speed increased and *JV1* passed through what submariners called the bathypelagic region and on into abyssopelagic, the transition coming at about 6,000 feet beneath the surface.

For the next five minutes the descent was remarkably smooth. But then, at a depth of 12,050 feet and less than 600 feet from the ocean floor, the sub started to shake. A loud cracking sound reverberated around the inside of the vessel. Kate shot her hand out, grabbing Lou's wrist.

'Nothing to worry about, guys,' Jane Milford called back to them. 'Just a bit of a rocky . . .'

The sub plummeted. It felt very similar to being in an airliner hitting severe turbulence.

Kate couldn't stop a small scream and she gripped Lou's wrist so tightly she broke his skin with her nails. He yelled and went to pull it away but Kate wouldn't let it go. She was staring directly ahead, eyes glazed with fear.

The sub slowed dramatically and started to rock from side to side. Another loud cracking sound reverberated around the inside of the machine.

'You guys OK?' It was Jerry Derham in the control room of the *Armstrong*.

'We are now,' Milford replied. 'Just hit a nasty patch. I think it was a vortex of some sort. I didn't pick it up on the sensors in time. We're fine.'

The touchdown was almost anticlimactic; a soft thud and a brief shudder and they were on the floor of the Atlantic, 12,600 feet beneath the waves. They heard the sound of the engines descend in pitch. Milford unstrapped her safety harness and came round to the rear of the small sub just as Kate and Lou were getting up from their seats. Lou was rubbing his sore wrist.

'Oh, stop being a baby!' Kate said, grinning.

'That's rich!'

'That had to be the trickiest landing I've ever had to make,' Milford declared.

'Did I hear you say we hit a vortex?'

'Yeah, we just clipped the edge of it, thank God. They present just about the biggest danger down here, apart from a hull breach. OK, I don't think we should waste any time. If you feel up to it, let's get suited up and out there.'

'How close are we to the planned landing site?' Lou asked.

'Bang on,' Milford responded. 'Look.'

She pointed to a monitor. It showed a schematic of the surrounding area. 'There's the hold.' She indicated a small rectangle on the right of the screen. 'We're here.' Milford ran her finger down to a spot about five hundred feet south-east of their destination. Back there is the bow section of the *Titanic*.' Then she indicated with her thumb and nodded to port. 'On the schematic, it's here.' She stabbed at a large white shape.

'This is the fissure?' Lou said, tracing a jagged line down the monitor. Magnified, it appeared irregular, a random gash in the ocean floor.

'Unfortunately it's between eighty and one hundred feet across. It doesn't narrow very much anywhere along this stretch.' Milford ran her finger over the ragged line covering about ten miles within the dimensions of the schematic.

'Sod's Law.'

'Yeah, maybe. But let's hope Sod's Law has played out enough for this mission. The problems have been stacking up. We deserve some good luck.'

Milford turned towards the locker room and the LMC suits.

36

JV1's massive lights illuminated the ocean floor in a pool of radiance that extended some two hundred feet in every direction. But even these, the three knew, would not produce much light beyond that circle, so that by the time they reached the crevasse the only visible illumination would come from the powerful torches on the arms of their suits and built into their helmets.

They stood outside the hatch for a few moments to get their bearings.

'*Armstrong*?' Milford called through the comms. 'We have left *JV1*. We're on the surface.'

'Wilco, commander.'

'Let's go,' she said to Kate and Lou. 'Not a second to waste.'

Milford had the nano-carbon bridge in a pack on her back, her oxygen tank tucked between it and her body. Lou was carrying a pack containing cutting equipment in case they needed to break into the hold. In Kate's pack she had a specially designed device for retrieving the documents they hoped to find.

The ground was firm underfoot, but they were

constantly aware of the fragility of this region of the ocean floor.

The light from *JV1* dimmed gradually as they progressed and after ten minutes they had reached the point where the light began to give way to darkness.

'Time to put on the headlamps,' said Milford.

On the right arm of their suits was a control panel. They tapped in a code and immediately the lights came on, nine between them, producing about one tenth of the luminescence they had close to *JV1*.

The ocean was devoid of all marine life, just as it had been on their earlier visit. The only sign that anything had once lived here in this vast stretch of ocean was the sprinkling of dead and rotting creatures caught in the lights.

Milford stopped suddenly and put a hand up. Lou and Kate halted immediately. 'There,' the commander said flatly, 'the crevasse. About fifty feet directly ahead. See it?'

Kate and Lou strained their eyes and could just make out a deeper blackness in the void ahead of them. It was the leading edge of the chasm.

'Got it,' Lou said.

'We must proceed very carefully now.'

From the left sleeve of her suit Milford withdrew a miniature sonar device similar to the one Jerry Derham had used on the mission inside the *Titanic*. It produced a steady pulse audible in all their headsets; a beat that would change if they encountered any subterranean irregularity close to the surface of the ocean floor.

They took it slowly, the sonar keeping up its regular comforting rhythm. As they approached the crevasse their light beams lit it up. They could barely see the other side.

'Believe it or not, this is the narrowest point for miles,' Milford said through the comms. She tapped the panel on her right sleeve. '83.67 feet.'

Lou peered over the edge and saw nothing but uninterrupted blackness; no sign of light or shade, no movement, nothing. It was like a crack leading to Hell itself. It filled him with a nameless terror. It wasn't just a physical fear, it was existential. Here, at the bottom of the ocean in the region marine scientists called the 'abyssal zone', or simply 'the abyss', lay a massive crack in the earth.

He recalled the stats from the briefing. The chasm was fifty-two miles in length, and varied in width between thirty and two hundred feet. And its depth? Well, no one could be sure. Researchers had stopped measuring after their sensors, stretched to the limit, had given up at a depth of over eleven miles.

He couldn't help himself – he imagined falling over the edge, falling, falling for what would feel like an eternity, until something happened. What? The pressure would grow so intense his suit would be overwhelmed and he would be crushed in an instant. Or else he would become snagged on something and die slowly. Or perhaps he would puncture his suit and simply implode.

He shuddered, forcing the thoughts away, stepped back and glanced round at Kate. She was still staring down into the chasm. Maybe, he thought, she was as obsessed with it as he was. In fact, he knew she was. She had the most powerful imagination of anyone he had ever met.

'Let's get started,' Milford's voice cut through the comms. She slipped the container off her back, opened the clasps and pulled out a cylinder about three feet long. She found a zip and pulled it back to expose an odd-shaped contraption. It was spindly and shimmered in the light from the torches.

'This,' Milford added, 'is the business end.' She pointed to a small box attached to the main body then placed the nano-carbon ladder flat on the ground two yards back from the edge of the crevasse.

'Lou, could you secure the end for me, please? Just lean on it. I'll set the controls.'

He crouched down and held the ladder in place as Jane Milford ran her fingers over a keypad on the rectangular box. She straightened. 'Stand back.'

Lou and Kate complied and they heard a cracking sound. Metal bolts shot from the base of the rectangle, punching through the sand and into the bedrock beneath.

Milford ran the sonar over the box and studied the screen. 'Excellent. Worked like a dream.' The anchors went down three feet and now they are probing further under the surface, the nanobots biting their way through the rock. They'll stop at about – here they go – seven feet.'

She leaned forward and gripped the box at the end of the nano-carbon ladder, trying to dislodge it, but it was as solid as an anchor cemented into a dozen feet of concrete.

'Now . . . stage two,' she muttered, touching the screen on the box again and pulling herself upright. The other two just watched expectantly.

For a few seconds nothing happened. Then a chunk of solid material levered up from the strange contraption. It swept through the air, growing as it moved. In a moment it was extending over the edge of the crevasse.

Kate and Lou looked on astonished.

'Nanotechnology is a wonderful thing,' Milford commented dryly.

The ladder grew before their eyes, stretching rapidly across the opening. After a few moments it stopped extending and lowered slowly into place on the ocean floor beyond the far side of the crevasse. The end of it was just out of sight.

'I've never seen anything like that!' Kate exclaimed.

'It's pretty cool,' Milford replied. 'You two ready to crawl across?'

'I guess,' Lou responded.

'Think of it as a normal ladder laid flat. Don't look down. Just keep focused on the far end.'

She paused for a moment and opened the link to the control room on the surface.

'*Armstrong*?'

No response.

'*Armstrong*? This is Commander Milford. We have established the nano-carbon bridge and we are about to cross the crevasse.'

Nothing.

'*Armstrong*? Captain Derham? Come in.' She glanced at the two scientists.

Then a sound, an electronic hiss.

'That's odd. The line is still open.'

She gave up and stepped onto the end of the ladder, found her centre of gravity and started to move forward. 'We have to go one at a time. Kate . . . wait until I reach the far side and come after me. Lou . . . you go last.'

He checked his watch. They had been out for twenty-nine minutes fourteen seconds.

Looking up, he watched the commander scramble along the extended ladder. The structure was absolutely rigid. Milford moved fast. In a minute she had traversed the span and was standing up on the other side. They could just make out the shape of her LMC suit. When her voice came over the comms she sounded slightly out of breath.

'Made it. Kate, you go . . . keep staring ahead.'

She stepped onto the ladder, crouched and gripped the first rung with both hands. Half a dozen steps on, she started to move out over the blackness of the ravine. Staring straight ahead, she scrambled forward with surprising speed, one hand over the other, a bit like a kid in a playground, her boots finding purchase and propelling her forward through the water.

'Almost there,' she declared, and with a last rush forward she was on the far side of the chasm straightening up.

'OK, Lou,' Milford said. 'Go!'

But he could not move. He was staring across the bridge to where the two women stood and saw the shadows transform, a black shape, the outline of a shark bearing down on Kate and Milford.

'Lou, come on.'

He could not speak; could not move a muscle.

'Lou?' Kate said much louder. 'What's wrong? LOU!'

Kate's voice snapped him out of the horrible delirium; the mirage dissolved.

Lou was on the ladder in a couple of seconds. It was difficult to manoeuvre in the cumbersome LMC suit, but after a few moments he established a rhythm, using the repetition to direct his thinking, to shake off the panic, the phantoms.

He saw a flash of light at the extreme edge of his vision. It lasted only a moment. He kept going, growing more confident. But then ... the view through his helmet seemed to judder. It was the oddest sensation. He had felt something like it once before, in Los Angeles, five years ago when he had experienced a 6.3 earthquake that had shaken his apartment block. He knew instantly what it was – the ocean floor was moving.

He froze and heard a strange grinding sound over the comms. Gripping the rungs with all his strength, he glimpsed Kate and Jane Milford stumble and lose their footing. The bridge shook. He felt the vibration shoot along his spine, along his arms. He slipped forward, one hand sliding from the rung in front of him as he tumbled. His helmet hit the nano-carbon structure and his suit yielded, just as it was meant to do, reshaping itself around the ladder.

Then came another violent jolt. Lou saw Milford pull herself to her feet, lose her balance again and trip forward, breaking her fall with her hands.

The bridge rocked again. Lou rolled to one side. A third, more violent tremor crashed around them. He tried to bring his arm round, grabbed at a rung, missed and slipped. Swinging slowly through the water, he tried to grasp the edge of the bridge, failed and fell under the nano-carbon struts with just his left foot hooked over a rung.

He heard Kate scream in his headset. All he could see was the featureless gash of the crevasse; his whole world turned black. His helmet light had shut down. His arms flapped, sending small bobbing rings of illumination all around.

And in that moment Lou suddenly felt relaxed. He was staring into the black void. It was featureless, immense, stretching on and on into oblivion. But he no longer feared it. Part of him wanted to embrace it. Part of him wanted to simply twist his ankle and he would fall, slowly, slowly through the ink-black water. He would fall miles and he would never again see light.

He felt his ankle move. It was involuntary. He was shifting in the current. But then he realized a hand was holding his calf and pulling him upward. He twisted, swung an arm, and touched the side of the bridge.

'Keep swinging, Lou.' It was Jane Milford. 'Swing like a pendulum, get some momentum going, then get hold of the bridge.'

Her voice seemed to be coming from far off, but the words made perfect sense. Of course that was what he had to do. He did as he was told and saw the void move, the blackness sweep around . . . a flash of the far wall of the crevasse, a torch beam, the shimmer of the nano-carbon in the sorry light. He touched the ladder with a finger, fell back, swung forward, clasped the rung, wrapping his arm around it. Then he brought his other arm about, grabbed the strange lambent material and swung his leg over so that he was once more in a stable position on the bridge.

'Hurry!' Milford bellowed in his ear, 'it won't hold both of us for long.' And she was pummelling the rungs, bouncing ahead of him back along the remaining forty feet of bridge. Lou sprang into action and followed her as fast as he could.

Thirty feet . . . twenty. He caught sight of Milford as she reached the far side and rolled over onto the ocean floor. Staring down, he saw a gash appear in the left strut of the bridge. The nano-carbon crackled along its entire length. He pushed onward, adrenalin swamping him, propelling him forward with phenomenal speed.

His foot slipped through a broken rung. His helmet hit the ladder hard, jarring his head, but he was almost there. He stretched out his right arm and Kate caught him. He moved his other arm forward. His foot fell through another rung. Jane had pulled herself up and between them the two women hauled him to the edge and he scrambled across the ocean floor, kicking up whirlpools of water and sand as he went.

37

'Oh, fuck . . . oh, God . . .'

Lou had slivered across the floor at the edge of the crevasse and now lay on his back.

'Take deep breaths. Try to calm—'

'God!'

'Lou . . .'

'We've lost the bridge, Kate. What the fuck are we going to—'

Milford was trying the control room again. There was nothing but static. 'Lou . . . Please calm down. Panicking won't help,' she snapped.

'Easy for you to say,' Lou shot back. 'It makes me feel better, actually.' Then he stopped and breathed deeply as he knew he should do. 'OK . . . OK . . .'

He looked around. Kate was leaning over him, offering a hand up. He could see Jane Milford tapping at the comms control on her arm.

'What the hell caused that?' he said.

Preoccupied, Milford said nothing.

'Any luck?' Kate asked.

The commander shook her head and tried again.

'*Armstrong, Armstrong*, come in, please.'

Nothing but a soulless hiss.

'Captain Derham. Come in, captain. This is a Code Red. I repeat . . . Code Red. Please acknowledge.'

No response.

Milford cursed again.

Lou glanced at the small computer screen on the sleeve of his suit. The numbers '4 . . . 1 . . . 5 . . . 6' shone on the monitor.

'Oh, Christ,' he hissed. 'We've been out almost forty-two minutes.'

'I'm aware of that, Lou.'

'So what now?'

'Only one option: we have to get into the hold and hope we can breathe in there without the suits. The radiation level inside the metal hold should be much lower than it is out here, but we won't be able to last long, even if the air is breathable. It'll at least give us a chance to recharge the suits. Maybe the guys up top will get to us in *JV2*. Come on.'

Lou glanced back at the crack in the ocean bed. The nano-carbon ladder was dangling from its anchor point on the far side. The end that had been perched on their side of the ravine had fallen away, lost in the blackness of the terrifying opening. A remaining few pieces lay scattered over the sand.

'We're still a long way from the hold,' Milford said. She flicked a look at her monitor as she strode on. '356 feet to be precise.'

They marched on, adrenalin pumping through them.

As they covered the uneven surface, they began to let go of the fear of seismic activity. With less than twenty minutes of life left in their suits they had to take the chance.

'The time limit was measured under lab conditions,' Kate said breathlessly as she hurried along. 'It could be inaccurate.'

Neither Lou nor Jane Milford replied. They each knew the obvious . . . the lab results could indeed be inaccurate . . . but either way.

The commander checked her monitor. Eighteen minutes, twenty seconds left. 'Come on, gotta move faster,' she snapped, gasping for breath.

'*Armstrong, Armstrong* . . . Come in, please. *Armstrong* . . . Is anyone there?' she called through the comms link to the surface. 'This is a Code Red . . . I repeat . . . a Code Red. We need immediate help. Do you read?'

Static.

'*Armstrong* . . .' Milford was on the point of exhaustion.

Then they saw the hold. It appeared suddenly in their torch beams sitting on the hardened sand, a silhouette of sharp edges and ragged, rusted sides.

Lou checked his screen. Thirty-two yards to go and seven minutes, sixteen seconds left for the suits.

The metal box looked more dilapidated than the images had made it out to be. Close up, they could see how the sides were covered in a thick layer of rust, and strange deep-ocean crustaceans. Chemicals had leached out of the alloy of the container's walls and run down the rutted sides in potently coloured streaks. It creaked, a sound similar to the one they'd heard as they approached the *Titanic* three days ago. This was quieter, weaker, but it was the sound of containment under strain, bolts slipping inexorably from nuts, rivets moving a tiny fraction of an inch. It was the sound of imminent collapse.

Milford dashed to the door in the front of the cargo hold. It was covered with rust, but the oblong outline could just be seen in the beams of their torches. To one side at waist height was the opening mechanism, a large wheel that sent a bolt into a plate on the wall. It was tempting to imagine they could simply break the mechanism with a crowbar or some special gizmo designed by the DARPA eggheads, but that wasn't an option because if they got it open they had to reseal the door, so they could operate the air lock inside, pump out the water and enter the hold itself.

Milford leaned on the wheel. It didn't move even a fraction of an inch, as though it had been welded into place. 'Lou, Kate. Come on.'

It was difficult for them to find a position in which they could all exert force on the wheel to open the door; their suits kept getting in the way. But finally they managed it. Lou positioned himself behind Milford and stretched over to the wheel. Kate slipped into a space beside the commander and just got her hands to it.

Lou saw the numbers on his sleeve display: '3 minutes 2 seconds.'

'On three . . . One, two, three . . . PUSH!' Milford bellowed through the comms.

They bore down on the wheel, but it was obvious from the feel of it that they hadn't even come close to loosening the mechanism.

They stood back, knowing there was no chance they could move the wheel this way. Lou unclasped the straps of the plastic container he'd been carrying on his back. Milford crouched down and opened it up.

'We need to cut around the wheel without damaging it,' she said and reached for a small pistol-sized device nestled in a foam tray inside Lou's pack. Not wasting a second, she spun round and lifted it to the rusted area around the wheel mechanism. 'It's a type of laser,' she explained and brought it close to the disfigured metal.

Lou checked his watch. '1 minute 24 seconds.' He swallowed hard and refused to let the panic take over.

Milford fired the laser. It produced an intense blue light that sliced through the metal around the wheel. Moving it with precise sweeps, she seared away the chemicals and the fused remains of dead sea creatures jamming the mechanism. Slivers of jagged metal scattered and tumbled through the water to the ocean floor.

Kate saw the time on her screen: '54 seconds.'

'All right,' the commander said, snapping off the laser and letting it float down to the sand. 'Again. Take up positions . . . as before.'

'One . . . two . . . three . . . push.'

Nothing happened.

'Again. Push.'

The three of them heaved forward in unison, bearing down with all the strength they could muster. None of them needed to look at their screens now.

The wheel would not budge.

'Again!' Milford screamed. And finally . . . some movement. It was slight, but enough to fill them with hope and renewed energy.

'Step back,' Milford commanded. 'Take a deep breath. And push . . . PUSH! . . . PUSH!'

The wheel freed and they stumbled forward as it rotated half a turn. Milford moved the wheel round; it was stiff, but she was charged up, filled with a primal power, a drive to survive. The wheel began to move faster. It reached the end of its run and they all pulled on it, stepping back as the door began to ease outwards.

'Yes!' Lou exclaimed. 'Yes!'

When the sound came through the comms, Kate and Lou had no idea what it was. It was a sound like no other they had ever heard in their lives. But then they felt a vibration through the water and subconsciously they knew what that meant.

Spinning in unison, they saw that Commander Jane Milford had turned to a solid block of carbon.

38

Approximately 600 miles SE of Newfoundland.
Sunday, 13 April 1912.

Fortescue had ordered a second breakfast, this one for himself. When the steward arrived with it, the scientist made a big fuss about how insatiably hungry he was feeling. The man, who had also brought the first tray to the room half an hour earlier, gave him a puzzled look that quickly transformed into a polite smile and he retreated with the remains of the first breakfast, the one Billy had consumed.

It was over his third slice of toast that Fortescue decided he would not wait until he reached New York to talk to Billy's relatives. Satiated with a pair of kippers, fine pastries and a pot of tea, he pulled on his jacket and headed out of his room en route to the barber's one deck up on B. He had just reached the end of his corridor and was emerging onto the main reception area close to the Grand Staircase when he was almost thrown off his feet by a fast young body charging straight into him. He looked down to see the petrified face of Billy O'Donnell.

'What the devil?' Fortescue exclaimed.

'Mr Wick . . .'

Fortescue saw a steward in a badly stained white uniform pick himself up and dust himself down. Then turning, he watched as a maintenance worker arrived breathing heavily. 'You little 'orror!' he exclaimed and made a grab for Billy.

Fortescue stepped forward, gently manoeuvring the boy to one side. 'It's quite all right,' he began.

At that moment, a man in an officer's uniform arrived. It was Herbert Pitman, the ship's Third Officer. He stood a few feet away from the tableau, hands on hips, a pained expression beginning to spread across his face. He took a step towards Fortescue. The stricken young steward who had been carrying the breakfast tray was clearing up the mess.

'I'm so sorry, sir,' Pitman began, turning to Fortescue. 'This little ruffian has been causing trouble all over the ship.'

Billy clutched at Fortescue's elegantly tailored black jacket.

'You get your filthy hands off the gentleman!' the maintenance man exclaimed and Pitman went to pull the kid away.

Fortescue raised a hand. 'Stop,' he commanded. 'It's quite all right.'

Both men froze and Pitman gave Fortescue an odd look. 'Sir, I don't think you fully under—'

'Of course I understand, Mr Pitman, but I can vouch for this young chap.'

The maintenance man pulled back, his arms folded, and Pitman simply stared at Fortescue. 'Vouch, sir? The little brat shouldn't be outside the Third Class area. I need to take this up with the boy's parents and perhaps even the captain.'

'There will be no need to trouble yourself, Mr Pitman. By the way, the boy has a name. It is Billy O'Donnell. He is travelling with his uncle and aunt. I invited him to First to run

me a few errands. It is regrettable that he has caused trouble.'
He looked down at the scruffy kid. 'What do you say, Billy?'

The boy was quick to react. He doffed his cap. 'I'm most
sorry, sir,' he said to Pitman.

The officer turned to the steward. 'Smalles . . . bugger off!'
The steward spun on his heel. Pitman simply glared at the
maintenance worker. He got the message and retreated without
a word. 'This is most irregular, sir,' declared Pitman.

'The boy has apologized, Pitman,' Fortescue retorted. 'I
shall not let him out of my sight until I return him to Third.
For your part, I would like you to let the matter drop. Now,
does that sound reasonable?'

'Very well, sir. But, I'm afraid if I see this young man
around these parts of the ship at any time between now and
our docking in New York, I will have to go through the company
procedures.'

'Quite so,' Fortescue said. 'You hear that, Billy?'

The boy looked at Fortescue then at Pitman and nodded.

'Good. Now, Mr Pitman, if you will excuse us, I shall take
the boy directly to Third.'

'You've no need, sir,' he said. 'I can take him there.'

'I actually have some business with his guardians, Mr
Pitman.'

The officer touched his cap and took a step back as Fortescue
encouraged Billy to walk on towards the door to the outside.

*

During the past few hours, the weather had changed. It had
grown colder thanks to a strong breeze coming down from the

icy wastes in the north, and Fortescue pulled his flimsy jacket close about his chest.

'I need to tell you something, Mr Wickins,' Billy said, the sound of his voice tossed around in the air.

'What's that, Billy?' Fortescue asked, crouching as they headed aft at a brisk pace.

'Need to tell you something.'

'Not now, young fellow. Too cold. Tell me a bit later . . .'

They reached a flight of stairs down to E-Deck and descended the steps, turned 180 degrees and proceeded along a narrow passage to a doorway. A sign above it said 'F-Deck'. Through the door they took another flight of stairs, Fortescue leading the way.

'Which cabin are you in, Billy?'

'You don't need to go any further, Mr Wickins. I won't trouble you again. A promise is a promise.'

Fortescue stopped and turned. He bent down and held Billy's skinny shoulders. 'I would like to speak to your uncle and aunt.'

'But I said I wouldn't.'

'Not about that nonsense, Billy,' he nodded towards the bow. 'I would like to talk to them about your astonishing ability.'

The boy looked panic-stricken. 'But you said that would be when we docked.'

'I think I should bring it up before then.'

'But they won't understand, Mr Wickins. They're not the sort—'

'Billy, please leave the discussion to me. I've talked to lots of parents before now.' And he gave the boy a reassuring smile. Billy did not return it but gazed down at his shoes.

'They won't listen,' he mumbled.

'Well, we'll see about that, won't we?'

*

The advertisements for the White Star Line boasted the merits of the Third Class accommodation aboard Titanic, *but even so, the difference between Third and First was startling.*

Billy led the way along a narrow corridor, down a short, dark staircase to one of the lowest decks of the ship. Everything here was smaller, narrower, shrouded in shadow and illuminated with dull light. The rooms off these corridors were almost at the waterline and many did not even have the benefit of portholes. There were no liveried staff, no plush carpets. The walls were painted a rudimentary pale green; the metal floor in the public areas was often left bare or covered with inexpensive and hardwearing carpet.

The boy stopped outside a room marked G10 and tapped quietly. The door opened and they saw a thin, callow-eyed woman, her bony fingers encircling the edge of the door. A musty, sweaty odour emanated from the room. Fortescue could hear at least four voices all talking at once, the cry of a young child.

'Billy.' The woman peered suspiciously at Fortescue.

'Aunt. This gentleman is Mr Wickins. He's a teacher.'

'What's up, Mary?' A gruff baritone came from the room. The door opened wide. A short, pugnacious-looking man in a stained black suit stood just inside the cabin.

'You weren't at chapel, me lad,' he said to Billy and then lifted his black eyes to Fortescue, looking him up and down. 'And you are?'

Fortescue extended a hand. The man looked at it then back up at his face.

Fortescue straightened his back. 'You must be Mr Spindle. I've just brought Billy here back from First Class.'

The man produced a mocking laugh. 'The little bastard causing trouble again? Upsetting the toffs?'

'I was wondering if I might talk to you about Billy.'

Spindle stared at him blankly. 'Get in,' he said to his wife and yanked her arm. She disappeared into the room. Spindle half-closed the door.

'What d'ya want to talk about?' His eyes narrowed.

Fortescue was not sure where to begin, how to explain that the boy was a genius.

'May I?' he indicated the door.

'No, you may not. We ain't got much room.' He stepped out into the corridor and nudged the door shut. 'We can talk 'ere.'

Egbert cleared his throat. 'Your ward, Billy, has a remarkable gift.'

'Gift for thievin',' the man hissed. 'Comes in 'andy, though, just so long as the little shit don't get caught.'

'He's actually a very talented mathematician, Mr Spindle. I'm a teacher and I think he should be given every chance to develop his abilities.'

The man looked into Fortescue's eyes, his face completely expressionless. Then he broke into an unpleasant smile. 'Mathematics, eh? Well, he must get that from his aunt.' He cackled.

Fortescue and Billy looked at him in silence.

'So what you saying, mister?' Spindle went on sarcastically. 'You expecting us to put the lad into a school for the gifted? I imagine it would be a little pricey . . . I might have to sell off a few shares.'

Fortescue held the man's gaze. 'I was going to offer to help.

I think Billy has a remarkable talent. It would be a crime to let it go to waste.'

Spindle considered the scientist. 'Did I 'ear right that you're a teacher?'

Fortescue nodded.

'So you could teach 'im.'

'Up to a point, but I have important business in America. I have to leave New York soon after we dock.'

Spindle nodded slowly and looked Fortescue up and down again. Fortescue sensed something had changed. The man's expression had turned from sarcasm to an odd blend of disgust and avarice. 'So, this "mathematical talent",' he said, 'would be worth paying for, right?'

Fortescue looked confused. 'I would be happy to pay for Billy to receive special attention,' he said and glanced at the boy. Billy looked from one man to the other.

Spindle's face was rigid, his black eyes held Fortescue's. 'Special attention . . . yeah.' He was nodding slowly again. 'That comes expensive.'

'I'm not sure I'm making myself clear.'

'Oh, it's very clear, Mr . . . Wickins was it? We knows all about special attention . . . ain't stupid.' And he touched the side of his nose.

Suddenly Fortescue got it. The man thought he was fabricating a story about Billy's skills and that he was really interested in the boy for nefarious sexual purposes. He felt a frisson of revulsion. 'I don't know how you have reached the conclusion I think you have reached, my good man . . .'

Spindle gave Fortescue a look of utter contempt. 'I ain't your good man, guvnor, and don't play me for a fool. I know what all you toffs are like. Mathematical ability, my arse . . .'

Fortescue felt a fury building. He glanced at Billy and then back at Bert Spindle. Trying to keep calm, he said, 'I assure you, you have it all wrong.'

'Five quid and you can have the little bleeder.'

'What?'

'Five now, five when we get to New York and I'll keep me silence too.'

Fortescue had a sudden overwhelming urge to strike the man. He took a step forward and saw a glint of metal. Spindle had a flick knife in his left hand. He made a grab for Billy with his right, but the kid slipped away and darted along the corridor behind Fortescue. Fortescue had his hands half-raised level with his chest. He realized he was suddenly breathing heavily.

'I'm afraid there's been a misunderstanding,' the scientist began, eyeing the knife.

'You reckon, do you, Mr Wickins? I don't think I've misunderstood nothing. I think I have the measure of you, mate . . . seen it plenty a times before. Empty your pockets.'

'What?'

'You 'eard me.'

'But this is preposterous!'

Spindle moved the knife forward six inches. Fortescue reached into his pocket and withdrew a few coins. Spindle grabbed them, pushing his face close up to Fortescue's. 'I've got your name,' he said. 'This ship's a small place . . . I'd watch out. Touch the boy without paying for 'im and I'll slice you ear to ear before you go overboard.' And he was gone.

Fortescue realized he was shaking. He peered down at his trembling hands. Lowering his arms, he took a couple of deep breaths, hardly able to believe what had just happened. He looked at the door to G10 for a long moment, then turned. There was no sign of Billy O'Donnell. He walked along the corridor and up the steps, seeing no one until he reached the top and the passageway onto D-Deck.

He heard a sound from behind. 'Mr Wickins.'

He spun round but there was no one there. Then he saw a hand beckoning him from behind a pillar. He walked over.

'I'm sorry about that,' the boy said.

'It's not your fault, Billy.'

Along the deck he spotted a pair of middle-aged women testing the air. They ducked back inside.

'Look, there's something I was trying to tell you.'

'A bit late now, isn't it, Billy?'

'It's not about me uncle and aunt.'

'Go on.'

'It's just . . . well, earlier, I was running away from something, something terrifying.'

'What do you mean?'

The boy looked down at his scuffed shoes and shrugged his shoulders. 'You'll probably think I'm lying.'

Fortescue shook his head. 'I won't. Tell me.'

'I was exploring and I got cornered. Had to duck into a storeroom. Then guess what happened? I'm behind some crates and this couple come into the storeroom and start whispering . . . schemin'.'

'Billy, you've lost me.'

'They was talkin' about you.'

'Who were?'

'That brother and sister pair you've been hobnobbing with.'

'Frieda and Marcus?'

'That may be the names they gave you.'

'What are you saying?' Fortescue was utterly exasperated.

'The woman, her name's Frieda. The bloke, he's called Charles and he's as English as you are.'

'They're Swiss!'

'So they says.'

'Billy.' Fortescue could feel his patience draining away. 'I've really had enough drama for one day.'

'They are trying to steal something from you.'

'Look, just stop!' Fortescue's temper had finally snapped.

'But . . .'

'I said stop!' He realized he was yelling and looked along the deck left then right. A man was walking a dog about fifty feet away. Fortescue's voice had been swept about by the wind and the man was oblivious to them.

He looked down at Billy and the boy could see the fury in Fortescue's eyes.

'It's true,' Billy persisted.

Something snapped in Fortescue. He could simply not accept that the woman he had made love to last night was deceiving him. The boy must be lying deliberately.

He raised his hand to strike the boy and at that moment a door opened behind him a few yards along the deck. He reacted quickly, glanced round, lowered his hand just in time. An elderly couple, both wrapped up in overcoats, slipped past him. The man was wearing an old-fashioned top hat which he lifted a fraction from his head as he passed.

Fortescue offered a brief 'Good morning' and turned back to where Billy O'Donnell had stood and caught a flash of jacket as the boy slipped out of sight.

39

Fortescue was in mental turmoil; the events of the past few days had suddenly caught up with him. He had not realized what a creature of habit he was. Out of the environment he was so used to – the laboratory he shared with Rutherford, his apartment, his small circle of friends and the remnants of his family in Surrey – he felt utterly lost.

Who was he to believe? How could Frieda and Marcus be anything other than what they appeared to be? Should he believe the word of Billy? Until now he'd had nothing but admiration for the boy and his talent, but in all honesty should he really have trusted a kid who skulked around the ship, admitted stealing as a pastime and whose uncle was a thug?

But then again, he was here on this ship for a reason, a deadly serious reason. He should never forget that. He was not John Wickins, he was not a barrister, nor was he a school-teacher with a rich father in America. He was Dr Egbert Fortescue, a researcher at Manchester University, but he was also Egbert Fortescue the co-discoverer of a priceless secret.

The previous evening someone had snooped around his cabin. He was sure of that. There could be no doubt that if the secret was known to enemies of England then his life would be in *danger and forces would have been mobilized to find and steal his work. That much had been made clear to him during the briefing session immediately before leaving Manchester. And now, of course, there was even more at stake, for he had moved onward with the endeavours he and Rutherford had started. He had reached far beyond accepted theory.*

Pulling himself up from his armchair, Fortescue walked over to the bed, crouched and put the combination into the safe. Dragging out the metal boxes, he removed his briefcase containing his notes.

Placing the papers on the desk, he added to them the work he had been doing during the past three days at sea that dealt with his new revolutionary discoveries. He pulled up a chair, removed his jacket, folded back his sleeves and began to write.

It took him almost an hour to make a fair copy of what amounted to twenty-seven pages of notes, then he spent a further thirty minutes double-checking every expression, every plus and minus sign and every set of parentheses.

Fortescue stood up, collected together the copy of the entire set and placed this in the inside pocket of his jacket. Then, sifting through the original collection of papers, he carefully separated out random pages to create two neat piles on the desk. Both of these contained pages of equations and numeric descriptions, but each only told a part of the story. The substance of each interwove, but he had parted them, a mathematical expression here, a line of notation there. He then placed the right-hand pile in his briefcase, slipped that into its metal box and returned it to the safe beside the isotope box before spinning the combination lock. He gathered up the second heap of notes, found a couple of elastic bands and a large envelope in the desk drawer. Securing the papers into a small bundle, he placed them in the envelope, strode to the door and out into the passage.

It was the obvious and logical way any sensible person would protect their work, he mused . . . Make a copy to keep on one's person, separate out the original into two random collections and hide these in different places.

It took no more than a couple of minutes to reach the main reception. The purser's office stood close to the Grand Staircase. It was a small room with a hatch opening onto the reception area. The window was unmanned. Fortescue rang the bell and a few moments later a young man in a white uniform appeared. He was out of breath, his face ruddy.

'Apologies, sir,' he gasped. 'Had to deliver a parcel to one of the gentlemen on A-Deck.'

Fortescue put the envelope on the sill. 'I would like this package placed in the hold.'

'Certainly, sir.' The young man looked at it then checked a logbook opened on the counter. 'Okey dokey . . . I can put this item . . .' He tapped it. '. . . into Security Box . . . Let me see . . . 19A . . . AS, in cargo hold number 4. How does that suit?'

Fortescue shrugged. 'I don't mind, just so long as it is safe.'

'Couldn't be safer, sir. Now, if ever you need to retrieve the item, just drop by. If I'm not 'ere, tell them Security Box . . .'

'Yes . . . 19AS, cargo hold 4. Very well, thank you.' Fortescue placed a sixpence on the counter and walked away.

*

Back in his cabin, Fortescue called for the steward, and while he waited he wrote a brief message on a piece of ship's stationery: 'Please join me for luncheon. Yours, John.' He then slipped the note into an envelope. When the man arrived, Fortescue handed it to him.

Twenty minutes later the reply came back. I thought you would never ask!

*

Frieda looked enchanting. She was wearing a pale-blue dress, her hair up in braids. He saw her seated at a table before she spotted him and he remembered her face in the dim light of her cabin very early that morning.

'You look more beautiful every time I see you,' he said as he reached the table and took her hand in his.

'Oh, goodness, you know all the right things to say.' She beamed at him. 'So what have you been up to? Sleeping, like me?'

He felt a spasm of anxiety, but smiled nonchalantly. 'I couldn't. I was up on deck to see the sunrise.'

'Goodness me . . . I didn't realize!'

'It was almost a religious experience,' Fortescue went on. 'If you happen to believe in such things.'

'John!'

'I'm sorry. I didn't mean to offend . . .'

'I shall pray for you.'

He nodded solemnly.

The waiter approached and they ordered: shrimp followed by lobster for Frieda; salmon and steak for Fortescue. The wine waiter poured each of them a glass of Château Lafite 1909.

'So tell me more about working with Georges Méliès.'

'You're really interested in this?'

'I am. I think he is a genius.'

'I do too. Well, where do I begin? What do you want to know, John?'

'Oh, I don't know . . . How does it all work? How does he make "the magic" happen?'

She took a sip of wine and replaced the glass decorously. 'Méliès is a genius, but he is also a dirty old man!'

Fortescue had a mouthful of wine, swallowed it . . . just . . . and guffawed. 'I imagine it comes with the artistic temperament.'

'Quite so . . . at least that's what the other ladies at the studio said to convince themselves. But, look, don't get me wrong . . . he is a sublime artist.'

'And, to be honest, I cannot blame him for his good taste,' Fortescue commented.

She looked at him under lowered eyelids. 'You are an agent provocateur, Mr Wickins.' And she beamed.

The food arrived and they ate in silence for a while.

'And what about you, John? Seeing as we are playing twenty questions.'

'Oh, Good Lord, Frieda. As I told you and your brother the other night, the last thing you want to know about me are the details of my profession. I would far rather create the impression of an artistic son of a wealthy industrialist . . . life as a lawyer is so deathly dull I simply refuse to discuss it.'

'Very well, but what about your love life?'

'Ah, well, admittedly, that has been slightly more eventful.'

'Oh?'

'But I do not wish to talk about other women when I'm in the presence of the most beautiful of the species I have yet encountered.'

'John Wickins . . . you are positively incorrigible . . . do continue!'

As the wine started to take effect, Fortescue found himself letting loose the suspicions Billy had engendered. He became once again transfixed by this young woman who seemed so interested in him. He wanted to believe in her, he wanted to be seduced.

And seduced he was. The main course arrived, was consumed; dessert followed, then brandy and a champagne for Frieda, and soon they were walking as though in a dream towards the lift, where a young attendant stood at the controls and smiled at them benignly. From there they were in the corridor leading to Frieda's cabin. They stopped, kissed, their tongues probing and exploring. Into the room, and onto the bed; clothes shed, skin touching skin, their breath mixing, bodies melding. They found each other and were lost to the world.

40

Fortescue awoke. It was dark and for several long moments he could not recall where he was. He had never slept so deeply and now he felt groggy. He pulled himself up in the dark and heard noises, a confusion of voices, someone shouting instructions. Then it all came back to him – the lunch, Frieda. He put a hand out across the bed. He was alone, the bedding ruffled. He fumbled for the electric light switch, found it, flicked it on and shielded his eyes.

'Frieda?'

No reply.

The room was decorated in what the brochure had called Georgian style. He could see recessed alcoves, paintings of neo-classical beauties and spear-carrying Adonises. The floor was covered with a rich green carpet, the bedspread a lush red weave. He stood and dressed quickly. The sounds outside were growing louder, closer, but he could not make out a single word. Then he felt a hard jolt and a spasm of panic shot through him. What the hell was that? *Another violent judder.* It seemed unimaginable that a vessel this size could be shaken by anything . . . but it had . . . twice in the space of a few seconds. He felt a vibration stutter across the floor, gripped the ornately carved bedstead and headed for the door.

A woman rushed past him in the corridor. He walked quickly towards the reception area close to the Grand Staircase. A group of passengers had gathered there. He approached the closest person, a man in a dinner suit pulling on a lifejacket.

'What in heaven's name is going on?'

The man turned, his face flushed with excitement. 'Hit an iceberg, old boy. Not supposed to be too serious.' He glanced down at the lifejacket. 'A precaution apparently.'

Fortescue said nothing, spun on his heel and headed for the door leading out to the deck.

A small group of First Class passengers had gathered on the main promenade. A member of the crew was talking to them animatedly. Some people were in their nightclothes; others were still wearing dinner suits and gowns. One of the group, a large man in a top hat and smoking a pipe, headed towards the bow. Fortescue started to follow him, passed a bulkhead, and there it was.

The Titanic had pulled away from the iceberg. Fortescue could feel the ship turning tightly to port. The iceberg floated now a hundred yards to starboard, but it still looked massive, towering over the gigantic vessel. The slopes of the ice mountain were jagged, the lights from the ship illuminating its bladelike edges, frozen rivulets, and the pits and channels in its blue-tinted ice. Between the ship and the iceberg the water churned black. Fortescue went over to the rail and looked at the water. He could see dots of white, flecks of detritus.

'Nothing to get too excited about, I'm told,' the man with the pipe commented.

Fortescue hadn't heard him properly. 'What?'

'The berg, old chap, the officer over there,' and he pointed *towards the gathering with his pipe, '. . . assures us the ship is unharmed. Close call, though.'*

Fortescue said nothing, just looked down at the water again, a deep sense of foreboding growing in the pit of his stomach. Pulling away from the rail, he sped back towards the door into the ship.

A clutch of scared passengers were squeezing out and he was obliged to stand aside to let them through, but then he plunged inside, stopped and suddenly realized he had no idea what he was doing or where he was going. He took the stairs down to C-Deck, pulling out his key as he dashed towards C16. Turning a corner, he almost knocked over an elderly lady and her younger companion. Apologizing, he helped to steady the lady who grunted and glared at him.

'The ship may be going down, young man,' she hissed, '. . . but there's no need to lose one's head.'

Fortescue caught a brief smile flickering across the younger woman's lips. He apologized again, gave the old lady a quick bow and proceeded at a slower pace.

The door to his cabin hung open a fraction. The lock had been broken, flecks of wood lay scattered across the carpet.

Fortescue stared at the handle, transfixed, a sudden flash of fear froze him to the spot. 'My God,' he hissed.

He eased the door inwards, every nerve alert. Keeping close to the door, he surveyed the scene, his heart pounding in his chest.

The room had been ransacked, the bed stripped, linen and pillows strewn randomly. His desk had been swept clean of papers; a crystal inkwell lay on its side, the contents spread in a royal-blue puddle across the inlaid leather surface. The cushions of his armchair had been pulled off, slashed open and the stuffing cast about. Then Fortescue caught sight of the safe under the bed. It had been forced open, the door pinned back, and the metal boxes containing the isotope and his briefcase had both been taken.

Fortescue simply stared at the empty insides of the safe, at its bare, featureless walls.

He walked slowly to the centre of the cabin. A sound came from the door behind him. He whirled round. Marcus was standing a few inches inside the room.

'Marcus!'

The man smiled and shook his head slowly. 'The name's Charles Grantham, John . . . Or should I say, Egbert? We all seem enamoured with pseudonyms, do we not?' His accent was cut-glass English.

'What is this all about?'

The man's smile seemed to have been painted on, unchanging as he spoke. 'Well, you see it's like this. Frieda and I . . . Yes, her name is Frieda. However, we are not siblings, nor are we in the film business. And we are certainly not Swiss! We both work for Frieda's government.'

'Which would be based in Berlin.'

'The German government was alerted to your work at Manchester University through a junior assistant in the Chemistry department. The young man was ordered to keep his eyes and ears open. I then took over the project. I've stood closer to you than I am now, old boy. But you obviously did not notice!'

'You're English.'

'Well spotted.'

'A traitor.'

He shrugged. 'If you insist. My mother was German actually. I loved her more than I cared for my father.'

Fortescue felt oddly calm. He was not trained for espionage or to fight. He was a scientist, an intellectual. But now, faced with a real spy, his cover blown, strangely he felt none of the terror he might once have imagined feeling.

'So you have the isotope and my papers?'

Grantham fixed the scientist with cold eyes. 'Yes, we do.'

'But you're crazy. The isotope is deadly. Even brief exposure . . .'

Grantham had a hand up. 'I studied physics at Cambridge, began my doctorate . . . So, please do not patronize me, I know perfectly well the capabilities of the ibnium isotope and I also quite understand the significance of your theoretical studies. You are a very capable man, Dr Fortescue.'

'You stole them earlier today and hid them somewhere.'

Grantham took two steps further into the room. 'Correct.'

The ship shook. It felt like a violent tremor close to the bow had reverberated the entire length of the ship. Fortescue almost lost his footing.

'So why come back? Why expose your real identity to me?' Egbert asked.

Grantham took three steps closer and drew a blade from an inside pocket of his jacket.

'What the devil?' Fortescue's former cool evaporated. He squinted in disbelief at the knife held waist high, shifted to one side, bracing himself.

Grantham moved quickly. Fortescue stumbled back, coming up hard against the edge of his desk. Grantham lifted the knife. Fortescue grabbed the man's wrist but knew immediately that his assailant was far stronger than him. He pulled back as the knife came closer and tried to push his arm forward with all his strength; but the knife kept coming, inching towards his face.

Fortescue put his left hand flat onto the surface of the desk, his fingers wrapping the edge to give him some leverage. The crystal inkwell felt cold on his wrist and his hand almost slipped in the ink. Acting on impulse, he let his hand move back a few inches. He grasped the inkwell, swung round and slammed its leading edge into Grantham's left temple.

For a second, the man had no idea what had happened. He was still moving forward, the knife slipping closer to Fortescue. Egbert pulled his arm back, brought the crystal inkwell round in a shallow arc and slammed a second blow to almost the same spot on Grantham's head.

Grantham's hand stopped moving, his eyes rolled upward, and he crumpled almost vertically to the floor, the knife sliding from his limp fingers.

Fortescue could not move. He was panting, gasping for air, shaking. Swallowing hard, he lowered his gaze to the body at his feet, crouched down and moved Grantham's head back. A huge dark patch had appeared close to the man's left eye, the edge of it an inch from his hairline. There were flecks of ink on his jaw and across the bridge of his nose, a trickle of blood appeared at the corner of his eye and spilled out onto his cheek.

Fortescue gazed in silence at his right hand. He still had the crystal inkwell gripped in his ink-stained fingers, his skin white in the dull electric light. A loud bang came from somewhere deep within the bowels of the ship and along the corridor a woman screamed. He jolted upright and tried to rationalize. He let the inkwell drop, took several deep breaths, leaned down and grabbed Grantham's hands. Twisting him round, he dragged him towards the bed. Laying him level with the edge, the legs straight out, Fortescue managed to roll the body halfway under the bed. He had to kneel down to finish the job, turning the dead man over twice to secure him from view.

He straightened and felt an almost obsessive need to wash his hands. Leaning over the basin with the beautiful ornate mirror positioned above it, he yanked on the hot tap and grasped the soap. Running the water over his hands, he massaged the Pears bar, dug his nails into the orange cube and wrung his hands with the foam and the oily soap. Then he threw water over his face, letting the hot liquid sting his eyes. He dried his hands and face, and then stared at himself in the mirror.

'You have killed,' he muttered, watching his lips move. A cold shiver passed down his spine. He took a deep breath, pulled an overcoat from his wardrobe and marched out of the room.

*

The first thing he noticed was that the ship was listing to starboard. He hadn't realized it in his room, but here in the corridor it was obvious. That could mean only one thing. Whatever the man with the pipe had claimed up on deck, the ship was taking in water, and a lot of it. He glanced at his fob watch. It was almost one o'clock. He had no clear idea why he was heading to B-Deck, except for some vague notion that Frieda might have returned there. She must have the boxes from the safe.

He heard another scream, a loud crack from close by. Reaching the reception area on C-Deck, he saw there were dozens of passengers clustered around the Grand Staircase. Another jarring sound like the snap of a whip resonated around the open area.

'Ladies and gentlemen . . . It is all right,' came a man's voice. Fortescue looked over and saw one of the senior officers. He had got up onto a chair and held a megaphone in his right hand.

'Please . . . ladies and gentlemen . . . there's nothing to fear. That was just a distress flare.'

'If there's nothing to fear, why fire a distress flare?' a man shouted. He was just a few yards to his right, a stocky man with white whiskers. Fortescue recognized him but didn't know his name. A couple went past Egbert headed towards the exit doors. He turned and squeezed a way through the crowd to reach the foot of the Grand Staircase.

Up one level, he reached B-Deck. Here, a similar crowd of First Class passengers had gathered. Two more crewmen were trying to answer their questions. A woman was crying; another sobbed into the shoulder of an older man holding her tightly. Fortescue slipped around the edge of the throng, and into the corridor leading to Frieda's cabin.

He reached the door. It was closed.

'Frieda? Frieda? Are you in there?'

No reply.

He banged on the wood. 'Frieda.'

He stepped away and charged at the door, then fell back, a dreadful pain rushing down his left side. He looked around and saw a fire extinguisher attached to a wall bracket. He *dashed over, tried to yank it from the support but found it was held fast. Crouching down, he studied the mechanism, pulled on a clip and the metal extinguisher slipped free. He lifted it, one hand on the base, the other around the top. It was heavy but just about manageable. Staggering back to Frieda's cabin, Fortescue raised the extinguisher to chest height and swung it round, smashing it into the door. The wood splintered, but the panel held. Swinging the extinguisher a second time, it ploughed through the wood, punching out a hole a foot wide.*

He paused for a moment to draw breath. Lifting the extinguisher a third time, he landed another, harder blow that smashed the lock. One swift kick to the handle and the door flew inwards.

A man rushed past him in the corridor. He was wearing a life jacket and had another clasped in both hands. He barely noticed Fortescue and completely ignored the shattered door.

Stepping inside, Fortescue surveyed the room. It was just how he had left it. The bedding was a mess. Frieda's underwear lay scattered across the floor. Searching the cupboards offered nothing. Under the bed, just air. He retreated back to the corridor.

Think, *he said to himself, mouthing the words silently.* OK, so Marcus – Charles Grantham – stole the boxes while I was asleep in here. Frieda left me . . . God only knows when. Then Grantham came to kill me. Frieda would have expected him to complete the task, then what? Meet her. Yes, but where? Think, Egbert, think. *Then he had it.* Of course . . . the storeroom where Billy had seen them. Oh God, Billy . . .

He dashed back to the reception area, down the Grand Staircase, dodging the growing hoards of panicking passengers. As he approached the turn in the stairs there came another loud crack, another flash . . . another flare . . . The situation was clearly deteriorating.

He stood in the reception of C-Deck buffeted by the other passengers clustered around the exit onto the promenade; one of the crew was giving directions.

A young officer lifted a megaphone to his mouth. 'A lifeboat has been lowered,' he announced. 'If you could make an orderly . . .'

People close to Fortescue surged forward and suddenly everyone was rushing for the doors. He was shoved to one side, his head colliding with a painting of the Titanic's sister ship RMS Olympic. The picture slipped from its hook and crashed to the floor sending glass shards across the carpet. Fortescue pulled himself to his feet and looked around angrily.

'Please. Ladies and gentlemen!' shouted the young officer with the megaphone.

'Billy had been in a room off one of the corridors leading away from this reception area,' Fortescue said aloud and rubbed a hand across his forehead. His fingers came up wet with sweat. He paused for a beat feeling nauseous, leaned forward, his hands on his knees, and took several deep breaths. This was so surreal. Focus, *he thought.* Focus. I have to focus. I have to retrieve the isotope and the notes. Then after that worry about what the hell is happening to this damn ship.

He remembered how Billy had crashed across reception, colliding with the steward. He retraced the boy's steps, found the corridor and swung into it. Two men ran towards him; they were chefs from the First Class kitchen, their white jackets and striped trousers smeared with grease, faces streaked black. Fortescue stood to one side as they rushed past him.

Moving slowly along the corridor, he drew parallel with the kitchens and swung a pair of doors inwards. He could see no one. Then he spotted flames, a line of fire across the back of the room, an upturned barrel, a smudge of oil on the metal floor. A ball of fire roared towards him and he jumped aside, landing heavily against the door to the cold room, his back smashing into the foot-long handle. He cried out in agony and slid to the floor, scrambling away as a spray of flaming oil smashed into the door and across the wall.

Out in the corridor, he had the presence of mind to slam shut the heavy steel door into the kitchen. Gasping for air, he tried to push aside the pain as he checked left and right. No one around. He went to move and another thunderous explosion shook the vessel.

Half a dozen steps along the corridor he saw a door on the right. It was slightly ajar. The ship creaked and groaned. He edged forward cautiously.

The lights flicked off in the corridor. Snapped back on. He could just make out the sound of two, maybe three men far off, shouting loudly, their words indecipherable. He tried to steady his breathing, the pain in his back was almost overpowering.

He was about to move when he caught a flash of colour to his right. Frieda emerged from the doorway a couple of yards away. She had a pistol in her left hand. In her right hand she held the larger of his boxes; the small one containing the isotope was tucked under her arm. She lifted the gun a few inches, pointing it at Fortescue's heart.

He put his hands up involuntarily and felt the blood drain from his face as he stared at her. She stood like a marble statue.

'Where is Charles?' Her voice was barely recognizable as belonging to the woman he had made love to earlier.

'Dead.'

She blanched. 'Get in there.' She flicked the gun towards the doorway. Fortescue edged around the door, never taking his eyes from the barrel of the gun a few feet from his nose.

'Stop.'

They stood just inside the storeroom in an open space about ten feet square encircled by a jumble of crates and boxes. A few of them had tumbled over. One had split open, a spidery jumble of wires and lengths of metal just visible through the cracked side panel.

She put Fortescue's boxes on the floor and gripped the gun with both hands.

'Why are you doing this now?' Fortescue said. 'There's no hope. The ship's going down . . . fast.'

'I will get a lifeboat. It's always women and children first. Once I reach New York I shall be met by a colleague. You, though, will end up in the Atlantic just as you would have done had the ship not struck the damn iceberg.'

'But it won't help you. You won't know what to do with the isotope. That box,' and he flicked a glance at the larger of the two, 'only contains some of the information you need.'

'Liar.'

'I'm not lying.'

She shrugged dismissively. 'No matter. We have been spying on you and Rutherford for a long time; we know more than you think. Contrary to what you may imagine, we do have some rather fine scientists in Germany.'

She took a step closer. Fortescue could see her finger tightening on the trigger.

'I could help you.'

She held his gaze, trying to read his expression.

'I have the rest of the theory in my cabin.'

'No, you don't. Charles would have retrieved it.'

'Too well hidden.'

'You take me for a fool? No, I'm sorry, John . . . Egbert.' She tugged on the trigger and Fortescue tensed, waiting for the inevitable. The gun went off, a fantastically loud boom resonating around the metal-walled room. He closed his eyes involuntarily and felt a thud in his guts that knocked the air from his lungs as he fell backwards against a pile of crates two feet behind him.

He opened his eyes and saw Frieda stumble to the floor, her gun twisted sideways about her finger. The bullet had hit the metal floor and ricocheted, sending off a random spray of shrapnel. And there, close to where the woman had stood, was Billy O'Donnell, a thick metal rod in his hands.

He lowered his arms and Egbert took a step towards Frieda's prone form. Blood gushed from a massive laceration across her neck. Her head was twisted unnaturally. She was quite dead.

41

Fortescue ran over to Billy. The kid looked stricken and started to shake. Fortescue crouched down, grabbed his left arm, lifted the weapon from the boy's grip and tossed it aside.

'Billy. Billy, listen to me.'

He stared past him, eyes glazed in shock.

'Billy. We have to get you onto a boat.'

He seemed suddenly to snap back to reality and grabbed Fortescue's shoulder. 'Is she . . .?'

'She is, Billy. But you saved my life. That was an incredibly brave thing to do.'

His face was still blank.

Egbert withdrew a wad of paper from inside his jacket. 'Billy,' he said. 'Now listen to me very, very carefully. This ship is going to sink. Many people will die. I probably won't survive, but you have a chance.'

'But—'

'No "buts", Billy. I am not who I said I was.'

The boy looked confused.

'What—'

'I'm a scientist, I have been sent on a very important mission. I have to deliver a special chemical and my notes on how to use it to a team of American scientists. I can't explain any more. But I know I shan't make it. You must make sure this document –' and he held out the bundle of pages '– reaches the right people. I've written the name and address on the reverse of the title page.'

The ship shook violently. Fortescue almost lost his footing and Billy fell sideways against one of the storage crates, just breaking his fall in time.

'Mr Wickins . . .'

'My name is actually Fortescue, Billy. Dr Egbert Fortescue.'

The boy swallowed hard, trying to hold back his tears.

'Follow me. No time to waste. Please, just take the papers and pass them on for me. You understand?' He thrust them towards the boy, but could not risk giving him the isotope. It was far too dangerous.

Billy nodded solemnly and pocketed the notes. Fortescue turned and picked up the boxes.

From beyond the passageway came a confusion of sounds – shouts, screams, the grinding of metal on metal.

They ran towards the end of the corridor and out onto the First Class deck. A few yards to stern a group had gathered about a lifeboat. There were at least sixty or seventy people clustered around it, including half a dozen crewmen issuing instructions.

'Women and children only . . . Just women and children,' one of the crew hollered.

Fortescue tucked the smaller box under his arm and, grasping Billy's hand, they rushed over to the railings. Peering over the side, they could see the ocean churning. A packed boat was in the water; a young officer stood in it surrounded by *seated women and children. He was trying to manoeuvre the boat away from the ship to make room for another fully laden lifeboat sliding down on cables towards the waves.*

They turned back towards the crowd of terrified passengers, each of them trying to find a place on the remaining lifeboat. 'My uncle and aunt,' Billy said. In the light from the stricken ship his eyes looked huge.

'There's nothing we can do, Billy. They'll have to fend for themselves.'

'But they'll drown!'

Egbert looked down into the boy's face. 'There's nothing I can do,' he said. 'If you don't get on this boat, you will die too.'

They reached the edge of the crowd. It was so tightly packed he could not see the lifeboat, just the cables holding it. Then he heard a terrible wailing as women were separated from their husbands and grown-up sons. He could see couples shoving their children onto the boat and stepping back. Then came the cries of the young ones as they realized their parents were not going with them.

'Excuse me,' Egbert called. No one noticed. 'Excuse me!' he yelled. 'I have a youngster here.'

Still nothing. He let go of Billy's hand for a second and grabbed the shoulder of a man in front of him, pulling him back none too gently.

'Curse you!' the man exclaimed, but Fortescue's blood was up. He ignored the man, reached for Billy and squeezed forward. Together they made some headway, and in a few moments Egbert had forced their way to the front.

'Sir . . . Hang on a second.'

Fortescue looked up and met the eyes of Third Officer Pitman. The man was clearly petrified but was doing a gallant job of disguising it.

'Mr Fortescue. It's women and . . .' He looked down and saw Billy.

'I'm well aware of that, Pitman!' Fortescue shouted and shoved Billy forward.

'But, sir, the boy's from Third!'

Fortescue glared at the man. 'Don't you even dare think about it . . .'

'Sir, I cannot allow . . .'

Fortescue let go of Billy again and raised his fist to within an inch of the officer's nose. He hadn't felt such rage for many years.

A middle-aged woman stood beside Fortescue. He recognized her as Lucy, Lady Duff Gordon, whom he had been introduced to at Frieda Schiel's party. 'There's no need for that, Mr Fortescue!' she said loudly. 'Mr Pitman, you shall let this little boy onto the lifeboat.'

'But—'

'Now!' She was so aggressive it made Fortescue jump, and suddenly Billy was being pulled away and carried towards the boat.

Lady Duff Gordon, her face almost spectral, was close behind Billy and stumbling towards the others in the boat. Fortescue caught a glimpse of Sir Cosmo Duff Gordon off to one side, his expression wooden.

Billy found Fortescue's face in the crowd. 'I won't fail you, Mr Wickins!' He held up the bundle of papers and was about to lower them again when a gust of freezing wind swept along the deck. The top page of notes flapped, separated and flew up into the air. Billy went to grab for it, but it shot up, twisting and flapping out of reach. The lifeboat slipped down a dozen feet, shuddered to a stop, swung on the support ropes and began to slide towards the water again.

Fortescue looked on in disbelief. He pushed forward, but was met by a solid wall of humanity, a crowd four deep pressed hard up against the metal rails of the ship. 'It needs to reach Professor Lewis!' Fortescue shouted. 'Department of Physics, University of . . .'

But Billy could not hear him. Egbert saw the boy's lips move. 'What?' he was calling back. 'What? Mr Wickins?' The sound lost in the wind.

'Professor Lewis . . .' The words bounced straight back at him and the lifeboat disappeared into shadow.

*

Fortescue was groaning, a horrible note of despair deep within his throat, a tortured cry of pain. He barged his way back through the throng and eventually reached an open space on the deck close to the doors. Pausing, he drew breath. The pain in his back was excruciating, but he had to ignore it. Then he felt a new shot of agony along his left side. He lowered a hand and brought his fingers up covered with blood. Looking down, he saw that his shirt and jacket were soaked. He ran his fingers along his side and found the nexus of the pain. A solid object was protruding from his body – a piece of shrapnel had lodged there.

He started to feel sick and felt his face grow cold. He could *not stop now. He still had one thing to do. He had to leave a record of where the other half of the notes were to be found, especially now Billy had the full set but had no idea who to take them to. Edging towards the door, he felt incredibly weak and noticed in the light from the ship that he was trailing blood along the deck.*

As he reached the door, it swung outwards, almost knocking him off his feet. He managed to grip a handle with one hand and keep hold of the precious metal boxes with the other. A couple of young men charged out onto the deck.

Inside the reception area there was the same medley of human and mechanical sounds. He looked around and for a moment he could not work out which way to go. Totally disorientated, he found a chair and sat for just a few seconds. He remembered he was on C-Deck, close to his room. That, at least, was something.

He heard an incredibly loud crash, looked up and saw a wall of water rushing straight towards him across the reception area. Jolting to his feet, he turned and ran towards the corridor.

He reached it just as the water completed its sweep across reception. It flowed back out onto the deck through the main doors. Fortescue heard a cry and caught a glimpse of one of the young men who had slammed through the door a few moments earlier. The wave of water picked him up and propelled him over the rail.

Water slewed into the corridor and was spraying up the walls, bringing down paintings and signs. It rampaged towards him and he stumbled, falling face first onto the carpet. He twisted and turned under the three-foot-high swell, the icy water so cold it felt as though it was cutting through him. He felt the box containing the isotope start to slip from under his arm and just managed to catch the handle. And as the water lost some of its power he pulled himself up and let it rush over his lower half.

Wading through the torrent, Fortescue reached the door to his cabin. Water cascaded into the room and spread out across the plush carpet, lapping around the legs of the chairs and the bed. He watched as the seawater flowed hungrily under the bed where Charles Grantham's corpse lay.

Rushing over to the desk, he wrenched open a drawer and tugged out a dry piece of paper. He found his pen in the inside pocket of his coat, leaned over the desk and scribbled something on the sheet of paper. It was in a code he had created for himself when he was an undergraduate at Cambridge; it described where missing elements of his work could be found – Security Box 19AS, Cargo Hold Number 4. He lifted the boxes to the table, pulled the briefcase from the larger of the pair, stuffed the note inside, returned the bag, slammed shut the lid of the box and locked it.

A loud boom shook the cabin. Fortescue could hear metal grating against metal, the floor shifting under his feet. He gripped the desk with both hands and felt the room vibrate. More water rushed in from the corridor and swept about his knees.

He went to his wardrobe, opened the door and water cascaded in. He swept his clothes along the rail, grabbed under the water for any remaining shoes and accessories and pushed them away. At the base of the wardrobe was a wooden panel. From a pocket of his jacket he took his door key. Leaning down, in the dim light, he could not see the base of the wardrobe through the grey water, but he could feel his way. He slipped the key along the back of the panel, found a small concealed groove, slid the key into it and levered up the wooden base.

Lifting the larger box, he shoved it into the opening in the base of the wardrobe, just managing to squeeze it inside by shuffling it along under the main part of the raised cupboard.

He felt the cabin shudder. Looking down, he noticed the water about him was red with his own blood. Strangely, his wound no longer hurt.

He wrapped his fingers around the handle of the small metal box containing the ibnium isotope and started to pull it towards the wardrobe under the water. He felt a sharp pain in the back of his left knee. Something submerged in the murk had stabbed him, he crashed into the water and lost his grip on the isotope box.

Scrambling around frantically, the water up to his thighs, Fortescue spun round and staggered back towards the desk. The cabin reverberated with another horrendous crash. From far off, he could hear terrible screams. He looked up and saw a metal beam slide through the ceiling plaster. It flew downwards and speared the bed. He was thrown to one side, before twisting and landing heavily, spread-eagled and face down across the desk, smashing his nose and teeth.

The desk was almost submerged. He slipped off and crashed into the water, hitting his head on something hard and immovable. Vomit rose up into his mouth and he swallowed a mouthful of water and teeth. Grabbing the edge of the desk, gasping and groaning, he pulled himself up and filled his lungs with air.

The room was poised at a terrifying angle. A roaring sound came from above. It built and built like a massive creature charging towards him from the darkest reaches of his worst nightmare.

Then he heard something new, something he had never heard before, something he could never have imagined hearing. For perhaps two seconds he could not understand what it was. Then suddenly he knew. It was the sound of a thousand voices calling out to God.

From the corner of his eye Egbert Fortescue caught a glimpse of movement. A bulkhead slammed through the cabin wall. It struck him side-on, sending him through the water. The last thing he saw was the bulkhead twist and buckle as it came down on him and he added his own sad lament to the dying chorus of his fellow doomed passengers.

42

12,600 feet below the Atlantic Ocean. Present day.

Lou and Kate jumped back as the swirling water tipped the frozen form of the commander to one side. She teetered on one leg then fell slowly to the ocean floor, bouncing twice on the hard sand.

The horror lasted only a second and then they clicked into automatic survival mode. Kate was first to the opening. She eased it back another couple of inches and they both squeezed inside. Lou dashed for the inner lock, a wheel that was a twin of the one outside, and pulled the door shut. Lou whirled the wheel round and the lock bolt shot horizontally into a groove in the wall of the hold.

Kate spotted the water evacuation pump on the wall. It was a hand-cranked hydraulic device. Grabbing the handle, she pulled down. Lou stood close by to her left. Silently the lever began to rise and the pump started to suck out the water.

'Can't wait,' Lou snapped through the comms. 'I'm going to open the inner door. So what if we get a little water in the hold?'

Before Kate could respond, Lou had reached for the inner door lock, his suited fingers gripping the handle. He turned it, first left, then right. It wouldn't budge.

'SHIT!' he cried and glanced at Kate, her pupils huge behind her visor.

'Oh my God, oh my God!' She started to panic and felt vomit rise up into her throat.

'Hang on,' Lou said. 'It will work but not while there's water in the airlock. It's a safety mechanism.'

The water was down to their knees now.

'Come on!' Lou hissed and tried the handle again. 'Come on, you fucker!'

They could no longer look at each other. The only thought in their minds was that the suits would go, that any second, any single moment, their puny soft human bodies would be crushed to oblivion.

Lou wrenched the handle for a third time; hard left, hard right. It was stuck rigid.

Kate began to sob. Lou looked at her, saw tears slithering down her cheeks. He pressed his visor against the front of hers.

'I love you.' They said it simultaneously.

Lou pulled away, took a deep breath, turned again to the metal handle. He could see the last of the water between his feet, hardly more than a puddle. He turned the handle far left.

Nothing.

'Aggghh!' he screamed and leaned on it with all his weight, pushing it to the right.

It gave. The door swung inwards. Lou stumbled

through into the hold, landing awkwardly on his front.

Kate dashed inside, pushing the door shut and pulling the lock into place.

'Switch off the suit, Lou,' she commanded and reached for the control panel on her sleeve, tapping in the code and deactivating her suit.

Lou didn't respond. She felt a terrible panic rush through her as she pulled back her helmet. Her suit deflated and she crouched down, dreading what she might see.

Lou was out cold. She pulled him round, found the computer screen on his sleeve, ran her hands over the touch pad, dumping the code into the system. Lou's suit switched off.

She shook his shoulders, pulled his deflated helmet over his head, slapped his face. No reaction. She hit him again, much harder.

'Lou! Lou! Wake up!'

He opened his eyes and drew breath from his tank mouthpiece.

'Wow!' he spluttered, pulling himself up. Then he vomited over his front.

43

The six mercenaries had been holed up with Sterling Van Lee in the 297 square feet of storage area 45, Corridor F, Deck 3C for twenty-six hours. They had limited rations and no sanitation; it was dark, the air stale. Even with their training and experience it was a trial without precedent.

Van Lee spent most of his time running through the operation plans over and over again, looking for flaws, searching for potential problems. He had requisitioned a corner of the cramped space and when he was not surveying the ship's schematics, cleaning his weapons by torchlight or studying the mission plan on an iPad, he gazed periodically at a GPS readout. In this way, at every moment, he knew precisely where they were so that when the time came he would be ready to give the word to strike.

At exactly 23.20 Van Lee opened the door to storage area 45; the assault team fanned out along different routes to the control room on the bridge.

Van Lee and his partner, former SEAL Chris Tomkin, were last out. They turned right along Corridor F, then up a flight of stairs to Deck 3B, all senses alert, adrenalin pumping.

The first to hear the crewman approach was Van Lee. He pulled in behind a bulkhead, Tomkin a fraction of a second behind him. They let the man pass, then Van Lee came up behind him, pulled the garrotte about his neck and jerked it back. The man struggled, gurgled and died. The team leader let the body slip to the floor. Tomkin had moved along the corridor, found a door to a cupboard and helped drag the corpse along the floor.

From there, the two men had a clear run up to the boat deck on the port side. Van Lee checked his watch. Delayed by the crewman they had so efficiently dispatched, they managed to catch up a few seconds as they ran fast along the exit corridor.

Nearing the bridge, the two men slunk along the deck and up the first set of steps. In a few seconds they were just yards from the control room. Van Lee caught a glimpse of the other two teams. One was poised close to the door into the room, the other had held back from the starboard exit.

Van Lee checked his watch again, raised his arm and gave the signal to go. Tightening his grip on his G3 assault rifle, he turned the handle on the control room door and charged inside.

There were six men in the room. Two heard the door open and turned. They each received a bullet between the eyes. Van Lee darted in, firing as he went, killing another crewman. One of the officers dived for cover, pulled his weapon and went to fire. Tomkin blew the man's chest apart with his G3.

The remaining two sailors, a young guy who looked as though he had only just left his teens behind, the other a man in his thirties, a couple of stripes on his sleeve, raised their hands. Two of Van Lee's party were already at the controls of the ship.

'Down,' Van Lee hissed at the two crewmen.

They lowered to their knees, their hands on their heads. Van Lee walked behind them and shot them in the back of the neck. They fell forward onto the metal floor.

The team leader nodded to Tomkin, who stepped over to the main control panel. At the door he called to his men at the starboard exit. 'Secured . . . Clean up the rest of the ship.'

They turned without a word and slipped away.

'The captain isn't here,' Van Lee said as he came back onto the bridge. 'Grainger, find him.'

Phil Grainger turned from the control panel and left, his G3 at waist height.

*

Captain Derham was in the galley kitchen a short distance from the bridge and had just filled his mug with strong black coffee when he heard the first shots. He pulled his revolver from its holster and fell back to the door.

Straining to hear, he discerned at least four voices, some belonging to his own crew, some he did not recognize. Then there were more shots. He heard a pair of loud thumps coming from the bridge and went out into the corridor.

Derham slid along the wall, reached a junction and heard a man giving instructions. He ducked behind a bulkhead.

Phil Grainger was a big man, six foot four and 250 pounds of solid muscle, but he could move like a leopard. He emerged from the control room, took a right and then a left, turning on his heel every three steps, scanning the corridor. He reached the passage leading to the galley. He had no idea Derham was poised to spring.

The mercenary took two paces along the corridor and a fist slammed into his face with such force his nose cartilage shattered. He fell back in a spray of blood, but got up as Derham stepped forward with his gun pointed at his forehead. Grainger swung out his right hand as he straightened and connected with Derham's wrist, sending his gun flying. The captain fell back and Grainger was on him.

Slipping a hand behind his back, Derham found his commando dagger in its sheath on his belt, pulled it round and shoved it into Grainger's side, aiming for his heart. He leaned back so he could shift his weight and twisted the man over onto his side, caught sight of his gun a few feet to his left, reached it, and swung it round just as Grainger, his front drenched in red, levelled his assault rifle.

Derham fired and dived to one side almost simultaneously. He heard the dull thud of a bullet hitting flesh and straightened to see the side of Grainger's head gaping open, his right eye socket obliterated. The man's G3 went off as he fell back, his dead finger jammed on the trigger. The gun waved around, bullets spraying the ceiling and ricocheting along the corridor.

Derham jumped up, pulled the assault rifle away, found a full magazine tucked into Grainger's belt and listened for anyone approaching. Satisfied, he slunk to the end of the corridor.

*

In the control room Van Lee stood behind Tomkin, watching him manipulate a row of keypads. In front of them above the nearest control rack stood a large monitor. It offered a murky image of the ocean floor 12,600 feet beneath the ship. In the centre of the screen stood the deep-sea submarine *JV1*, its lights splashing a puddle of radiance around it.

'I've cut comms,' Tomkins said. 'This image,' and he pointed to the screen, 'is from a remote camera on the tether line that contains the fibre-optic cables.'

'What's the status of the sub's crew?'

'The vessel is empty. They're all out on the ocean floor.'

Van Lee raised an eyebrow. 'You have the electro-static charge ready?'

'A few more seconds.' Tomkin ran his fingers over the keypads, paused to check a display then resumed the tapping. 'Ready.'

'Do it.'

Chris Tomkin punched in a series of numbers and poised a finger over the return key. The other two mercenaries stopped what they were doing and came over. He hit the button.

A loud screech came from a speaker above the control panel. There was a blinding flash of yellow on the monitor and *JV1* exploded, 12,600 feet beneath *Armstrong*. The fragments flew outward as if in slow motion. Under the water and at a pressure of almost 500 atmospheres, the burst of flame lasted only a fraction of a second.

44

Derham heard gunfire from far off, towards the stern. Stopping for a second, he pulled back against the wall. He needed to take stock. There had been six crewmen in the control room when he left to make coffee. By now they might either be dead or out of action. That meant that out of the crew of twelve, there were, at best, only six others active on the ship. It had been a surprise attack and so it was unrealistic to hold out much hope for the rest of his men. In fact, he could well be the only one left alive.

He moved along the passageway. A closed door stood to his left . . . the secondary comms hub. He went back against the wall, G3 held vertically, the side of the barrel close to his nose. Springing forward, he jerked on the door handle and with one smooth action swung round into the room, sweeping his assault rifle around.

A man was leaning over the control panel. He had his rifle slung over his right shoulder, finger on the trigger, tapping a keyboard with his free hand. He started to straighten. Derham sprayed the room with bullets and the man flew backwards against the wall, torn apart.

Derham dashed over to the panel, ran his fingers over the keys and heard a crackling sound over the monitor. He leaned in. '*Mayday . . . Repeat Mayday . . . This is* USS Armstrong *. . . we are boarded and under attack . . . Repeat, we are boarded and under attack.*'

More static. Then a muffled voice. Derham could not understand a word. He cut in. 'Cannot hear you. Please repeat. Over.'

More unintelligible words, static. Then a loud hum and the line died.

'Shit!' Derham exclaimed. 'They must've cut comms in the control room.' He was about to try to reroute the system when he heard voices from the corridor. He dived behind the console.

The door eased open. Through a tiny slit in the corner of the console, he could see two men in black fatigues, faces in shadow, weapons ready. They slipped into the room.

Derham jumped up, unleashed a spray of bullets and ducked back down. Leaning forward, he peered through a crack.

'Drop the gun.'

The voice came from behind him.

Derham let the weapon fall to the floor.

'Get up.'

Derham rose to his feet, felt the man's rifle against the nape of his neck and knew he was a dead man.

'Sergei. Stop. I want him alive for a while longer.' The voice came from the doorway.

A man with steely blue eyes crossed the room, his

rifle lowered at his side. The man with the G3 at his neck hissed and Derham felt the barrel pull away from his skin.

'Who are you?' Derham snapped.

He ignored the question and stopped a few feet away from the console. 'You are Captain Jerry Derham. I've read a lot about you.'

'Why are you here? What do you want?'

'Well, captain. You are here to retrieve an artefact from the wreck of the *Titanic*, while our job is to stop you. My employers would rather whatever it is you are looking for stayed put.'

Van Lee stepped forward and removed Derham's pistol and knife. Then he spun him to face Sergei, pulled some twine from a pouch in his combat trousers and bound the captain's hands behind his back.

Van Lee led the way out into the corridor. They took a right and followed a straight narrow corridor to the steps up to the control room.

Derham surveyed the carnage and forced himself to say nothing, to remain icily calm.

Two of the mercenaries were still at the console. 'Steve, Al,' Van Lee snapped. 'You traced the sub's crew?'

'Nothing yet,' Al replied without looking up.

Van Lee swung round to Derham. 'Excuse the mess.' Then he kicked one of the corpses close to the control panel where Chris Tomkin stood. He pointed to the monitor. 'I thought you'd like to see this,' he added. 'The wreckage of your clever submarine.'

Derham blanched.

'The crew are out on the ocean floor, but they won't last long, of course.'

Derham held Van Lee's stare. Without warning, he spun round, raised his leg and landed his boot square in the throat of the man called Sergei standing a few feet behind him. They all heard his windpipe snap. He dropped his gun and brought his hands to his neck, gasping for air.

As Derham whirled back round Van Lee took a step back and slammed his fist hard into the captain's face, knocking him backwards into the injured gunman. The two men fell to the floor in a tangle of limbs.

Van Lee forced Derham up and onto his knees, totally ignoring his colleague writhing in his death throes. He landed a kick to the captain's chest, causing him to double up in agony. A second kick to the jaw sent Derham sprawling back across the cold metal floor. Van Lee stepped forward; Chris Tomkin came round behind Derham.

'Get up, you fuck!' Van Lee screamed.

Derham slowly struggled back to his knees, his hands still tied behind him. He was reeling in pain and blinded by blood running into his eyes. Tomkin grabbed his hair and yanked his head back. He pulled an Ek Commando knife from his belt and brought the blade round to Derham's throat. Glancing up, Tomkin held Van Lee's eyes, waiting for the order.

'Lower your weapons.' The shout came from the door into the control room. Four men charged into the room, HKMP5 sub-machine guns at their hips. Two more came in a second wave and charged across the room, side-stepping the corpses and taking up position close to the control panels. The men were dressed in assault armour, helmets and goggles, with badges bearing the impression of a winged dagger and the words 'Who Dares Wins' on each sleeve.

The four mercenaries froze. The SAS leader took two paces over to where Derham knelt, Tomkin's knife still at his throat. He stood behind the mercenary, bringing the barrel of his weapon to the back of his head. 'Drop the knife and back away,' he said calmly.

Tomkin barely moved a muscle, but the soldier sensed instantly what he was about to do. With stunning speed the SAS officer grabbed Tomkin's knife hand and pulled the trigger of his HKMP5.

A soldier helped Derham to his feet, and the SAS commander whirled on Van Lee and the other two. 'Drop your weapons, or you can follow your friend.' He flicked his assault weapon towards Tomkin's headless corpse.

45

'I'm OK,' Derham snapped as one of the SAS men helped him to his feet. Three of the British soldiers had stripped Van Lee and the two other mercenaries of their weapons, bound their hands and had started to escort them out.

Derham dashed over to the control panel and stabbed at the keypad. 'Commander Milford . . . do you copy?'

Nothing but an electronic hiss.

'Milford, come in.'

Derham turned a dial and the speaker emitted a high-pitched whine.

'The bastards have cut the comm link,' Derham spat and slammed a palm down onto the control panel.

'Captain?' The leader of the SAS team was standing beside him.

Jerry turned and saluted. 'Captain Derham.'

'Major Graham Davenport. We were shadowing you . . . received your Mayday.'

Derham exhaled. 'I'm extremely grateful, sir,' he said. 'But three of my people are down there on the ocean floor.'

The major looked at the screen. 'The sub has gone.'

'Yes, but they were already some way from it . . . I hope.'

'How is that possible?'

Derham glanced at a clock above the control panel. 'I can't explain. We have a second sub. I have to get down there.' He spun round. 'I would like you to assume command of the ship. I hope some of my men have survived.'

'We'll begin a search,' Davenport said and watched Derham race to the door.

*

There was no time to run through the routine checks, but *JV1* and *JV2* were kept on standby 24/7. Derham had no comms between *JV2* and *Armstrong*, so he would be riding solo the whole way with no navigational aid from the surface.

As the sub shot away from beneath the ship, Derham let it accelerate to maximum speed. He glanced at the depth gauge, watching the digits change rapidly as on the screens the light began to fade.

*

The monitors displayed an image of the area around where *JV1* had stood. *JV2* was still too far away to make out anything other than blurred clumps of dark and light marking out the cargo hold and other large pieces of the *Titanic*.

Derham was working robotically. He could not contemplate the thoughts trying to seep into his consciousness. He could not accept that Jane Milford, Kate and Lou were dead. But at the same time he was processing the situation logically. The only way the three of them could still be alive is if they had made it to the cargo hold and got inside before their suits gave out. He had to hang on to that hope.

He adjusted course with short bursts of the engines. The on-board computer was guiding the ship automatically but he was able to override manually to compensate for random fluctuations in the currents. He glanced at the image on the control panel monitor and noticed it had cleared. Now he could just make out individual features and spotted the wreckage of *JV1* strewn across the ocean floor.

The cargo hold stood to the right of the screen. He swivelled the bow camera thirty degrees to starboard. It showed up scattered chunks of debris. Then he found the ravine, a black gash in the earth running north–south, the ends disappearing beyond the range of the camera.

'There's only one way to do this,' Derham said aloud. He leaned forward, tapped at the controls and brought up a management screen on one of the monitors. In the bottom-right corner was a set of parameters . . . speed, depth, position and half a dozen other stats. Inputting a series of command codes, he overrode the entire automated piloting system, and running expert fingers over the keypads, he transferred control to manual and focused on the bow camera.

The submarine was remarkably manoeuvrable. He brought it round so that it sliced through the water horizontally sixty yards above the ocean floor, then he slowed the vessel to a sedate twenty knots. On the view screen the terrain streamed past, the compacted sand and shingle a muddy grey in *JV2*'s powerful beams.

Derham was approaching the ravine. He knew the team had used a nano-carbon bridge to cross it . . . assuming they had reached that far. *JV2* would have to be set down on the far side of the crevasse and he would have to use the bridge to reach the cargo hold.

Using the sonar Derham could tell that he was closing on the location of the nano-carbon bridge. One hundred yards west . . . fifty yards. He guided the sub to port. The sonar told him the bridge was now ten yards away . . . five.

He reached it and circled slowly, adjusting the camera under the vessel and changing focus so he could get a clear image. Then he saw it, the tattered ends of the nano-carbon bridge, shredded lengths stretching down out of sight into the ravine.

Panning the cameras, he tried to find clues, bodies, anything that could tell him what had happened. On the second sweep he caught a glimpse of some metal shards.

He adjusted a toggle on the control panel and rose ten yards. Realigning the camera, he could make out the shape of the cargo hold. According to a set of stats in the bottom right of the screen, it was 106 yards west of the ravine.

Moving *JV2* slowly over the ocean floor, Derham checked the sonar, adjusting it to probe the sand. The computer displayed a map of the seismic make-up of the terrain between the ravine and the cargo hold. It appeared as a series of curved lines a little like contours on an elevation map. The information was incomplete but more accurate than anything they had pictured from the surface.

Pulling back on the throttle so that *JV2* drifted in the current, Derham leaned forward to study the flowing lines on the monitor. He ran a finger along the glass tracing the contours and analysing the stability of a patch of ocean floor about twenty yards square. He stopped and stabbed the screen.

'There!' he said aloud, and knew even this, the most stable spot around, could easily be a deadly place to put down. But there was no choice. This was life or death. If there was any chance of rescuing the team from *JV1*, he had to land there.

Flicking the toggle on the panel, he turned to port, punched in a set of nav figures and pulled away from the crevasse, one eye on the camera showing the sand.

The landing was a masterclass in manoeuvring the *JV2* and it came to rest with an almost imperceptible bump. On the screen, Derham could see the outline of cargo hold 4. The monitor told him it stood precisely thirty-seven yards to port.

46

Lou got to his feet and looked around.

The cargo hold was about three yards to a side. The air was breathable, but they had no idea how long it would last. As soon as the suits were deactivated they began to feel the temperature drop. The water outside was close to freezing point.

Some of the sensor and comms systems of the LMC suits were functioning even when the main systems had been powered down. Lou tapped the screen on his arm and scrolled down.

'Radiation levels are high, but we can survive for a while. Luckily most of the remaining radiation is alpha and beta particles which can't get through the skin of the cargo hold. There is some residual gamma ray radiation.'

'How long, Lou?'

He double-checked. 'The radiation would get us first . . . forty minutes, maybe forty-five until we get a fatal dose. The cold? I reckon a bit longer. The air? Anyone's guess. Or maybe the whole thing will collapse first.' He looked around at the corroded hold. 'Take your pick.'

'Some choice! How long do the suits need to recharge?'

'No idea. I think we're in completely uncharted territory now, Kate.'

The air stank of rust and rotting organic matter. Three of the walls were lined with hundreds of lockers and safety deposit boxes. Some of these had corroded; doors hung off rusted hinges exposing crumbling contents; ragged papers and other detritus lay scattered across the rusted metal floor. The hold creaked, old brackets and joints feeling the strain of a century spent at the bottom of the Atlantic Ocean.

'God, this place feels so creepy,' Kate commented as they walked over to the nearest wall of boxes. 'I never imagined I could feel claustrophobic on the ocean floor!'

They could just make out some numbers attached to the doors of the security boxes: *13BS . . . 28BS*. Kate turned towards the right adjacent wall and scanned along the rows and columns of boxes until she could make out a number.

'37AS,' she called over to Lou and crouched to study some of the lower boxes. Eventually she found another label – 56AS – straightened and surveyed the boxes higher up. Lou came over and they took an end each.

'Got it,' Lou called. Kate joined him. He was pointing at a row about shoulder height. '16AS.' He ran a hand along the box fronts. '21AS . . . Too far.' He stopped, backtracked. 'This must be 19AS.'

The hold shook. Kate started to fall and grabbed at Lou. He put his right hand against the wall of boxes to steady himself. A loud grinding sound came from their left.

'It's not happy!' Lou commented.

'Come on.' Kate stepped forward and tried the handle of deposit box 19AS. It was stuck fast. 'Typical!'

Lou rummaged in a pouch on the belt of his suit and lifted out a small plastic cylinder. Depressing a button on the side, a blade shot from one end. He leaned in towards the door of the box and slipped the blade along the edge.

The hold shuddered again. The knife slipped from his fingers and fell to the floor. Kate stumbled, made a grab for the wall of deposit boxes and landed on her front.

Lou ran over.

'You OK?'

She nodded and tried to stand. 'Ow! My God!'

'Here,' Lou said and helped her up.

Kate tried to put weight on her left leg and screamed in agony.

'Sit,' Lou commanded. 'Stay still.'

Another massive jolt far more violent than the last reverberated around the walls. It went on for several seconds.

Lou froze. 'Shit! It really isn't happy!'

A horrible crunching sound came from the corner of the cargo hold. Kate swivelled round and they both saw the wall start to distort, water cascading down one corner of the hold.

'It's going!' Lou screamed and dived to the floor next to Kate. 'Pull up your helmet!' He was tugging his on. 'Reactivate the suit, Kate.'

'But . . .'

Lou had his helmet on and locked. Kate couldn't move.

'KATE!' Lou grabbed her helmet and pulled it into position, flicked the clasp and stabbed at her wrist control panel. Pulling back, he did the same to his own keypad. The suits made low hissing sounds; a row of lights on each arm flicked on, blinked orange and then green. The liquid metal carbon expanded rapidly.

Kate tried to stand up again.

'Stay put, Kate!' Lou shouted. 'I can do this.'

The floor started to buckle. Lou lost his balance, tried to grab at the boxes and stumbled into them.

The entire hold began to shake as if it were about to launch from the ocean floor. Kate screamed, the sound coming loud through their comms.

Lou scrambled to his feet, but for a moment he couldn't get his bearings. He pulled himself along the wall using the gaping doorless holes and found 26AS. Grabbing his way a few feet further, he reached Fortescue's deposit box.

They both heard the sound at the same moment, turned and saw the inner door of the lock start to open inwards. A figure appeared at the opening.

'Thank God!' came a voice through their comms.

'Jerry!' Lou exclaimed.

The captain rushed over to them. 'Where's Jane Milford?'

'Her suit . . .' Lou started to say.

Derham sighed and looked down. 'OK, Kate?'

'I think I've broken my—'

The hold rocked and the sound of snapping metal came from directly overhead. A crack appeared one end of the roof and stuttered across the length of the cube, zig-zagging like a fissure on a frozen lake. The walls shook. A torrent of water poured in. Lou grabbed the nearest locker to steady himself and saw Derham struggling to keep upright.

'Come on!' the captain screamed above the noise.

'But the box. I can get it,' Lou cried. He looked down searching for his knife. He couldn't see it – it was now under a foot of swirling dark water.

Derham was easing Kate to her feet.

Lou hammered on the door of the security box. 'Damn you!'

'Lou . . . Gotta go, man!' Derham hollered. He turned and with his spare hand tried to pull Lou round, but Lou shrugged him off and slammed his fist into the front of the box again.

'Shit! . . . You . . .'

The water was now up to their knees.

'Lou! . . . Please!' Kate screamed. But he seemed oblivious.

A metal panel broke away from the roof and swung down, screeching as it buckled and contorted.

Derham pulled Kate to him and headed for the door.

'No!' she screamed. 'Jerry . . . NO! LOU . . .!'

Tears of frustration ran down Lou's cheeks, blurring his vision. He took a gasp of air from the tanks of his suit and hit the door of 19AS one last time. It held, stuck fast.

He felt Derham's hand grab his arm and this time he did not resist. Spinning on his heel, he stepped forward, grasped Kate's arm and the three of them hurtled to the airlock door as the cube began to fold in on itself.

47

Five miles outside Lyon, France. Following day.

Five minutes before leaving for a state banquet in Paris, Glena Buckingham was dressed in a pale-blue sequinned cocktail dress her stylist really should have advised her against. She had never possessed much in the way of sartorial sense or style. If she were three billion euros poorer, she would have been viewed as the same nerd she had been at school and at Cambridge University. Jewels, Versace and professionally applied make-up helped, but they did not do a thorough enough job.

She sat with Hans Secker on the balcony adjoining the drawing room. Between them stood a table with a pair of partly consumed gin and tonics. Before them stretched a magnificent view of the Rhône Valley. Glena Buckingham was smoking.

'So,' she said, lifting her glass, blue smoke rising from the end of the Cuban cigar in her other hand. 'We can chalk up a victory, I suppose.'

'Why the reserve?' Secker replied. 'I actually think we should be very pleased with ourselves. A substantial chunk of the Fortescue material has been lost for ever; the rest is at least partially in the public domain and incomplete enough to stop any clever clogs from developing cold fusion within a decade, minimum.'

Buckingham nodded sagely. 'More through luck than skill,' she said, turning dark eyes upon her executive assistant and drawing on the cigar. 'Our best man, Sterling Van Lee, singularly failed in his operation. If the Gods had not been on our side, those two pain-in-the-ass scientists, Wetherall and Bates, would have retrieved the rest of the Fortescue documents and the game would be up. Someone would have developed cold fusion within two to three years, and you and I would be out of a job.'

'But that did not happen, did it, Glena?'

'There's always the danger that given enough inducement, Van Lee or one of his men will blab,' Buckingham responded icily.

'Measures are in place to prevent that from happening. Van Lee and his two surviving buddies will not see the sunrise tomorrow.'

'And Newman?'

Secker took a sip of his drink to cover his unease. 'We will find him.'

Buckingham exhaled quickly through her nose, drank some more of her gin and tonic, resting its base in her palm. With the cigar clenched between her teeth, she said: 'I have always been a glass half-full type, Hans.' She pulled away the cigar and produced a faint smile.

'And so I accept that we have won this fight. It was a close shave, but we did win.'

Then she lifted her drink again. 'To victory,' she said and drained the glass.

48

Kota Kinabalu, Indonesia. Next morning.

Professor Max Newman was seated at a table in the Coconut Bar close to the edge of the beach watching the gentle turquoise waves roll across the white sand.

It was early and quiet in the bar. An old TV stood on a shelf in a corner near the bar, the sound barely audible.

Newman twirled the contents of his cocktail glass and took a sip. He had arrived only the previous night, reaching the hotel on the beach in a rickety cab just as a tropical storm broke. And even though he had been helped from the car by a pair of porters with umbrellas, by the time he had reached the reception desk, he was soaked through. Sleeping late, he had enjoyed a full breakfast, armed himself with sunscreen and a straw hat and wandered down to the beach.

The desperate escape from the United States had taken him to Bangkok, Damascus and Tripoli before he backtracked east to Jakarta and then the short hop to Kota Kinabalu. He knew he could never rest and relax, not completely. Not only had he stolen from his own government and passed on sensitive material to a rival state, he had taken large sums of money from the Chinese, and they would not be happy with him now they knew they had paid a fortune for material that had gone public within a matter of days. He could admit to betraying America, he told himself. But he could not be blamed for upsetting the Chinese. It wasn't his fault that forces beyond his control had accessed the same material and handed it over to the public. Not his fault at all.

He was draining the cocktail glass when he noticed something new appear on the TV: a rather unflattering photograph of Sterling Van Lee.

He got up from the table and walked closer to where the set was perched so he could hear it properly.

'Another, sir?' the barman asked.

Newman shushed him and flapped his left hand irritably.

'. . . was the leader of the team who stowed away on the *Armstrong*, killing most of her crew,' a reporter was saying as the image changed to show the faces of Van Lee's accomplices. 'But now, the three who survived the SAS assault on the vessel, Steve Heynerman, Al Brillstein and Van Lee himself, are dead. They were being held in three separate cells at a military detention facility outside Washington. Each of the three men was poisoned. A thorough investigation has begun . . .'

Newman stood transfixed, feeling his heart race. He suddenly felt a desperate urge to urinate and for a horrible moment he thought he was about to wet himself.

'Bathroom?' he asked the barman. The man pointed to a door just beyond an overhanging shade at the front of the bar.

Newman walked quickly over to the washroom, pushed on the door and rushed to the urinal. He heard the door swing open again behind him but was too engrossed in relieving himself to take any notice.

Jing Bojing, Secret Police designation Chai454, moved silently across the floor to stand two feet behind the man he had followed from Kota Kinabalu airport the previous night. He lifted the garrotte and slipped it around Newman's neck.

Newman struggled, his brain trying, through the pain and terror, to understand what exactly was happening. He caught a glimpse of his assailant in a faded and fractured mirror above the urinal and seeing the man's features, he knew which of his enemies had caught up with him first. The last of the air in his lungs left him, the wire of the garrotte caught his jugular and for a few seconds he saw blood spray from his neck before the light darkened to nothing.

49

Norfolk, Virginia. Twenty hours later.

Kate was wearing a loose-fitting top and baggy running shorts, her hair tied back as she sat up in bed in her apartment, late afternoon sun streaming through the drawn curtains. Her leg in an aluminum cast was held in a support at a forty-five degree angle.

Jerry Derham had done everything he could to make her comfortable. When she had insisted on being allowed home, the navy had provided her with a private nurse.

Even so, she felt physically and emotionally drained. Her body needed to recuperate, but the real pain came from her sense of loss, the terrible things that had happened to her godparents, the horrible death of Jane Milford. She knew that she needed to get back to work to help eradicate the pain.

She touched the screen of her iPad and her BBC World News app appeared. A reporter was standing aboard a naval vessel, the ocean wind ruffling his hair.

'The story has been a hundred years in the making,' he said, 'but only during the past few days has the astonishing truth emerged.' The picture changed to a faded sepia photograph of a stiff-looking Egbert Fortescue in a round-collared shirt, tie and raffish bowler.

'. . . and we know, of course, that Fortescue's amazing theories were several decades ahead of their time,' the presenter was saying over the picture. It cut to a montage of images from Manchester University to Los Alamos and the devastation of Hiroshima.

'After official complaints from Russia, China and a number of Middle Eastern states, and the mobilizing of Chinese naval forces earlier this week, NATO has agreed to place the findings and the documents recovered from the wreck of the *Titanic* with an international body tasked with the job of deciphering Egbert Fortescue's complex mathematics. This has appeased several nations who were incensed by the partisan behaviour of the Western allies in establishing the Exclusion Zone when the radiation from the vessel was first detected a week ago.'

There was a tap at the door and Kate turned to see Lou and Jerry, each with a bouquet.

'May we?' Lou asked.

She beamed and switched off the iPad.

'Thank you, they're beautiful,' she exclaimed taking the flowers.

Kate's home nurse came in behind the men. 'Shall I put those in water for you, Dr Wetherall?'

Kate inhaled the fragrance. 'Yes, please.'

Lou kissed her on the cheek. She patted the edge of the bed and he perched there, an arm along the top of her pillow.

'So, how you feeling?' Jerry asked. He pulled over a chair and sat down.

'Fine,' she replied. 'I still can't believe I damaged my leg so badly.' She flicked a rueful glance at the cast. 'But then I think we're all lucky to be alive. Has Jane Milford's body been recovered?'

Derham nodded. 'And I've heard talk of a special commendation.'

They fell silent for a second.

'The story is everywhere,' Kate said, trying to break the mood.

'Yes, there are some people who are not very happy about that, but the decision was taken out of the government's hands . . . The UN Security Council forced the issue. The Chinese were particularly aggressive.'

'Can't say I blame them,' Lou commented.

'And what about the saboteurs on the *Armstrong*?' Kate asked.

'The CIA are still coming up empty in their efforts to find out who they were working for.'

'There must be some suspicions.'

'There are rumours MI5 know more about who is involved than they are letting on.'

Kate raised an eyebrow. 'And Professor Newman? Nothing on him either?'

Derham shook his head. 'Appears to have simply vanished from the face of the earth.'

'He must have been paid some serious money,' Lou commented.

'Sure, but somehow I don't think he will enjoy it

much knowing that his scalp is wanted by the British and US governments as well as the Chinese, not to mention whoever he was working for originally . . . the mysterious organization who employed Van Lee and his thugs. The chances are he'll turn up dead before long.'

'I guess,' Kate mused. 'So what now? I saw on the news the material from the wreck is being placed with an international non-political body.'

'The only compromise the Security Council would accept,' Derham said.

'But we only have half the material anyway,' Lou said glumly. 'The documents that were in cargo hold 4 have been lost for ever.'

'That's assuming they had not already crumbled to powder in Box 19AS,' Derham replied.

Lou sighed and nodded resignedly. Kate gave him a gentle smile and ran a finger along the top of his hand where it lay on the pillow close to her cheek.

Her cell phone trilled. Lou reached over to the side table and handed it to her. She glanced at the number, but looked blank.

'Hello?'

'Is that Dr Kate Wetherall?'

'It is.'

She heard a brief sigh down the line. 'Kate, it's Professor Geoff O'Donnell. We met at a conference in Houston last year . . .'

50

Princeton, New Jersey. Same day.

Professor Geoff O'Donnell pulled onto the drive of his late parents' house and sat for a minute listening to the end of the news on the radio. The top story was the amazing account of how scientific documents from a century ago had been retrieved from the wreck of the *Titanic* along with a radioactive source. He'd been following the story closely as he did anything connected with the famous shipwreck. The *Titanic* had been constantly fascinating for him ever since he was ten years old and learned that his grandfather had been a survivor.

'Wow!' he said quietly to himself. 'Kate Wetherall.' He remembered they had met at a conference in Houston last year and he had liked her straight away.

The bulletin ended, Geoff plucked up the roll of rubbish sacks he had gone to the store to buy and trudged up the drive. His sister, Amanda, had already made a start on sorting out the kitchen. Geoff walked in. She waved and blew at a strand of hair that had slipped from under her baseball cap. He placed the roll of rubbish sacks on the counter and went up the stairs.

Reaching the landing, he wandered into the bedroom he had once slept in. Until he had left for university, this house was the only home he had known. He and Amanda now had a mammoth task ahead of them sorting out two generations of accumulated possessions. Both his parents and grandparents had been hoarders.

Then he recalled something long forgotten. His father, Thomas O'Donnell, had told him that Grandpa Billy had kept a box of papers and pictures from his earliest days as an immigrant in New York. He had never seen this box and had often wondered what had happened to it. He hadn't dared to ask him because everyone in the family knew Grandpa Billy always refused to talk about the *Titanic*. But what if his grandfather had passed on the box of memorabilia to his son Thomas? Geoff mused.

'Hey, Mand,' he called down the stairs. 'Gonna start with the attic . . . go top down.'

His sister came to the foot of the stairs. 'Ever the logical one,' she said with a smile. 'You need a hand?'

'No. You start at the bottom and we should meet in the middle . . . in about a month!'

In all the years he lived in this house he had ventured into the attic just once, and had put his foot through the ceiling of his parent's bedroom. It was the only time he had been beaten by his father and he had never considered returning.

The attic ladder slipped down easily. Geoff clambered

up and flicked on a single naked bulb hanging from a rafter. He could see at least a dozen tea chests stacked neatly to one side of the space.

Pulling a torch from his pocket, he began to look around. Removing the lid from the nearest wooden box, the first thing he saw was a neatly folded college scarf.

'Wow!' he exclaimed. 'I'd forgotten I ever had that!' It was his scarf from UCLA, pale blue and yellow. He had bought it the first morning there. That day he had embarked on what was to become a life in academia. Six years ago he had been awarded the chair of Marine Studies at the University of Tampa.

He closed the lid and panned round with the torch beam. The rafters were hung with cobwebs and the air smelled of old books. He noticed a couple of piles of what looked like encyclopedias stacked against the towers of tea chests. He lifted the top one, blew away the dust and read: *Encyclopedia of Natural Science, Vol. 4*.

Turning to his right, he spotted the water tank, heard it gurgle, and made a mental note to switch off the water at the mains. He cast the torch beam around and was about to swing back to the old boxes when the light caught a large faded leather trunk. He recognized it vaguely as being one of the massive trunks his father would strap to the roof rack of the Oldsmobile before the family headed towards the freeway and their regular holiday spot in the Catskills.

Geoff picked his way over, ducking under a low beam and crouching in front of the trunk. It was covered with a thick layer of dust and he could see a few patches of mould at one end of the lid. The brass lock at the front had tarnished. He knelt down and went to release the lock. It was a little stiff, but gave, and he eased up the heavy top, letting it rest back against the brick wall behind it.

It was almost completely empty. To the right lay a wooden box, a cheap mass-produced container with gaudy beads around the rim. He lifted it and opened the lid. Inside lay an old pen, an inkwell and a few inexpensive bracelets. He returned it to the trunk and spotted an ancient teddy bear propped up behind a stack of books. It was Gerald, his favourite toy when he was six.

A biscuit tin rested on top of the books. It looked incredibly quaint, edged in a tarnished gold pattern, the lid carrying the image of a woman in a flour-speckled apron, her hair pulled back, sleeves rolled up. Many years ago this tin had been in the kitchen. He had a clear image of himself sneaking a biscuit from it one morning before leaving for school.

Geoff laid it on the attic floor and prised open the lid. Inside was a pile of old black and white photographs. He lifted them out.

The first was a picture of his parents. They looked young. He guessed it had been snapped around the time they were married. Then there were half a dozen photographs of him and Amanda at various ages: playing in the yard, on a rocking horse, winning a three-legged race at school. He placed them carefully back in the biscuit tin and noticed at the bottom of the pile a very old photograph he had never seen before. It was of a short, slender man in a suit and tie. He was standing on the corner of a street, an old-fashioned car parked behind him. It looked like the picture must have been taken in the late 1920s, maybe early 1930s. Then he recognized the face. It was his grandfather, William.

William, or Billy as he was called in the family, had died in 1981. Geoff was nineteen at the time and he had loved the old man dearly, but he felt as though he had never really known him as well as he would have liked. There was always some sort of barrier there. It was a feeling others in the family shared. His mother, Margaret, Billy's daughter-in-law, had once told him that she had felt the same thing. She loved Billy, but she sensed he could never give all of himself to anyone and put it down to the traumatic experience that had shaped his life . . . his rescue from the *Titanic* when he was twelve years old.

Geoff shook his head. 'So many memories,' he said aloud and surveyed the other end of the trunk. He saw a square of moth-eaten brown velvet, and lying beneath this another box. This one was made from what looked like mahogany. Geoff had no recollection of ever seeing it before. He lifted it, eased it open and held it up to the light. A roll of papers wrapped in a frayed and faded red silk ribbon lay inside. Intrigued, Geoff lifted it out, pulled off the ribbon and unfurled the pages to reveal a wad of papers covered with closely packed mathematical symbols. On top of this was a letter. The paper was desiccated, the ink faded to an orange-brown. He started to read.

August 7, 1945.

Yesterday, my country exploded an atomic bomb over Hiroshima, while this morning, my eldest son, Thomas, has been accepted into Yale. For me, these two events share an odd synchronicity.

I don't ever speak of the Titanic, *and even my beloved wife Geraldine knows only parts of my story.*

I was coming up to my thirteenth birthday when my aunt and uncle told me they had decided that we would be leaving for America and a hoped-for new life of opportunity.

We travelled Third Class, of course, and even getting the 32 pounds and 10 shillings to pay the fare for a family of nine must have been a task in itself.

I remember I was a bit of a tearaway and I had a fondness for exploring the ship. It was a game evading the crew, sneaking around First Class. That was how I met Mr Wickins.

Well, he told me his name was Wickins and that he was a schoolteacher. It was only later, just as we said goodbye for the last time, that he confided in me that his real name was Dr Egbert Fortescue and that he was actually a scientist.

He was an extraordinary man and he had an extraordinary tale to tell. He was on a mission to take what he called 'a special chemical' to America and he had some notes on his theories that he was to pass on to another scientist there. When he knew that he could not survive, he gave me the notes and wrote on a sheet of paper the name and address of the person I should give them to.

Sadly, fate took a hand. I remember it as though it were yesterday. I was being lowered into a lifeboat. Dr Fortescue, almost lost in the crowd, was waving farewell from the deck. The front page of Egbert Fortescue's notes flew off into the Atlantic breeze before I could read it. At that moment, I knew that history had taken a strange and unexpected turn.

The six hours that followed are lost to me. The next memory I have is of the sun breaking over the horizon as though nothing had happened. I was in a lifeboat squeezed together with forty or fifty others and I saw a rescue boat slicing through the water headed straight for us. Within an hour I was aboard the Carpathia, *the ship that came to the rescue of those who had survived the sinking.*

We all arrived in New York around the time we had originally expected, but under very different circumstances, of course. Thousands of people lined the shore as the ship pulled into Pier 54. Some reports in the newspapers said there were over forty thousand well-wishers there that day.

I was accosted by reporters, old ladies with ideas of taking me home with them, and photographers wanting to take my picture. I even saw a man with a movie camera.

I know some people made fortunes from the disaster; others traded on it and used the fact that they had survived to help them secure jobs and to forge careers, but I knew that was not for me.

I had Egbert Fortescue's notes, but I had no idea what to do with them. And, to be honest, at first, there were more pressing matters to deal with. I had to find work and a place to sleep. I found a laboring job pretty quickly. Uncle Bert had been right all along in his belief that America would be a land of opportunity. I was one of the thousands of men who worked on the Woolworth Building on Broadway . . . all fifty-seven floors of it!

So, for several years I was preoccupied with trying to make a decent living and just getting on with my new life. I kept Fortescue's papers safe, but did nothing with them.

The war swept everything up in its path. In 1917, I was conscripted into the army, but the fighting was over before I could be sent overseas. In 1918, I went back to the construction industry and my old job. I worked hard, became a foreman and then a site manager, but I never forgot about Egbert Fortescue and the papers he had entrusted to me.

Then, in 1921, I married and moved into a larger apartment. Packing away my few possessions, I rediscovered the notes from Fortescue and suddenly felt guilty that I had not done enough with them. And so I began visiting the public library on Fifth Avenue, and I gradually started to piece together anything I could find out about Egbert Fortescue and what he had been doing on the Titanic.

That was how I eventually unearthed the true story of the man I had met briefly. There was an old report in The Times of London detailing the sad news that the scientist had died in a mysterious drowning accident in Manchester in April 1912. I thought this was an unnecessarily macabre *decision on the part of the men who wove the fiction, but at least I now knew a little more. The identity of the fellow in the photograph accompanying the piece was unmistakably the man I had met on the stricken* Titanic. *But, of course, there was no clue as to what Dr Fortescue, a physicist who had worked with Professor Ernest Rutherford, had been doing on the ship, nor where the precious cargo he had with him ended up.*

I spent many long hours pondering what Egbert Fortescue had written in his set of notes. But, although I've always had a gift for math and could follow the steps he was taking, I had absolutely no idea what it was the mathematics described. Every weekend I would visit the public library to study mathematical texts and I finally began to realize that the work was something to do with the new science of atomic physics.

I read everything I could find on the subject. There was not a lot during those days – it was all very new. I managed to find some scientific journals, but the first few I discovered were written in German. One journal was called 'Annalen der Physik'; another was 'Zeitschrift für Physik'. Eventually I located an English magazine, 'Nature', and spent a long time working out what was meant by the new science of atomic physics and matching this with the mathematics Fortescue had written. I finally concluded that he had been working at the cutting edge of the discipline. Indeed, although I understood only a tiny fraction of the work, it was clear that the man I had met on the fateful voyage of the Titanic *was a leader in his field.*

Eventually I reached a decision. I would have to show Fortescue's work to someone who would fully appreciate it, and it occurred to me that the best person would be the most famous scientist of the day, Thomas Edison.

I was pretty naive! I wrote to the great man and waited three months for a reply from a secretary who said that Mr Edison was too busy to see anyone but that if I wanted to travel to the Edison laboratories in West Orange on 3 September at 2 p.m., I could meet up with a Professor Frank Usoff who assisted the famous inventor.

Usoff worked in a laboratory crammed with odd-looking equipment, test-tubes and glowing glass bulbs. He had a rather poky little room at the back and a young man in a white coat led me through the lab to meet the professor.

I realized immediately that Usoff was feigning interest in what I had to say and looked at me with growing scepticism as I described the set of papers that had come into my possession.

'Mr O'Donnell,' he said, studying my face. 'What is your area of expertise?'

'I'm sorry?'

'Your discipline? Which university department do you work in?'

I wasn't sure whether he was being serious or extremely rude. I decided he might not have been correctly informed. 'I'm not an academic, sir.'

'Oh, so what is it you do?'

'I'm a site manager in Manhattan.'

Usoff looked confused. 'I see. Very well, let me peruse the papers you mentioned in your letter.'

I handed them across the professor's desk. He spent several minutes surveying the equations.

'I have done a little research myself,' I said.

Usoff looked up. 'You have?'

I could see the suppressed amusement clear in his face. But, undeterred, I went on. 'Yes, I think it is something to do with atomic energy.'

'Ah, yes,' the professor commented, turning back to the pages before him. 'I imagine there is quite a call for experts in atomic science on construction sites.'

I bridled and Usoff shook his head slowly. 'Where did you get these?' He nodded at the papers.

I felt a knot in my stomach and realized I shouldn't have ventured here. I looked into Usoff's face and tried to weigh up what I should do.

'Well?' he said as though talking to an errant child.

'I was given them to look after by a fellow passenger aboard the Titanic.*'*

Usoff's mouth opened and it seemed that for several moments he did not quite know what to say. He took a deep breath. 'Well, they make little sense,' he said finally. 'I'm not sure what you expected.'

'The first part is a simple enough description of a set of experiments . . .' I began.

The professor held up a hand. 'Please, Mr . . . Mr O'Donnell. I really think this is a matter for gentlemen of science . . . do you not?'

He had chosen his words carefully and I understood immediately the implication . . . the emphasis on the word 'gentlemen' rather than 'science'. I knew what this arrogant sonofabitch was thinking . . . What can some uneducated Irish laborer know about science? Who is this Mick trying to fool?

I got up from the chair. 'I understand,' *I said.* 'I won't be wasting anymore of your time, professor . . .'

He was standing. I went to take back the papers. He put his palms on them.

'I would like to take a further look at these,' *he said firmly.*

'I'm sure you would now,' *I replied.*

He glared at me and gave me his most intimidating look, but I would have none of it.

'I'm sorry,' *I said,* 'but they were entrusted to me by a friend.'

'On the er . . . Titanic,' *Usoff replied sarcastically.*

I grabbed Fortescue's notes and stacked them neatly, while the professor stood rigid behind his desk.

I didn't say goodbye, just turned and strode into the laboratory. A man was walking towards me, a big bulky fella. I recognized him immediately . . . Thomas Edison.

He nodded to me and I nodded back. He walked into Usoff's office and I heard him say: 'Who was that?' *Usoff replied:* 'Oh, just another crank, sir.' *And they both laughed.*

As I headed back to New York on the train I watched the trees and the buildings, the fields and the low clouds stream past. A long time before this moment, I had come to accept my lot in life, to accept the fact that I had been born into the wrong family at the wrong time and that I would never have an opportunity to achieve my full poten-

tial. 'Men like Usoff,' I said to myself 'see it as their right to be superior.' It was an affectation Egbert Fortescue never showed, and I believe he was not that way inclined. He had possessed a truly great intellect and yet he had been a man with no need to put on airs and graces, a man confident enough in his own abilities and with too kind a soul to put others down.

And then I started to think about the legacy he had left and entrusted to me. And for the first time, I began to realize what a terrible responsibility had been placed on my young shoulders. The most dreadful war in human history had just ended. There could be no hiding the extent of human savagery that had been unleashed. What horrors, I pondered, would the wrong people create with Fortescue's knowledge? For it had not escaped me that atomic science could be used for good and for evil. What if there was another towering genius out there who could correctly interpret what Egbert had written and utilize what I had recently begun to appreciate could be the most powerful force in Nature?

And so here I am on August 7, 1945, the day after something similar to Fortescue's science has been unleashed upon the world. I have kept the man's work hidden for thirty-three years and I do not plan to show it to anyone again. I will keep it quietly tucked away, for I could never destroy these papers. Perhaps someday someone will rediscover them and they will read them in the light of a bright day; and they shall be understood by people more enlightened than we sorry men.

William M. O'Donnell.

His hands trembling, Geoff O'Donnell lowered the letter to the pile of papers covered with equations. Then he reached for his cell phone, found Kate Wetherall's number stored there from the Houston conference and tapped the speed dial button.

extracts reading groups
competitions books new
discounts extracts
competitions
books new
events books
extracts
new reading groups
interviews
events extracts
discounts
new books events
events new
discounts extracts discounts
www.panmacmillan.com
extracts events reading groups
competitions books extracts new